BETTER LATE THAN NEVER

# BETTER LATE THAN NEVER

## Jenn McKinlay

BERKLEY PRIME CRIME
New York

BERKLEY PRIME CRIME
Published by Berkley
An imprint of Penguin Random House LLC
375 Hudson Street, New York, New York 10014

Library of Congress Cataloging-in-Publication Data

Names: McKinlay, Jenn, author.
Title: Better late than never / Jenn McKinlay.
Description: First edition. | New York : Berkley Prime Crime, [2016] |
Series: A library lover's mystery ; 7
Identifiers: LCCN 2016019630 (print) | LCCN 2016024007 (ebook) |
ISBN 9780399583735 (hardback) | ISBN 9780399583742 (ebook)
Subjects: | BISAC: FICTION / Mystery & Detective / Women Sleuths. |
GSAFD: Mystery fiction.
Classification: LCC PS3612.A948 B48 2016 (print) | LCC PS3612.A948 (ebook) |
DDC 813/.6—dc23
LC record available at https://lccn.loc.gov/2016019630

First Edition: November 2016

Printed in the United States of America
1   3   5   7   9   10   8   6   4   2

Cover art by Julia Green
Cover design by Rita Frangie
Book design by Laura K. Corless

*My library career has been full and rich, allowing me to work in a wide variety of libraries over the years with so many truly amazing and brilliant people. So, this is my shout-out to all of those libraries and the remarkable people who work in them: East Lyme Public Library, Cromwell Belden Public Library, Andalucia School Library, Phoenix Public Library, Maricopa County Public Library, Desert Botanical Garden Research Library and Scottsdale Healthcare Medical Library. I believe all the way to my soul that libraries are the heart of their communities, the backbone of our society and the place where every man, woman and child can discover the elemental truth that is—if you can dream it, you can be it.*

# Acknowledgments

As always, I have such a wonderful team of people getting me to the finish line with my stories there will never be enough champagne or chocolate to thank them for all that they do. So here are my humble thanks to my wonderful agent, Christina Hogrebe; my fabulous editor, Kate Seaver, and assistant editor Katherine Pelz; the amazing artist who does my covers, Julia Green; and the entire team at Berkley Prime Crime who have been so supportive of me for all of my series. I consider myself very lucky to have you all in my corner.

BETTER LATE THAN NEVER

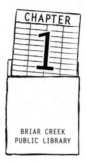

**CHAPTER 1**

BRIAR CREEK
PUBLIC LIBRARY

"Let the wild rumpus start!" Beth Stanley cried as the cart of books she had stacked to bursting abruptly regurgitated its contents all over the Briar Creek Public Library's main floor with a loud rushing noise followed by slaps and thumps as the books landed on the ground.

"Shhh!" Ms. Cole hissed. She was an old-school librarian—nicknamed "the lemon" because of her frequently puckered disposition—who was in charge of the circulation of materials for the library located on the Connecticut shore.

"Sorry, I tried to stop it but I couldn't hold it in," Beth said. She was wearing a crown and carrying a sparkling scepter, which was really a bejeweled cardboard tube from a roll of wrapping paper with a tissue-paper flower sticking out of the end.

Lindsey noted the tail pinned to the back of her yoga pants and the pointy ears poking out beneath her crown.

With her short, dark hair styled in wild disarray, Beth bore a remarkable resemblance to Max, the character she was representing.

"*Where the Wild Things Are* for story time?" Lindsey guessed.

"Best story time book ever," Beth said.

"Brilliant! I love Maurice Sendak," Paula Turner said.

"No one asked you," Ms. Cole said. Her glance was frosty as she took in her part-time clerk with undisguised suspicion.

Paula was the library's newly hired clerk, and with her sleeve of colorful arm tattoos and long hair dyed a deep purple, she had been a challenge for the conservative Ms. Cole to supervise from day one.

"That'll do, people," Lindsey Norris said. She was the director of the small library and tried to maintain some semblance of order. "We have three more loaded book trucks coming in. We need to make room behind the desk."

"There is no more room," Ms. Cole said. Her tone was as dry as butterless toast, and if she were anyone else Lindsey might have thought she was teasing. Ms. Cole was not.

A monochromatic dresser, Ms. Cole was in all black today, as if she were in mourning. Lindsey figured she probably was, given that they were holding their first annual fine amnesty day, which went against everything in which Ms. Cole believed.

She was a punitive sort who enjoyed using fines and shushing to curb their patrons' naughty behavior. Lindsey had been trying to get her to roll with the times for a couple of years now. It was a battle.

"Why don't we get the crafternoon ladies to help?" Beth

suggested. She was picking up the books that had fallen off of her cart. Lindsey and Paula helped her. Ms. Cole did not.

"In what way?" Lindsey asked. She stacked the books back on the cart.

"They can fine-sort the book trucks that are already checked in, which will make room for the new ones," Beth said. "In fact, if we wheel the trucks to the meeting room, we can do that while we discuss our book of the week."

"They are not cleared to work in the library," Ms. Cole protested.

"Drastic times," Lindsey said. She looked at Paula and Beth. "Let's wheel the checked-in carts to the crafternoon room to make room for the incoming."

"I really must protest," Ms. Cole said.

"Of course you must," Lindsey said. She met Ms. Cole's upset gaze with her own and tried to channel her inner calm. "Answer me this: Do you have a better idea?"

"You mean aside from never having another fine amnesty day ever again?" the lemon asked. "No."

"Then to the crafternoon room it is," Lindsey said.

She, Beth and Paula each took a cart and pushed it to the back room where the crafternoon ladies met every Thursday afternoon to eat, discuss a book and work on a craft.

As they entered the room, they found Nancy Peyton and Violet La Rue already in place on the comfy couches placed in the center of the room. Violet had been in charge of the food today, so it was ham and cheese sliders, potato soup and a veggie platter.

Lindsey felt her stomach rumble. She tried to remember the last time she'd eaten. It must have been last night because when she'd arrived at the library this morning, the book drop had been full to bursting. She'd skipped breakfast to help unload it and hadn't had a chance to think about eating since.

"What's this?" Nancy asked as the parade of carts appeared.

Nancy was Lindsey's landlord as well as one of her crafternoon buddies. A widow, Nancy had inherited her old captain's house when her husband, Jake, went down with his ship many years ago. Nancy then turned it into a three-family house and rented out the top two floors. Lindsey lived on the third level while Nancy's nephew Charlie Peyton was the filler in their house sandwich and resided on the second floor.

"How married are you to the idea of doing a craft today?" Lindsey asked.

"Not very. Why?" Violet asked.

She was dressed in her usual jewel-toned caftan, which made her dark complexion glow. A retired Broadway actress, Violet had an innate grace and flair that, despite her gray hair, which she wore scraped into a tight bun at the back of her head, made her seem eternally youthful. Truly, she could command a room like nobody's business. Right now, her tone was cautious. Smart lady.

"I'm throwing myself on your mercy," Lindsey said. She bowed with her arms out in obeisance just so they would know she was sincere. "We are so far behind on sorting the books that have been returned we may never catch up. Would you ladies be willing to help us get these trucks in order?"

Nancy and Violet exchanged a glance. The two ladies were longtime best friends and Lindsey knew they communicated without words. It was no surprise to her when they both faced her and answered at the same time.

"Yes, of course," they said together.

"Is Ms. Cole going to come in here and yell at us for eating near the books?" Violet asked. "Because that would be a problem for me."

"So long as we don't eat over the books, I think we'll be okay," Lindsey said.

"Food, I need food!" Mary Murphy hustled into the room with Charlene La Rue right behind her.

"Girl, every time I see you, you are either eating or napping," Nancy said. "Are you feeling all right?"

She moved to stand beside the food table and loaded a plate for Mary before the woman even had her jacket off.

"Oh, yeah, I'm fine," Mary said. "Just storing up for winter, you know, like a squirrel."

"It's May," Violet said. "You keep packing it in like this and you'll be able to hibernate for two winters."

"Heh heh." Mary laughed uneasily and her gaze darted to Lindsey.

Lindsey smiled at her to let her know her secret was still safe. The truth was Mary was pregnant with her first child. Lindsey had figured it out, but the others were still clueless. Lindsey had promised Mary she wouldn't say a word to anyone, including Mary's brother Sully, who Lindsey had an on-and-off-again sort of relationship with, so Mary's news and the fact that Lindsey knew about it and Sully didn't made things a teensy bit complicated.

Charlene La Rue paused beside her mother, Violet, to kiss her cheek. Charlene had inherited her mother's slender grace and beauty but instead of going into theater, Charlene was a television reporter in New Haven. With the career and the husband and kids her schedule was packed to bursting, but she kept her crafternoon Thursday commitment because it was one of the few times she got to spend with her mother and talk about something besides the children.

Thankfully, everyone was on board with fine-sorting the books while they discussed their book of the week, Nathaniel Hawthorne's *The Scarlet Letter*.

It took three trips to bring all of the extra carts into the crafternoon room, but once they were in, they all took a cart and began arranging the books for shelving.

"Question," Charlene asked. "How far do I go following the Dewey number?"

"Meaning?" Beth asked.

"Can I just lump all the 398.2 books together or do I go all the way to the letter that follows?" Charlene asked.

Lindsey glanced at Beth and said, "I still believe in 398.2, how about you?"

Beth laughed. Mary and the others frowned.

"I don't get it," Nancy said.

"I do." Charlene glanced up from her cart. "Judging by these books, 398.2 is the base number for fairy tales. Won't Sully and Robbie be happy to know that she still believes in happy ever after."

"Ah, yes, but who will be her Prince Charming?" Violet asked.

"Oh, no," Lindsey said. "There is no charming anyone for me. Thank you very much."

She shook her head back and forth to emphasize her point. She'd been keeping her personal life on the down low and had no intention of sharing any information until she knew where it was going. "We are not discussing my love life or lack thereof, not when we have Beth's new relationship to dissect and discuss."

"Way to throw me under the gossip train," Beth said. Then she grinned. "But since you asked, Aidan is wonderful. He's funny and smart, handsome and kind." She sighed. "I've never been happier."

The woman positively glowed and Lindsey was pretty sure her crown sparkled for real. The other ladies all sighed with her and Lindsey was relieved to have successfully distracted them.

"Has the 'L' word been used yet?" Mary asked through a mouthful of ham and cheese.

"Not yet," Beth said. She fretted her lower lip between her teeth. "Should it have been? We've been dating for three months. Who says it first? Should I say it first? I don't know if I'm ready for that."

"It should just come naturally," Nancy said.

"She's right, but I'd wait and let him say it first," Charlene said. "I knew I was in love with Martin after the first two months, but I let him take the lead on the 'L' word. Men can be pretty skittish about declarations of love."

"Ian said it first," Mary said. "Of course, I didn't really have a chance since he said 'I love you' the very first moment he saw me. I think our meeting went something like me saying, 'Hi, I'm Mary,' to which he replied, 'Yes, I'll marry you. I've been madly in love with you since you walked through the door five seconds ago.'"

Lindsey laughed. She could see Ian doing just that. Mary was a lovely woman with thick curls of red-brown hair and sparkling blue eyes, and Ian was, well, not so much of a looker. But he had personality by the bucketful and he adored his wife, which Mary never took for granted.

"Speaking of the 'L' word and relationships, here's my

question about the book," Nancy said. "What does a strong female like Hester see in a spineless sniveler like Dimwit?"

"Dimmesdale," Violet said.

"Whatever," Nancy said. "I hated him."

"I think that was the point. Hawthorne portrays him as weak and Hester as strong even though she's treated very badly for adultery while he hides behind his position and does nothing to protect her," Charlene said. "What did you think of him, Mary?"

"Huh?" Mary asked through a mouthful of soup.

"What did you think about Dimmesdale?"

Mary looked chagrinned. "No idea. I didn't finish the book. Frankly, when I got to Hawthorne's eighth use of the word *ignominy*, I quit."

Beth started to laugh and the others joined in.

"I'm serious. That word does not roll through my head," Mary said. "Every time it cropped up, I had to stop and sound it out and it never felt right and then I was just irritated, so I quit."

"Hawthorne loved that word," Lindsey said. "I read a critique where it said he uses *ignominy* sixteen times in the book, *ignominious* seven times, and *ignominiously* once."

"Ugh." Mary looked pained as she spooned more soup into her mouth.

The rest of the crafternooners shared amused looks but no one chastised Mary for quitting on the book. They weren't very strict about that part of being a crafternooner, or any part of being a crafternooner for that matter.

"Lindsey, can I talk to you for a second?"

Lindsey turned to see Paula standing in the doorway. She was holding a book in her hands and looked excited.

"Sure, what is it?" Lindsey asked as she crossed the room.

"This book," Paula said. "It's my sure thing. It has to be the winner for the category of most overdue item."

To keep the staff entertained during the flood of incoming materials, Lindsey had offered up prizes for the staff member who found the most overdue item or the most abused material. The prize was a free pizza because Lindsey had discovered during the past couple of years as director that food was always a motivator for her staff.

"Really?" Lindsey took the book and glanced at the cover. It was *The Catcher in the Rye* and it looked to be in good shape. "How overdue is it?"

"Judging by the slip that was left inside, the book was due on October twenty-third, nineteen ninety-six." Paula pointed to a yellowed piece of paper. "Twenty years."

"No way," Lindsey said.

"Way," Paula said. "So, I'm down for the free pizza from Marco's Pizzeria, right?"

Lindsey pointed to the clock. "The contest goes until closing time today, but so far it looks like you're in the lead."

Paula pumped her fist.

"Did someone say pizza?" Mary asked. She had moved from the soup to the veggie platter but her eyes lit up at the word *pizza*.

"Not for you," Lindsey said. "Go put your name and the book's name on the leader board, Paula. I'd like to keep the book though."

"Will do," Paula said. She left the room with one more pump of her fist.

"Wow, twenty years overdue, what ILS were they using back then?" Beth asked.

"Dynix?" Lindsey guessed. She glanced at the book, which looked to have been well taken care of over the years. "Remember we learned about that integrated library system in grad school? Let's see, if we calculate the fine at today's going rate of twenty cents per day for twenty years, we're looking at . . . help me out, somebody."

"About seventy-three dollars per year, which would be fourteen hundred sixty dollars," Mary said.

They all looked at her.

"What?" she asked. "I'm good with numbers."

"Impressive," Nancy said.

"As opposed to ignominious," Violet joked.

"Good thing you're having an amnesty," Charlene said. "Can you imagine paying that fine?"

"We'd never charge more than the cost of the book, but you're right it's steep, although not as bad as Keith Richards's library fines I'll bet," Lindsey said.

"Keith Richards the rock star?" Violet asked.

"The one and only," Lindsey said. "Apparently, he was quite the library lover in his youth. In his autobiography, he said the library was the only place he would willingly obey the laws, like silence. And he admitted he was a bookworm who checked out books but never returned them. He has something like fifty years in fines racked up in Dartford, Kent."

"Ha! Can you imagine Ms. Cole taking on Keith Richards?" Nancy asked. "I'd pay to see that."

"Me, too," Violet snorted.

"Who do you suppose had this book checked out for twenty years?" Charlene asked. "And why return it now?"

"I'll bet the lemon knows," Beth said. "She never forgets an overdue book."

"She can't have kept the records that far back, can she?" Lindsey asked.

Beth pointed her scepter at her. "Only one way to find out."

Lindsey shrugged. Holding the book close, she went to find Ms. Cole.

CHAPTER

2

BRIAR CREEK
PUBLIC LIBRARY

"Ms. Cole, may I interrupt you for a moment?" Lindsey approached the circulation desk with caution.

With carts of books all around her, Ms. Cole looked like a military general addressing the troops. She glanced at Lindsey and picked up three books that looked as if they'd exploded. The covers were warped and the pages were yellowed and wrinkled, indicating severe water damage.

"I think these swam ashore," Ms. Cole observed. She lowered her reading glasses and looked at Lindsey over the top. It was her I-told-you-so look.

"They are in less than ideal condition," Lindsey conceded.

"Less than ideal? They're a disaster. And look at this!" Ms. Cole held up a book for Lindsey to see. "This book smells like it smokes a pack a day."

She waved it under Lindsey's nose. The pungent smell of stale tobacco smoke curled Lindsey's nose hair.

"Discard pile," she said. "But on the upside, you're in the lead for most damaged item."

"Thrill me," Ms. Cole said.

Lindsey wanted to wave her hand in front of her face to dispel the stink of the damaged book but she resisted, knowing it would only please Ms. Cole to prove her point that amnesty day was a bad idea because now damaged materials were being turned in without penalty and patrons would not be billed for replacements.

Lindsey happened to think it was worth it to clear people's records and allow them to borrow again instead of holding them hostage for overdue materials and replacement costs. She and Ms. Cole were just going to have to agree to disagree, but the lemon wasn't quite there yet.

"Look at it this way," Lindsey said. "We are clearing up old records and gathering a list for replacements—"

"That will have to come out of our existing budget," Ms. Cole argued.

Lindsey sighed. They'd been on this merry-go-round since Lindsey had announced her plan to have an amnesty day. As far as Ms. Cole was concerned there was no brass ring. Lindsey knew there was no way she was ever going to convince the lemon that the one-day return forgiveness with no questions asked was a good idea. Fine. Time to move on.

"We did get a return that might interest you," Lindsey said. She held up the copy of J. D. Salinger's book, which was in excellent condition. "Twenty years overdue judging by the due slip inside and still in excellent condition."

Ms. Cole gave her a suspicious look. She dumped the smoke-saturated book into a plastic tub for discards and held out her hand for the copy of *The Catcher in the Rye*. She turned the book over to examine it and thumbed through the pages. Then she looked at the due-date slip. Her lips compressed into a thin line and she turned and strode away from the desk leaving Lindsey to follow or not. Lindsey followed.

Ms. Cole tucked the book under her arm and led the way through the stacks to the storage room in the back of the library. This was where the library kept its odds and ends, holiday decorations, old wooden trucks that weren't broken but were heavy to push, extra step stools, vintage equipment like old library-card punchers that weren't in demand anymore but were still functional. It was also where the library kept files of old records. Or more accurately, it was where Ms. Cole kept her files of old overdue notices.

The lemon always wore her key to the back rooms of the library on a red spiral rubber cord around her wrist. It was the only fashion accessory that she ever wore besides the beaded cord for her reading glasses and her wristwatch.

She used her key to open the door and flipped on the light switch. The lone overhead fluorescent light sputtered to life and did its best to beat back the gloom in the windowless room. It didn't reach into the far corners and Lindsey had to suppress a shiver. She blamed Dean Koontz and his Odd Thomas series. Deep, dark shadows always gave her a jump scare thanks to him.

Ms. Cole strode through the room to the back, where the file cabinets lined the far wall. This was her domain, where she kept the old records sorted by due date. They went back a good thirty-five years, essentially, when Ms. Cole was given control of circulation. She opened the drawer that covered the mid–nineteen nineties and flipped through the half sheets of paper held together in bunches by paperclips.

She peered through her reading glasses while she searched, finally extracting a small stack of paper. She read through the stack until she found her match. She moved back under the light with the paper in hand. Lindsey watched her, wondering if she was ever planning to share.

Ms. Cole looked at the book and then at the papers. Her face drained of all color and she staggered to the side, clutching an old wooden cart to keep herself from falling over.

"Oh, goodness no," she said. When she glanced at Lindsey her face was stricken with shock and grief. "It was hers."

The book and the papers fell from her fingers and Ms. Cole listed to the side as if she didn't have the strength to remain upright. Lindsey jumped forward to grab her before she keeled over on the spot.

"Ms. Cole, what is it?" Lindsey asked. "What did you find?"

The lemon shook her head as if she couldn't put voice to the horror of what she'd just discovered. Lindsey put her arm around her and helped her sit on an old padded chair that had been surplused from the office when someone had spilled a cup of coffee on it, staining the upholstery beyond repair.

Lindsey knelt in front of Ms. Cole to study her face. She was deathly pale and beads of sweat dotted her upper lip. Despite the perspiration, she was shivering and looked like she might faint.

"Are you all right?" Lindsey asked. "Do you want me to call someone?"

"It's the book," Ms. Cole said. She pointed with shaky fingers to the book that was now facedown on the floor. "It was checked out to Candice Whitley."

Lindsey glanced at the book. She knelt to pick it up along with the overdue notices that had fallen all around it like scattered leaves on a chilly autumn wind.

"Candice Whitley," Lindsey said. "Why does that name sound familiar?"

Ms. Cole opened her mouth to speak but she couldn't seem to catch her breath. She was gasping and panting. Lindsey thought she might be choking but that made no sense. Her generous bosom was heaving but she didn't seem to be getting enough air.

"Ms. Cole, are you . . . Oh . . . You're hyperventilating!" Lindsey cried. She dropped the book and the papers on a cart and glanced around the storage room as if there might be something to help the situation. "Here. Put your head between your knees and try to calm down. I'll be right back."

Lindsey helped the lemon to lean forward then she bolted out the door, running through the library to the staff break room where she knew there were some paper lunch sacks. She yanked open the cabinet and grabbed one, sending all the other contents of the cupboard onto the counter with a crash.

"Lindsey! What's going on?" Milton Duffy, a library board member and one of Lindsey's favorite patrons, was standing in the doorway, wearing his usual tracksuit, looking shocked by her behavior.

"Ms. Cole is hyperventilating!" Lindsey cried. "Follow me!"

Milton was currently dating Ms. Cole. No one had quite figured out the attraction between the two opposites, but now was not the time to dwell.

Lindsey had known Ms. Cole for a while and she had never, never seen her come undone like this, not even when there'd been a dead body found in her precious library. The fact that she was hyperventilating made Lindsey feel like she might sympathy hyperventilate, almost like sympathy crying but with a lack of carbon dioxide and potential for passing out instead of tears.

Lindsey ran back to the storage room with Milton on her heels. The door was open just as she'd left it, with its flickering fluorescent overhead light giving the room a ghoulish glow. Ms. Cole was still in the chair, looking the worse for wear as she was panting and trembling.

"Eugenia!" Milton cried. He snatched the bag from Lindsey's hand, snapped it open and held it over Ms. Cole's nose and mouth. "Easy, my dear. Try to calm your breathing."

Ms. Cole nodded and used one hand to grasp his. It was an unusually vulnerable gesture from the unflappable Ms. Cole and Lindsey felt as if she was intruding on the tender moment between the couple, so she turned her back to them to give them some privacy. She gathered the book and the papers from the cart, trying to keep busy sorting them while Ms. Cole regained her equilibrium.

Finally, Milton removed the bag and Ms. Cole slumped against the back of the chair. She was still pale but not deathly so and she didn't seem quite as shaky as she had.

"There," Milton said. "You're getting your color back."

"Thank you." Ms. Cole took a slow breath as if to be sure she wasn't going to start wheezing again.

"What happened? You two ladies didn't get into a brawl over library policy, did you?" he asked.

Lindsey and Ms. Cole gave him reproving looks.

"We are not that uncivilized," Ms. Cole said. "We do not scuffle like rabble."

"No, of course not, but we all know the amnesty day has been a bone of contention between you two," Milton said. "Emotions have been running high."

"Be that as it may," Ms. Cole said, "this is much more horrible than encouraging people to continue their bad behavior."

Lindsey stopped herself from rolling her eyes. Barely.

"So what is it? What did you discover?" Lindsey asked. "I don't understand why you were so upset to see that this book was checked out by—what was her name?—oh, yeah. Candice Whitley."

Milton gasped. He glanced at Ms. Cole in shock and she nodded. Lindsey noted the matching looks of horror on their faces but for the life of her she couldn't figure out what the significance was about Candice Whitley.

"You're not going to start hyperventilating now, are you?" she asked Milton.

"No," he said. "Just give me a second."

He stood up straight in what Lindsey recognized as Mountain Pose. Milton was a longtime yogi, who frequently practiced in the library. She and Ms. Cole waited while he meditated through his upset.

"All right," he said. He relaxed into a casual stance and looked at Ms. Cole. "Are you sure it was checked out to her?"

"Yes, and it gets worse," she said. She reached out and gripped his hand in hers. "I counted the days back three weeks from the due date and I am quite sure it was checked out to her *on the day she was murdered.*"

CHAPTER

3

BRIAR CREEK
PUBLIC LIBRARY

**"M**urdered?" Lindsey asked.

"I'm afraid so," Milton said. He looked a little shaky and Lindsey grabbed a chair for him to sit down beside Ms. Cole.

"Wait," Lindsey said. She began to pace. Now she remembered the name. Candice Whitley. "She was the high school English teacher who was strangled and left for dead under the football stadium bleachers at the high school back in the nineties, right?"

Ms. Cole nodded. Her black attire seemed suddenly apt given the expression of grief on her face. Lindsey wondered how well Ms. Cole had known Candice Whitley, as she seemed to be awfully rattled by the subject of her death. Then again, it was murder, and that could shake the stoutest heart.

"And you're certain she checked out this book on the day she died?" Lindsey asked.

Again, Ms. Cole nodded, then she took a deep breath as if willing the words to come to her.

"The book was due Wednesday, October twenty-third, which, given our three-week lending policy, means it was checked out on October second, which was the day Candice was murdered," she said. Her voice was wobbly and Milton put his arm around her and drew her close.

Lindsey looked at the book in her hands and felt the hair on the back of her neck prickle with unease. She looked at Milton and Ms. Cole and knew they were thinking the same thing she was.

"So, it could be that someone found the book in their belongings and decided to return it," she said.

Milton ran a hand over his bald head and then stroked his neatly trimmed goatee. He looked as unsettled as Lindsey had ever seen him. She knew he was thinking the same thing she was.

"Or it could be that the person who returned the book . . ." Lindsey paused. The idea was so awful she wasn't sure she could say it out loud.

Ms. Cole's voice was very soft when she whispered, "Was Candice Whitley's murderer."

Lindsey felt her knees go wobbly, as if they had withstood enough of the scary stuff and were going to give out now. She stiffened her legs. She was not going to buckle on mere speculation even if it did seem bad, really bad.

She glanced at the papers in her hand and looked for the one that belonged with the book. There was no doubt that this was a very uncomfortable situation. She didn't like it, mostly, because she had come to realize over the past few years that unlikely coincidences usually weren't coincidences

at all. She had to do something with this book and its overdue notice. Give them to the police. Something.

"Come on," she said. "Let's get out of here."

She let Milton and Ms. Cole lead the way out of the room
and then switched off the light and locked the door behind
them. Together they walked back to the main part of the library.

"Paula just found this book with the slip in it. Maybe
someone checked it out after Candice," she said. "Do we have
any access to the old circulation records?"

Ms. Cole shook her head. "No. While I do keep a hard
copy of overdue notices, mostly for people who think they
can argue with me, I purge the database records for lost items
and expired library cards every two years. We've upgraded
to new systems three times since this book was checked out.
It appears this book has not circulated in a very long time."

"Is there any way to tell when it was returned today?"
Milton asked.

"Since it's no longer in the computer system, there'd be
no record for it," Lindsey said. "If Paula just found it, do we
know if the books she was sorting were recently returned?"

"No, she was working on the huge pile that was shoved
into the book drop last night. It could have been returned
any time since we emptied the drop at closing yesterday,
which was sixteen hours ago," Ms. Cole said.

Lindsey glanced at Milton and Ms. Cole. They both looked
wiped out, as if they'd been caught in an unexpected storm.

"Milton, would you take Ms. Cole into the staff break
room for bit? Maybe have some tea? I'll have Paula take
charge of the front for now."

The fact that Ms. Cole didn't protest told Lindsey just
how undone she was by the horrifying turn of events.

"If anyone needs me, I'll be back shortly. I'm going to take the book over to the police station and see what Chief Plewicki thinks about this. Hopefully, she can offer up a theory we haven't thought of that will make more sense."

"Good thinking," Milton said. "Emma is a very capable young woman and might have some useful insight for us. Perhaps we're just overreacting."

His voice sounded hopeful, but Lindsey could tell from the drawn look on Ms. Cole's face that she didn't think they were overreacting, and Lindsey didn't either.

I t was a beautiful spring day outside. The month of May along the Connecticut shore was something special. The days were warm, the nights were cool, frogs peeped, birds chirped and flowers bloomed. So long as it wasn't pouring rain, it just didn't get any lovelier.

At the moment, however, Lindsey was oblivious. She strode down the sidewalk to the police station, clutching the book in her hand. She had thought about calling Emma, the police chief, and having her come to the library, but with all the chaos of amnesty day, she figured it would be easier if she walked the book to her. Plus, she needed the fresh air to clear her head.

In the few years she'd known Ms. Cole, she'd never seen her lose her composure. To Lindsey that alone proved the importance of the item in her hand. She glanced at the book. The iconic cover art of a line drawing of a carousel horse over a splash of red with the title in bold yellow lettering was always how she pictured the novel in her mind.

She'd always assumed the artist had chosen the carousel scene in the book, where the young girl Phoebe rides the carousel in the park in the rain and her older brother, Holden, watches her and feels moved to tears. She'd always thought the horse on the cover was an overly dramatic rendition of the scene.

Did the artist mean for the horse to look as fierce as it did? Was it supposed to represent Holden running away? She'd read that the author, Salinger, preferred plain covers with little text so as not to distract the reader. She wondered what he'd thought of this cover.

She clutched the book closer. Why had Candice Whitley checked it out from the library? She was a high school English teacher, so this book should have been available at the school. Why go to the public library for it?

It was well known in library circles that Salinger's book was listed by the American Library Association as having been banned from some schools, but surely that wasn't the case here in Briar Creek twenty years ago.

Lindsey tried to remember if there'd been any books banned in her high school. She didn't think so. Having grown up in a college town in New Hampshire, her school had been very forward-thinking, a reflection of the community, which was made up of academics and their kind.

She turned onto the walk that led to the police station. She supposed she'd never know why Candice had checked out the book. The best she could hope for in this situation was to discover who had returned the book and hope that it really was just a random happenstance. She tried to ignore the prickle of unease she felt with the realization that Candice had been at the library checking out this book shortly before she was killed. She also tried to ignore the very real possibility that whoever had returned the book might be connected to Candice's murder, and in fact, might be her murderer.

Lindsey pulled open the glass door and strode into the station. Officer Kirkland was seated at the front desk. His freckled face broke into a wide smile when he saw Lindsey.

Big, raw-boned and tall, with a shock of fiery red hair that was trimmed into a flat top, Officer Kirkland was a presence that was hard to ignore, sort of like an overeager golden retriever. His toothy smile was always welcoming, and Lindsey knew he was considered a friendly face among the residents of the town.

"What have you got for us today, Ms. Norris?" he asked, rising from his seat.

"Lindsey," she corrected him.

"Yes, ma'am," he said.

Lindsey shook her head. Kirkland was only eight years younger than her but whenever he addressed her with a *Ms.* or a *ma'am* he made her feel like she could be his grandma. For months she'd been trying to break him of the habit with no success.

"Is Chief Plewicki in?" she asked.

"Yes, ma'am, she's meeting with Mayor Hensen and his right-hand man, Herb Gunderson," he said. He leaned forward. "Do you want me to call her? Is it an emergency?"

Kirkland's eyes lit up at the possibility of chaos and mayhem. Lindsey knew that the sleepy little town of Briar Creek probably wasn't the hotbed of criminal activity that the young officer hoped for. Still, they'd had their fair share of heinous crimes over the past few years, so he really didn't need to feel neglected in the criminal investigation sciences.

"Settle down, cowboy," she said. "I'm not sure what I've got just yet."

Kirkland flushed, duly chastised, and nodded at her.

"Sorry. It's just that we've had some burglary activity lately and I thought you might have a lead for us."

Given that the case Lindsey was interested in was over twenty years old, she doubted it would help them in any way.

"I think it's safe to say I'm here on an unrelated matter," she said. "But it might be of interest to the mayor, so if they could squeeze me in, that'd be great."

"I'll check," he said.

Lindsey wandered over to the bulletin board to study the missing posts for dogs, cats and a barbecue. She had been through the missing-dog thing herself recently when her puppy, Heathcliff, had wandered off, scaring about five years off of her life. When she looked at the missing pictures posted by her fellow residents, she knew exactly how desperate they felt. Well, not the guy missing his barbecue, but everyone else.

"She said to go on back," Kirkland said. He put down the phone and held open the half door that led to the back of the station. "They're in her office."

"Thanks," Lindsey said.

She walked down the short hallway and stopped before Emma's office. She rapped lightly on the wooden door and waited until she heard Emma yell, "Come in," before she pushed the door open and entered.

The office was spacious with a large desk and bookcase on one side and a round glass conference table with four cushy leather desk chairs on the other. Both the mayor and Herb half rose out of their seats when Lindsey stepped into the room, but Emma didn't. She was still in a big black boot for her recently fractured leg and Lindsey knew it was still giving her trouble.

"Afternoon, Lindsey," Mayor Hensen said. Dressed in his usual impeccably tailored suit with his dazzlingly perfect teeth, Hensen looked the part of the quintessential mayor.

"Hello, Lindsey," Herb said. Like a big looming shadow, wherever the mayor was, Herb was sure to follow. Lindsey had determined during her years of working with them that Herb's picky, pedantic personality was the substance to the mayor's flash.

"Good afternoon. I'm sorry to interrupt," she replied.

Emma gestured Lindsey to the vacant seat. "No, it's fine. You've got good timing. We were just wrapping up."

Lindsey settled into the chair and the mayor finished what he'd been saying when she had arrived.

"I'll need daily updates on the progress of the investigation," he said. "The sooner we catch whoever is doing this the sooner we can ease the minds of the residents."

"About that," Chief Plewicki said. "I was thinking we really need to let people know that there is a burglar in town. They're going to hear about it through word of mouth—you know how fast things spread around here—and it'll be worse if it isn't coming from my office. It'll go from being small burglaries in vacant houses to a crazed rapist in a clown suit breaking and entering with a flamethrower and handcuffs."

Lindsey snorted and both the mayor and Herb gave her dour looks.

"Sorry," she said. "But she's right."

Herb looked pinched by the colorful description, but they all knew Emma was right. When rumors flew through town unchecked, they took on a mythology all their own, which was one more reason why Lindsey was keeping her private life, well, private.

"I see your point," Mayor Hensen said. "I'll speak to the

editor of the weekly and see if he can run a news piece that disseminates the information accordingly without causing a panic."

Lindsey knew that what he really meant was to have the paper spin the story in the least damaging way possible toward the mayor's office, but she didn't feel the need to point it out.

Herb and Emma nodded as if they agreed and then Emma turned to Lindsey and said, "Kirkland said you have something of interest to us all?"

"Perhaps, or maybe I just need a second opinion," Lindsey said. She put the book on the table and Emma frowned.

"Oh, man, I hated that book," she said.

"What?" Mayor Hensen asked. "How could you? It's one of the best books ever written."

"Meh," Emma said. "Holden Caulfield is a whiner."

Herb glanced between them as if unsure of what opinion to offer. Lindsey narrowed her gaze at him. She'd seen that look before, most recently on Mary's face during their crafternoon.

"You've never read it, have you?" she asked.

"No." He shook his head but he looked relieved, as if he considered this the best possible answer under the circumstances.

"What about you?" Emma asked Lindsey. "You probably loved it."

"Why do you say that?" she asked. "Just because I'm a librarian I have to love all the literary classics?"

"Sort of goes with the job, doesn't it?" Emma asked.

"No," Lindsey said. "Honestly, I didn't love it or hate it. Mostly, I felt sorry for Holden that he goes through one awkward and miserable experience after another. It does capture the impetuous manic emotions of the age though, doesn't it?"

"Exactly," Mayor Hensen agreed. "It is so raw. It brings you right back to that time in life where you are not a child or an adult but something wedged awkwardly in between."

Lindsey was impressed. She hadn't thought Mayor Hensen was the type to get swept up in a book. She'd always assumed he was more of a non-fiction reader.

"There was too much angst," Emma said. "I loathe angst."

"In any event," Herb said. He glanced at the clock on his cell phone. "Why does the book bring you here, Lindsey? Have we had complaints about the library owning the book? Is someone asking us to reconsider it as part of the collection?"

"Blasphemy!" Mayor Hensen said.

"No, not that I know of at any rate," Lindsey said. "Actually, it's this particular volume that is the dilemma."

She sighed as she opened the book up and took out the overdue notice Ms. Cole had dug out of her file cabinet. She turned it so that the others could see it.

"It may be nothing, but this book was returned today during our amnesty day, and it came to our attention that it was checked out over twenty years ago."

"Excellent!" The mayor thumped his fist on the table. "So the amnesty is working."

"Oh, yes, materials are coming back in droves," Lindsey said. "But this one"—she paused to tap the cover—"this one is problematic."

"How so?" Emma asked.

"According to our file of overdue notices, it was checked out by Candice Whitley on the same day she was murdered," Lindsey said.

"What?" Herb Gunderson asked. He stared at the book

as if demanding an explanation from its pages. "That can't be. That's not possible."

His face went a sickly shade of gray and then it flashed a hot sweaty red as if in outrage. Lindsey had never seen so much emotion come out of Herb before. She glanced at Emma, who was also watching Herb with a curious gaze.

"Easy." Mayor Hensen put his hand on Herb's arm. He then turned to Lindsey and said, "I'm afraid I'm not following why a book being returned on a day we're offering to waive fines would be of any interest to our police chief. Wasn't the entire purpose of the amnesty to get people to return long-overdue items?"

"Yes, it was, but given that this book has no history that we can find other than being checked out to Candice Whitley on the day she died, we were concerned that it may have been returned by the murderer," Lindsey said. She pushed the book toward Emma. "If she had it on her at the time of the murder, it stands to reason. Don't you think?"

Emma opened her mouth to speak, but Herb interrupted with a sharp, "No! That is not possible, and I refuse to allow this unsubstantiated speculation to go any further."

CHAPTER

4

BRIAR CREEK
PUBLIC LIBRARY

"Excuse me?" Emma asked. "I'm sorry, when exactly were you made the chief of police?" She made a show of checking the badge on her left front pocket and then pointed to it. "Huh, that's my name, so I'm thinking this is my call."

"I just . . . it's . . ." Herb stammered, and Mayor Hensen held up his hand to signal for him to stop talking.

"I think what Herb is trying to say is that we have a rash of burglaries that are happening right now. They need to be the top of your priority list," Mayor Hensen said. His tone made it clear that he believed he was in charge of the police department and had the final say on how Emma spent her time.

Lindsey could have told him how that was going to go, but when it came to Emma, men seemed to have to learn the hard way.

Emma was a pretty woman with a heart-shaped face, full

lips, big brown eyes and arching eyebrows. Small in stature and very curvy with a mane of long dark hair that hung just past her shoulders, she was not what a person usually pictured when they heard the title *chief of police*.

Because she was so pretty, people, mostly men, frequently made the mistake of thinking she wasn't as strong-willed and self-directed as a man. Much like Herb and the mayor thought they could tell her how to prioritize her caseload right now. Big mistake.

"First, the last time I checked I answered to the town council, not the mayor's office, so unless there's been a power shift of which I am unaware, I would suggest you not try to direct me on how to do my job."

Mayor Hensen looked like he would argue, but Emma never gave him the chance.

"Second, there is no statute of limitations on murder," Emma said. Her voice was low and soft with a lethal hiss, like a snake about to strike. "So I don't give a damn if Whitley was murdered last night or twenty years ago. If there is a clue relevant to her case, which has never been closed, then I will follow it to the ends of the earth if I have to, and I will do it at the same time that my team and I investigate the burglaries. Am I clear?"

Herb and Mayor Hensen exchanged seriously unhappy matching looks.

"Of course," Mayor Hensen said. "I wasn't telling you how to do your job."

"I'm sure you weren't," Emma said. "Given that you're not my boss."

Mayor Hensen's lips compressed into a thin line. Lindsey knew he didn't like to be reminded of the limitations of his position.

The hierarchy had been a sticking point in the relation-ship between the mayor and the chief of police for years. Both reported to the town council and were considered completely separate departments, although the mayor's office had been lobbying to have the police department put under its supervi-sion for as long as Lindsey had been in town and she sus-pected for even longer than that.

The town council was intractable on the topic, feeling that the possibility of corruption was too great if the police were to report to the mayor, which Lindsey thought was a valid point. The mayor, however, felt that having the police under his supervision would help the two departments work more closely together.

So far, not one Briar Creek police chief had felt the need to work more closely with the mayor's office. No one in town was surprised by this, except perhaps the mayor.

Mayor Hensen checked his watch. He rose from his seat with the stiff posture of a toddler who'd gotten his sandcastle kicked back into the dirt.

"If you'll excuse us," he said, "I have a presentation to give this afternoon at town hall that I need to prepare."

Herb rose too, grabbing his notepad and pen. He looked at the copy of the book on the table and Lindsey put her hand on it. She wasn't sure why, but instinct told her not to let either man touch it.

"I'll be in touch about the burglaries," Emma said.

Both men strode toward the door, but Herb paused in the doorway. He looked uncomfortable and then he said, "I'd appreciate being kept up to date on the Whitley case as well as the burglaries."

"Of course," Emma said.

Herb nodded stiffly and left the room. Lindsey turned to

look at Emma. She knew she had one eyebrow raised just like Emma did, as if to say, *What was that?*

"Was it just me or was that weird?" Lindsey asked. She took her hand off the book.

"That's an understatement," Emma said. "I know Hensen can be a bit of a blowhard, but he has never tried to tell me how to do my job before."

"Did you see Herb's face?" Lindsey asked. "He actually looked nervous and angry, but mostly nervous."

"Yeah, that was odd. It was almost as if he was afraid," Emma said. "I think I'm going to pull the case file on the Whitley murder and do some reading."

"Need any help with that?" Lindsey offered. She knew Emma wasn't likely to take her up on it but it never hurt to offer.

"No." Emma took the book and the overdue notice. "But thanks for offering."

"Sure," Lindsey said. Sensing their meeting was over she rose from her seat and held out her hand to help Emma up. The chief of police accepted the help and Lindsey steadied her, allowing her to get her balance on the unwieldy boot.

"I can't wait to be done with this thing," Emma said. "When it comes off, I'm buying a dozen pairs of really cute shoes, pink high heels with sparkly bows and any other ridiculous footwear that I never appreciated before."

"That is an excellent goal, although platforms are not the easiest things to chase bad guys with," Lindsey said. "And you'll wind up back in a cast."

"I know." Emma shook her head. "Every time I watch a cop show and they have the female detective wearing high heels, I want to kick her in the patootie. I mean, really, who writes those shows? It just ruins it. Ruins it, I tell you."

"I'm guessing male writers," Lindsey said. "Male writers with superhero-chick fantasies."

"Huh, those boys need to be schooled." Emma grunted as she hobbled across the room to her desk, where she sat down and propped her foot up.

"What are you going to do with the book?" Lindsey asked.

"I'll have Detective Trimble from the state police take it to their forensic lab," Emma said. "They have the equipment to check it over for any evidence not visible to the naked eye—you know, tiny fibers, blood splatter, stuff like that. After so much time, however . . ."

She zipped the book into an evidence bag and put it in her outbox. Lindsey felt a pang of worry. She wasn't sure if it was for the book or the mystery surrounding it, but she felt an unsettling sense of loss and unease as she headed to the door.

"Oh, Lindsey." Emma called her back.

"Yes?"

"When you start reading up on the old newspaper articles about the Whitley murder, let me know if you find anything of interest," Emma said. "Particularly if they mention her whereabouts on the day of her murder and if she had the book on her at the time of the murder. It's unlikely, but you never know. If the reporter writing up the story was detail-oriented, we may get lucky."

"I wasn't going to . . . Okay, yeah, sure I will," Lindsey said. Then she grinned. "You know me pretty well, Chief."

"It's my job," Emma said and returned Lindsey's smile. "Photocopies of anything of interest would be most welcome."

"Roger that."

Lindsey left the police station feeling slightly better about the situation. The fact that Emma thought the book might be a clue in Candice Whitley's murder made her feel less paranoid, although she supposed it should actually make her feel more paranoid, given that it meant there could very well be a murderer in Briar Creek.

The question she couldn't let go of, however, was why? Why had the book been returned now? What had changed that the murderer wanted to bring attention back to the murder case, or had it just been a mistake?

She felt a shiver start at the base of her spine and shimmy up her back vertebra by vertebra, ruining the calm she'd felt moments before. If the book being returned was a mistake, what would the murderer do to get the book back?

Lindsey picked up her pace as she hurried down the sidewalk toward the library. Housed in a square stone building that was formerly a captain's home, the library overlooked the town park and the ocean beyond.

The Thumb Islands, an archipelago of more than one hundred islands if the person counting them included the big rocks, filled the bay, giving Briar Creek a first line of defense against the hurricanes and foul weather that blew in across Long Island Sound.

Today there was no need to fear the weather as the sky was a pristine blue without even a puffy white cloud floating by to block the sun. The breeze was light and tugged at the ends of Lindsey's long blond curls, snapping them just like it did the flags that flew high on the pole in front of the library.

Lindsey took a deep calming breath of the briny sea air. She glanced at the building before her. It was solid and strong, resembling a fortress of knowledge found in volumes and volumes of years of accumulated wisdom.

There. That made her feel better. She had no reason to panic. The answer to any question was always within reach.

And in this case, she might be borrowing trouble for no reason.

The book might not be the clue she feared it was. The person who returned it may have had nothing to do with Candice Whitley's death. Even if it was the murderer, they might not even realize they had returned the book. Truly, she was making herself nervous for nothing.

She stepped onto the rubber mat and the automatic doors whooshed open.

"Lindsey, help!"

She glanced up as she strode across the main room to see her library assistant Ann Marie Martin waving to her. She looked like she was signaling for Lindsey to throw her a life preserver in a choppy sea. Lindsey turned in her direction and picked up her pace.

Ann Marie had recently been promoted from a clerk position in circulation to a library assistant in reference. Lindsey had been training her for a few weeks, but with so many resources to learn, it really took six months to a year before a new hire could manage the reference desk without second-guessing their abilities.

"How can I help?" Lindsey asked as she circled the desk to join Ann Marie behind it.

"I know there's a resource that will tell us what every library owns, but I can't find it," Ann Marie said. She frowned at the computer as if it had betrayed her.

"WorldCat," Lindsey said. "It's at the bottom of the list of electronic databases."

"That's it!" Ann Marie said. She glanced at the patron who stood waiting on the other side of the desk. "I told you she was a book wizard."

"Book Wizard; I like it," Lindsey said. "Sounds snazzier as a job title than *Information Specialist.*"

Lindsey smiled at the patron and recognized Brian Kelly. He was new to Briar Creek, having moved here from Portland, Oregon, just a few months ago. He had the hipster look going, with the skinny jeans, wrinkled flannel shirt, uneven face scruff, black-framed glasses and a beanie that covered his short-cropped thick black hair. Lindsey guessed he was somewhere around her age, give or take a few years.

"Hi, Brian, how are you?" she said.

They had only spoken a few times, but Brian was rapidly becoming one of her favorite patrons. He was very well-read and, while they had dissimilar tastes in reading material, she always enjoyed hearing his recommendations.

"I'm chill, how you doin'?" he asked.

Lindsey smiled. "Not chill, but okay."

Brian tipped his head to the side as he studied her. "You know what you need?"

"Oh, boy, hit me," she said.

"Shteyngart," he said. "Particularly, *Super Sad True Love Story.*"

"I don't know. I'm off the dystopian stuff," Lindsey said. "It tends to leave me in very bleak places, especially if the ending is a bummer. I'm not really up for an existential crisis right now."

"I hear what you're saying, but the snark factor is high in *Super Sad,*" Brian said. "I think you'd dig it."

"Maybe," she said. "I'll take it under advisement."

Ann Marie glanced between them while she tapped away on the keyboard. "It's like you're speaking English and yet I can't understand a word of it."

Brian and Lindsey grinned at each other.

"Sorry," Lindsey said. "Book-lover's shorthand."

"I have so much reading to do," Ann Marie said. As the mother of two rambunctious boys, her reading had been limited over the past few years to picture books and children's novels, but now that her boys were older, she was planning to make up for lost time. She seemed to leave work every evening with a big stack of books. Lindsey had no idea how she managed to get through them all.

"That's the one curse of this job," Lindsey said. "As hard as we try, we can't read them all."

"Okay, I think I've found the book of poems that you're looking for in three local libraries," Ann Marie said to Brian.

Lindsey observed Ann Marie's use of the World Catalog, a resource to which libraries from all over the world contributed. It was the most comprehensive catalog for materials worldwide, and Lindsey used it frequently to track down materials in other libraries for their patrons.

Ann Marie swiveled the monitor of her computer so that Brian could look at the listing.

"That's it," he said.

Ann Marie smiled. "One of the libraries will let us borrow it for you using interlibrary loan, but it may take a few weeks. The other two own the item but don't circulate it," she said.

"No problem," he said. "I can wait."

"I didn't know you were a poetry fan," Lindsey said.

"It's an interest of mine," Brian said.

He looked sheepish and Lindsey suspected it was more than an interest. She wondered what it would take to get him to let her read some of his poetry. She figured she'd wait until the right time to ask, like when his book came in.

"Here's the form I'll need you to fill out," Ann Marie said. "Then I'll go ahead and process this request."

"Thank you," Brian said.

Lindsey knew that Ann Marie could take it from here. "I'm going to head into my office. Call me if you need me."

"Good luck getting in there," Ann Marie said. She glanced over at the circulation desk and then shook her head.

Lindsey followed her gaze and gasped. In the time she'd been gone it looked like a dump truck had arrived to unload more materials on the library. She couldn't see Ms. Cole through the towering stacks of books. She knew that couldn't be good.

"Oh, boy," she said. It was with a certain sense of doom that she walked over to the circulation desk to help.

CHAPTER

5

BRIAR CREEK
PUBLIC LIBRARY

**"I**s that my sweater vest?" Lindsey asked Beth.

"Maybe."

"What do you mean, maybe? Either it is or it isn't."

"It depends upon whether you agree to loan it to me or not," Beth said.

They stood in the staff break room, taking a few minutes off from shelving the carts of books that filled the circulation area. With the amnesty close to being over, Lindsey had emptied the book drop for what she hoped would be the last time that day. Surely, no one else could be hoarding any more overdue books.

"Okay, why would I be loaning you my most favorite purple vest?" Lindsey asked. "The last time I checked it was hanging in the small closet in my office. Did you go into my closet? You do know that's my go-to vest for when it's freezing in here, right?"

Beth pursed her lips and studied the ceiling and then

began to whistle the tune to the story time song *Ten in the Bed*. Lindsey was not to be deterred.

"Beth," she said. She tried to make her voice sound stern but that just wasn't her gift.

"I saw it hanging in there when the door was open and I couldn't resist trying it on. If I cinch it with a belt, it's a perfect fit." Beth demonstrated by putting her hands on her hips and pantomiming a belt. Lindsey frowned.

"I'm sorry," she said. "Remember when we roomed together in grad school and you used my black formal gown to play the part of Maleficent during a story time at your internship in the Hill section of New Haven?"

"Vaguely," Beth said. She did not meet Lindsey's eyes.

"The dress came back crusty with toddler booger and vomit," Lindsey said.

"Oh, yeah, that was the same outreach preschool that gave me the flu, twice," Beth said. "It's all coming into focus now."

"I love you, you know I do," Lindsey said. "But I really don't want my favorite vest to come back crusty."

"Understood," Beth said. "I was merely hoping to use it for one program."

"Will the program include spit-up, poopy diapers and a bubble machine?" Lindsey asked. "Because that would be bad."

"No, it isn't for a story time. I would be wearing it for a program for the teens," Beth said. "Aidan and I have decided to cohost a gamers' prom."

"A whater's what?"

"Gamers' prom," Beth said. "You know, with music from popular video games, decorations that are video-game based and food. Can't you just see *Pac-Man* cupcakes or *Destiny* cookies?"

"I'm seeing frosting ground into the carpet and Ms. Cole stroking out," Lindsey said.

"No, it'll be great. The teens can LARP their favorite characters—"

"LARP? That sounds illegal. Is that illegal?" Lindsey asked. She could feel her anxiety start to spike.

"LARP means *live action role play*," Beth said. "Honestly, I thought you were hipper than this."

"Me, too," Lindsey said. "I think I need to spend more time in the children's area and bone up on my youth skills."

"Here's a tip," Beth said. "Don't use the words *bone up* around teens ever."

Lindsey snorted. "Got it."

"Anyway, we were thinking the teens could dress up as their favorite game characters," Beth said. "And Aidan and I are going in costume as Link and Princess Zelda."

"If I understood the reference it would be romantic, wouldn't it?" Lindsey asked.

Beth turned a pretty shade of pink and said, "Yeah, Link has to save Princess Zelda from Ganon. Isn't it great? I finally get to go to the prom with a man who isn't going to spend the evening trying to get past second base."

"Would that be because he doesn't have to try?" Lindsey asked. She wiggled her eyebrows and Beth turned an even deeper shade of pink.

"Maybe," she said. Then she giggled. "And Zelda always wears a purple tunic sort of thing over a white dress. This sweater vest is perfect, especially when I bling it out with some gold sleeves."

"No blinging!" Lindsey said. "If you borrow it, it comes back exactly as it left me."

She would have been fiercer about protecting her favorite

vest, but it did her heart good to see her friend so happy. Beth had been looking for a decent guy for a long time and by all accounts Aidan Barker was a keeper.

Lindsey and the crafternooners had done a thorough background check on him. After all, what was the point of being an information specialist if you couldn't use your skills for good, like checking out the judicial branch website for the state of Connecticut to see if the guy your friend was dating had served time or had outstanding arrest warrants?

"All right, you can borrow my vest," Lindsey said. "But take care of it."

"I promise. I'll even get it dry cleaned when I'm done."

"Deal," Lindsey said. Beth grinned and disappeared with a wave back into her natural habitat: the children's section of the library.

Lindsey walked back to the front of the building. She wanted to check on Ms. Cole. There had been a lot of *harrumphs* and told-you-so's coming from behind the piles of books all afternoon, but Lindsey had also seen Ms. Cole at her most vulnerable. Despite the lemon's gruff exterior, Lindsey wanted to make certain that she was all right. She hadn't asked to go home, so Lindsey assumed she was okay, but she felt it was important to be sure.

Of course, she also wanted to ask Ms. Cole about Candice Whitley. The lemon had been so overwrought about finding the overdue book that Lindsey was curious about how close Ms. Cole had been to Candice Whitley. She seemed to have been genuinely fond of the young teacher, which was remarkable mostly because the lemon was not fond of very many people.

Lindsey glanced around the main room of the library. Most of the regulars had gone home for dinner. She knew there would be a small rush after six that would last until seven thirty and then the final half hour would be quiet until they closed.

Lindsey glanced at the clock. She only had a few minutes until she was done for the day. Curiosity caused her to throw caution to the curb as she approached Ms. Cole, who was manning the front desk.

"How are you feeling, Ms. Cole?" she asked.

Ms. Cole glanced at her over the top of her reading glasses. Her eyes were narrowed with suspicion. She was no dummy.

"Fine," she answered. She glanced at the book trucks behind her. "Considering the amount of work that has deluged us."

"I wanted to make sure you were all right after . . ." Lindsey let her voice trail off. She wasn't sure Ms. Cole would appreciate her mentioning her bout of hyperventilation.

Sure enough, Ms. Cole drew herself up so that her back was ramrod straight. "I can assure you I am back to normal now that the shock has worn off."

"Good. I'm glad to hear it," Lindsey said. She watched as Ms. Cole checked in a few items. When she didn't move away, the lemon looked back at her, again over the top of her glasses, which Lindsey had to admit was quite the intimidating look.

"Was there something else?"

"Yes, actually," Lindsey said. She forced a smile. Ms. Cole didn't return it. Not a big surprise. "I was wondering what you could tell me about Candice Whitley?"

"No."

"No?"

"That's what I said." Ms. Cole continued checking in materials.

"But why?" Lindsey asked. "If we gather enough information, maybe we can help figure out what happened to her."

"That's why I said no. You are a librarian, not a detective," Ms. Cole said. "You need to comport yourself with the decorum of an information specialist, not an officer of the law."

"But—"

"No."

Ms. Cole stared at her as if she was willing her to go away. Talk about a stonewall. Lindsey felt like she had run at full speed into the bricks at Platform 9¾ and had not been able to magically slip through. Ouch!

Lindsey pursed her lips while she studied the lemon. She knew there had to be a way to get her to tell her what she wanted to know; she just had to hit the right button.

"You're right, of course," Lindsey said. "I just was thinking that if Candice was a very active library borrower then maybe there was more than the one book checked out to her, or if she was chronically late, there might be other items floating around out there that are also twenty years overdue."

"She was," Ms. Cole said. "And she wasn't."

"Was and wasn't what?" Lindsey asked.

"She was an active borrower but she was never late with her materials," Ms. Cole said. "Candice Whitley was a lovely person, inside and out, and she was very respectful with her borrowed items. She treated library books as a privilege."

"I see," Lindsey said. No wonder Candice had been a favorite of Ms. Cole's. She had obviously been an excellent library patron.

"She was also an excellent teacher," Ms. Cole said. "Her students adored her." She glanced at Lindsey with an annoyed look, realizing she had said far more than she meant to. "And that is all I'm going to say."

"Just because she appeared to have it all together doesn't mean she did," Paula said.

She was sitting on the other side of Ms. Cole, sorting a book truck. Her hair was tied in a thick purple braid and her colorful tattoos were just visible beneath the three-quarter-length sleeves of her shirt.

Lindsey gave her a wide-eyed look. Was she really going to engage Ms. Cole?

"What's that supposed to mean?" Ms. Cole snapped.

"Everyone has secrets." Paula shrugged.

Apparently, she was. Lindsey opened her mouth to steer the conversation in a new direction but Ms. Cole got there first.

"You don't know the first thing about Candice Whitley," the lemon sputtered.

"No, I don't," Paula agreed. "But you don't either, not really. People let you see what they want you to see, like Holden Caulfield in the book that started all this. He doesn't share his inner turmoil with anyone, so does anyone in the book really know him? No, that's why he is so full of angst."

Ms. Cole rolled her eyes. "That's nonsense."

"Is it? If you think about it," Paula continued, looking completely unfazed by Ms. Cole's disdain, "you can never really know another person no matter how close you are, because you aren't inside their mind and heart."

"That's just . . . That's ridiculous," Ms. Cole argued. "Of course you can know people. You can tell what they're really like from how they behave, from what they say and do. It's actions that define a person, not their inner turmoil or angst. Some people don't have any angst, you know."

Paula glanced away and Lindsey watched a shadow pass over her face. She knew Paula had a past; Paula had alluded to it in previous conversations. But Lindsey didn't know the details and she hadn't shared what she did know with her staff. It was none of their business, just as it was none of hers.

She suspected it was her past that made Paula see things the way she did. Lindsey could understand that and she agreed with the young woman.

"I think what Paula is saying is that we all have an internal life that no one else has access to," Lindsey said. "What a person presents to the world might not be an accurate depiction of who they really are, for better or worse, and that includes Candice Whitley."

"Well, I say she was a lovely young woman who was murdered in cold blood," Ms. Cole said. "Whoever killed her strangled the life out of her. There was absolutely nothing she could ever have done to warrant a death like that."

"On that, we all agree," Paula said. "Her death is a horrible tragedy. You seemed to have known her and liked her. I am sorry for your loss, Ms. Cole."

The lemon stared at Paula hard for a moment and then she gave her a quick nod. "Thank you. Now let's get back to work. These books aren't going to check themselves in."

Crisis averted. Lindsey knew she had gotten more out of Ms. Cole than she thought she would, so she'd have to be content with it. She was debating whether or not to question the library pages, who at the moment were all busy shelving, when the front doors opened and in strode Herb Gunderson.

He looked ill at ease and when Lindsey waved to him, he gave a half wave back and scurried over to the DVD rack.

"That's odd," Ms. Cole said. "Herb always comes in on Fridays to check out movies, never Thursdays."

"His internal life must have dictated that he do otherwise today," Paula teased. "See? You never can tell . . ."

Ms. Cole hushed her. "He looks nervous and a bit twitchy. Do you think he looks nervous?"

Lindsey watched him cross his arms and tuck his hands

under his armpits. It seemed like a self-soothing sort of gesture. She'd never seen him do that before.

"Yeah, there's definitely some anxiety happening there," she said.

"Small wonder," Ms. Cole said. "Having that book show up after twenty years has got to be his worst nightmare."

"Why?" Lindsey asked. She was afraid to question Ms. Cole too deeply lest she clam up, so she tried to appear casual even as she hung on every word Ms. Cole uttered.

"Because Herb's younger brother Benji Gunderson was Candice Whitley's boyfriend at the time of her murder. He was also one of the primary suspects."

CHAPTER

6

BRIAR CREEK
PUBLIC LIBRARY

"Are you kidding me?" Lindsey asked.

"I never kid," Ms. Cole said.

"Yeah, what are you thinking?" Paula asked Lindsey.

"I wasn't," she said. She resisted the urge to do a face palm. "So that's why he was so weird when I brought the book over to Emma when he and the mayor were there."

"The Gunderson family has barely recovered their good name," Ms. Cole said. "Well, except for Benji; he never will."

"Poor Herb," Lindsey said. "I had no idea. He never said."

"Of course he didn't," Ms. Cole said. "The shame has dogged him his entire life. Why do you think he works so hard for the mayor? He's been trying to rid his family of the gossip ever since that horrible night."

Lindsey tried not to stare as Herb perused the DVD collection. She imagined that the very by-the-book town manager had to be rattled to the core, which was probably why he was here. Since he was looking at the movies a day earlier than usual, she suspected that he wanted more than movies from the library.

Ten minutes later, when he approached the desk, she was proven right.

"Lindsey, hi, how are you?" he asked with a feigned note of surprise, because finding the librarian in the library would be a real shock. Not.

"I'm fine," she said. "And you?"

"Good, really good. Say, could I have a word?" he asked.

"Sure," she said.

He glanced at Ms. Cole and Paula, and Lindsey got the feeling he didn't want to talk in front of them. She waited while Ms. Cole checked out the movie he handed her and Lindsey walked with him toward the door.

"What can I do for you?" she asked.

"I was just wondering if Emma told you what she was going to do with the book."

"Oh, the book," Lindsey said. She hesitated for a second but then decided that Emma wouldn't care if she told him. She certainly hadn't asked her to keep it a secret. "She was planning to turn it over to the state police to see if their forensic unit can find anything on it that might indicate if it was in Candice's possession at the time of the murder."

"Oh, I see. That's good, very good," Herb said. He sounded as if he was talking himself into believing it. "Excellent."

"She said it could take weeks or months before they get to it," Lindsey said. "And even then, after all these years they may not find anything."

Herb nodded. It was a quick, jerky motion, as if he was just trying to make it all go away. Lindsey felt bad for him but she also felt that she had done the right thing. Whether

Benji Gunderson was involved in the murder of Candice Whitley or not, she deserved justice.

"Well, I'll let you go," he said. He turned and left the library and Lindsey noticed that despite the pleasant evening, his shoulders were slumped as if in defeat.

She knew she shouldn't feel guilty, that she had nothing to feel guilty about, but still she felt bad for him. One of the things she had learned early on with Herb was that appearances were always so important to him. Following the rules even when they didn't make sense was his modus operandi in every staff meeting Lindsey had suffered through with him.

Maybe he'd always been like that or maybe it came after what his family had been through. She didn't know; she just knew that the case being reopened and his family being under scrutiny again had to be horribly uncomfortable for him.

If she'd been quicker-witted, she would have asked him about his brother Benji. It was probably a good thing she hadn't. Herb had looked worried enough without an inquisition.

She opened the door to the small room that housed the book drop to check it one more time. It was still empty. She would have cried with relief but she didn't want Ms. Cole to see her. As it was, she was pretty sure if she brought any more books to the circulation desk, Ms. Cole might stab her with a pen.

She switched out the light and closed the door. It was just about time for her to call it a day. She turned, slammed right into a solid male chest and yelped.

"Oh, sorry, didn't mean to get you in a fizz," Robbie Vine said. He caught her by the shoulders to keep her from toppling backward.

"Ugh." Lindsey blew out a breath. "Sorry. It's been one of those days."

"I heard there's been some excitement in the stacks today," Robbie said. "So, where do we start?"

"Excuse me?" she said.

She stepped out of his hold, trying to look casual about it, but judging by the twitch of his lips she failed miserably.

She gave him a stern look. Robbie was a handsome British actor currently residing in Briar Creek. He had gotten it into his head that he and Lindsey would make a fine couple, and while she did find him attractive, Lindsey knew that his life wasn't here and that he would be leaving sooner rather than later to resume his role as an actor, and that life just wasn't for her.

"Start what, exactly?" she asked.

"Our investigation, naturally. I heard a book was returned today, after twenty years, and that it had been checked out by a woman on the same day that she was murdered," he said. He shivered. "Makes my neck prickle just to think about it."

"Huh, looks like the rumor mill got that one right," she said.

"So." Robbie clapped his hands together. "What have you discovered about it so far?"

"What do you mean?"

"Please, love, I know you," he said. "This is going to nag you like a loose thread. I'd wager my last dollar that you've already started—"

"Hi, Dad!"

Lindsey and Robbie turned around to see Dylan Peet, one of her library pages, walking toward them.

"Hello, son," Robbie said. The affection in his voice was obvious as he regarded the teen.

Robbie had arrived in Briar Creek the previous year to help his longtime friend Violet La Rue with her community theater production of *A Midsummer Night's Dream*. In the process, he had reconnected with his son, Dylan, and was thoroughly enjoying his role as a father.

Lindsey glanced between them, marveling at their similarities. While Dylan's hair was a deeper auburn than his father's reddish blond, they shared the same green eyes and devilish grin, the sort that charmed good girls into all sorts of bad decisions.

"Are you ready for supper?" Robbie asked. "I made my specialty, bangers and mash."

"Excellent," Dylan said. "I just need to grab my backpack from the break room." He turned to face Lindsey. "I'll come in tomorrow for extra hours, if that's okay, and get these carts shelved."

"Okay?" Lindsey asked. "That would be outstanding."

Dylan grinned and it practically blinded her. She watched him walk away with a bounce in his step that reminded her so much of Robbie.

"He is more like you every day," she said. "Although if I remember right you used to have a few inches on him in height. He's closing the gap."

Robbie looked chagrined. "I know. He's almost an adult. I missed so much of his childhood. I can never get those years back."

"No, but you have each other now," Lindsey said. "And you arrived just when he needed you most."

"Ay, there's that," Robbie said. "He's a great kid. He's trying to figure out what sort of relationship he wants with his adoptive parents. I told him I'll support whatever he decides. I'm just glad to have him in my life."

Lindsey reached out and squeezed his arm. "You're a good dad, Robbie, and he's lucky to have you."

Robbie looped an arm around her shoulder and gave her a half hug. Then he kissed her forehead.

"Thanks," he said. His voice was gruff and he cleared his throat. When he spoke again, his voice had its usual teasing lilt. "I hear some women find the father thing very attractive."

He gave her a decidedly flirtatious look.

Lindsey shook her head at him. "No."

"No, what?" he protested. "I didn't even ask you anything."

"You know I'm not going to date you," she said. "Save your come-hither looks for women who will."

Robbie wrinkled his nose as if he smelled something bad.

"Is it Sully? That sailor boy of yours?"

"My personal life is none of your business," she said. "And he's not mine."

"Not my business?" Robbie gaped. "I got divorced for you."

Lindsey dropped her head to her chest. Over the past few months, she and Robbie had been over this and over this.

"I never asked you to get divorced," she said. "You and I have never really dated. We're just friends, and I think it's best that we keep it that way."

"So, it is the water rat!" Robbie said. Per usual, he completely ignored her words about them not dating ever. "What do you see in him?"

"Let me think," she said "He's good, kind, strong, funny, smart . . ."

"Okay, enough. I swear I'm going to puke," he said.

"Not on our carpet," she said with a laugh. "Take it outside to the bushes if you're going to be sick."

"You didn't say handsome," Robbie said. "You have to admit I have him beat in the looks department."

"He's handsome," she said. "And you know it."

"Oh, come now, there has to be something I've got that he hasn't," Robbie said.

He looked put out, and Lindsey couldn't help but take pity on him.

"You *are* more emotional than he is," she said.

"What, as in girly?" he cried. He looked appalled.

"No, like openhearted and emotionally available," she said. "Trust me, it's a good thing."

"So, what exactly is going on between you and Sully?" he asked. "I've been watching but I haven't seen any actual dates happen. Are you two dating?"

"I don't know." Lindsey shrugged.

It was the honest truth; she really didn't know. They'd begun spending more time together a couple of months ago, and it seemed to be going well, but she knew they were both being very cautious. By unspoken agreement, they hadn't said anything to anyone about the time they spent together, preferring to keep it private until they knew where they stood for sure.

She envied Beth's situation where she was free to just fall head over heels in love with Aidan. But that was more in Beth's nature than Lindsey's. Lindsey had always been more careful, a bit of an overthinker some might say.

"That's not an answer," Robbie said. He glared out the window toward the pier where Sully docked his water taxi and tour boats. "Tell me this: Are you in love with him?"

Lindsey blinked. There it was. The "L" word again. She and Sully hadn't gotten there yet. She hadn't even allowed herself to think about it. They were very much doing a baby-steps sort of thing with their relationship. To have Robbie ask her flat out, well, she just wasn't prepared.

"Um . . ." She didn't know what to say. She felt her face get scorching hot and she pressed her palms to her cheeks.

"Oh, Bloody Nora! You are, aren't you?" he cried. Suddenly, he staggered back, clutching his chest. He careened around the lobby, hunched over and moaning.

"Robbie, are you all right?" she asked. "Can I get you something? Water? Ice? Should I call a doctor?"

"No, no," he said. He waved her off and spoke through gritted teeth. "I'm sure it's nothing."

"But—" she began, but he interrupted with a groan as he grabbed the counter in front of Ms. Cole.

Ms. Cole looked at him over her glasses. She seemed singularly unimpressed.

"My heart," Robbie cried.

Lindsey's eyes went wide. "Are you having a heart attack?"

She rushed forward as he slumped to the floor. She caught him before his head connected with the ground and cradled his upper body in her lap with his head on her shoulder.

"Ms. Cole, call 9-1-1," Lindsey said.

"No," Ms. Cole said.

"He's having a heart attack," Lindsey said.

"No, he isn't," Paula said. She popped up beside Ms. Cole as they both peered over the counter at Lindsey and Robbie.

"The pain," Robbie moaned. "How does a heart withstand the deep cut from the sharp blade of apathy?"

"He's acting out the breakup scene from his last movie," Paula said. "You know, where the hero dies of a broken heart. Great death scene, really, top notch. It even made me cry, and I never cry."

Lindsey lifted one eyebrow and glared down at him. "Are you using a movie line on me?"

"That depends," he said. "Is it working?"

"You're impossible." Lindsey huffed and shoved him out of her lap.

"Impossibly cute? Impossibly charming? Impossible to resist? I'm not picky," he said. He propped himself up on an elbow.

"Just impossible," she said.

Robbie fell back into an undignified heap on the industrial carpet. He lay there, clutching his chest and moaning. Lindsey ignored him and stood up, brushing off her clothes.

The front doors slid open and a bark broke the quiet of the library. Lindsey glanced up to see her black fuzzball of a dog, Heathcliff, racing toward her at top speed.

"Hey, buddy," she said. She bent over to scratch his head while he hugged her leg with his front paws.

Following behind him was Captain Mike Sullivan, or as he was known locally, Sully. He was wearing his usual jeans and a T-shirt. His trim build and muscle-hardened physique were made for the casual attire. His reddish brown curls were windswept and his face and arms were tan from hours spent in the sun. He was smiling when he saw Lindsey but his smile went sideways when he caught sight of Robbie on the floor.

"Don't tell me he finally wore out his welcome and you brained him with the heaviest book in the collection," he said.

Paula snorted and Ms. Cole made a hiccupping noise that Lindsey thought might have been a laugh, but then again, Ms. Cole and Robbie both liked to perform in the theater so she could very well be commiserating with him.

"My heart is broken, if you must know," Robbie said.

"Really?" Sully asked. He frowned. "I thought you had to have a heart for it to be broken."

"Ah, and the hits keep coming!" Robbie clutched his chest and Heathcliff abandoned Lindsey to jump on him. He licked Robbie's face as if his dog spit was a magical elixir with healing powers that would get Robbie back up on his feet.

Robbie scratched the dog's ears and sat up. "Thank you, mate. At least someone cares."

"Your heart is not broken," Lindsey said. She held out a hand to him to help him rise to his feet.

"Of course it is if he's the one you're in lov—" Robbie began but, realizing what he was about to say, Lindsey stomped on his foot, effectively cutting off his words.

"Yeow!" Robbie cried.

"Oh, sorry, clumsy me." Lindsey turned back to Sully.

"Thanks for bringing Heathcliff by," she said. She smiled at him in what she hoped was a normally friendly way and not the panic-induced fit it felt like.

"No problem," he said. "Nancy asked me to bring him to you since she had self-defense class with Violet to attend."

"Oh, right, I forgot," she said.

Sully put a hand on the back of his neck, looking distinctly uncomfortable in front of the audience that was Ms. Cole, Paula and Robbie. "Did you want a lift home? I'm headed that way to visit my friend Tom."

"That'd be great, thanks," she said.

"What?" Robbie squawked. "He's giving you a lift when I'm clearly the one who is crippled."

"You're fine," Lindsey said. She turned to Sully and said, "Would you mind grabbing my purse from my desk while I help Robbie to a chair? I feel bad that I've injured him."

"I can help him," Sully offered. It was grudging at best.

"No, I don't think so," she said. "You might drop him on his head."

"Not the worst idea," Sully said. He gave Robbie a mock scowl and then whistled for Heathcliff to follow him as they went into Lindsey's office for her things.

"Dogs aren't allowed . . ." Ms. Cole's voice trailed off as both Sully and Heathcliff ignored her. *"Harrumph."*

Lindsey took Robbie's arm and led him to a nearby chair. His green eyes were twinkling at her.

"Sorry I stomped on you," she said.

"I'm not." His grin was full of mischief.

"What? Why?" she asked.

"You haven't told him yet," he said.

"Told him what?" She tried to play dumb, but Robbie was an amazing study of people and there was no fooling him.

"That you love him," he said. "You two aren't fooling me with this friends thing you're trying to pull off. Anyone with eyes can see that there is more going on here."

She heaved a sigh. "Not that it's any of your business, but we are just friends who are open to the possibility of more."

"Ha! So, he hasn't said it yet either!" Robbie bounced up from his seat, looking awfully chipper for a guy who had just been in the throes of death and nearly crippled. "Now I have hope."

"No, you don't," Lindsey said. "This changes nothing, because you and I are really just friends. Period."

"Actually," he said, "this changes everything. Mark my words, Lindsey Norris, I'll win you over yet."

Then he took her hand and kissed the back of it like it was the year eighteen sixteen not twenty sixteen.

Before Lindsey could utter a word of discouragement,

Dylan appeared from the back room. She didn't have the heart to chastise Robbie in front of his son. She merely shook her head at him and his grin deepened.

Dylan glanced between them, clearly bewildered by what was happening between his father and his boss. He wasn't the only one. Lindsey had a feeling Robbie was going to try her patience right to the end before she got through to him. Unfazed, Robbie threw his arm around his son's shoulders and strode out the doors of the library with a cheery wave and a wink.

"Did he really just kiss your hand? I think I might be ill," Sully said. He handed Lindsey her purse and stared out the door at Robbie's departing back.

"There seems to be a lot of that going around." At Sully's questioning look, she added, "Never mind. And don't worry. You know Robbie, he just likes to make an exit."

"Yes, but why does it never last?" Sully asked.

CHAPTER

7

BRIAR CREEK
PUBLIC LIBRARY

Lindsey laughed. "I think you'd miss him if he was gone," she said.

"Not even a little," Sully said. He gave her a side eye and then said, "Okay, maybe a smidgen, but that's it, and that's only because you have chosen not to date him."

"He grows on you."

"Like a fungus."

Lindsey grinned. She wanted to hug him, but they were still in public and they had been avoiding any sort of public displays of affection to keep the gossip on their status to a minimum until they were ready to share.

"Come on, I have so much to tell you about today," she said.

"Really?" he asked. "Now I'm intrigued. Let's go."

Lindsey glanced back at her staff. Paula waved and Ms. Cole gave her a curt nod. It was their night to close the building, so she knew she didn't have to worry.

That was the beauty of Ms. Cole. Despite her medieval librarian ways, she was a model of efficiency when it came to the policy and procedure of closing the building down. In the few years Lindsey had been here, she had come to rely on Ms. Cole to get the job done.

"Good night," Lindsey said. "Call me if you need me."

Beth popped up from behind the children's desk and waved. Sully paused in the doorway to clip Heathcliff's leash onto his collar and the three of them left the building in the very capable hands of Lindsey's staff.

"Dinner at my place okay?" Sully asked. "I have steaks to grill."

"Sounds perfect," she said.

He opened the passenger door for her and she waited for Heathcliff to jump into the pickup truck before climbing in herself. Sully shut the door after her and then strode around the front to climb into the driver's seat.

As soon as Sully turned on the engine, Heathcliff climbed over Lindsey's lap to stick his head out the window. She rolled it down and took ahold of his leash on the off chance he got overexcited and tried to leap out.

It was a short ride to Sully's house on the shore. As soon as Sully parked the truck, Heathcliff jumped out of the cab and began to mark his territory around the yard of the weathered gray house as if afraid in his absence another dog might have laid claim to the three-bedroom cottage.

"My curiosity is killing me," Sully said as he unlocked the door. "Tell me what happened today."

Lindsey and Heathcliff followed him into the tiled foyer, which gave way to the kitchen. Heathcliff went to patrol the house, again probably checking that his turf was secure, while Sully went to the fridge and grabbed a beer for himself and poured a glass of wine for Lindsey. As she dropped her handbag on the floor and took a seat at the granite counter, she took a moment to appreciate the sense of homecoming she felt being here with Sully.

He ducked outside to switch on his gas grill and when he came back, he pushed the glass toward her and said, "Talk."

Lindsey took a sip and settled in to watch him prep their dinner. She did love to watch him cook.

"Candice Whitley," she said.

Sully was foraging in his vegetable crisper for the fixings for a salad and when Lindsey said the name he jerked upright, smacking the back of his head on the top shelf of the refrigerator.

"Sorry!" Lindsey cried.

"It's okay." He turned around, holding the back of his head with one hand while cradling a head of butter lettuce with the other. "But I could have sworn you said—"

"Candice Whitley," they said together.

"I did," Lindsey confirmed.

"The same Candice Whitley who was murdered twenty years ago, the high school English teacher found strangled to death under the football bleachers?"

"That's the one."

Sully put down the lettuce and picked up his beer. He eyed Lindsey over the bottle while he took a long drink. Then he shook his head as if trying to shake off a passel of bad memories.

"Okay, I'm ready now," he said. "Explain."

"Today was our first library fine amnesty day," Lindsey said. "Any overdue books or other materials were accepted no matter their condition and fines were wiped clean. We got way more books than I anticipated, but that's okay."

Sully nodded. "I noticed the pile behind the circulation desk. Plus, Ms. Cole appeared to be battling an eye twitch."

Lindsey smiled. "Yeah, there was that. Anyway, one of the returned books was over twenty years overdue, so I had to know who had checked it out. Ms. Cole keeps all of those records, so we looked it up and it had been checked out to Candice Whitley."

"Whoa."

"It gets weirder. It was checked out to her on the day she was murdered."

Sully glanced down at his forearm and then rubbed the hairs that were standing up. "Chills. I just got chills."

"We all did," she said. "Ms. Cole actually hyperventilated. Thank goodness Milton was there to help me calm her down."

"She recovered enough to stay at work," Sully said. "Then again, I imagine it would take more than hyperventilating to get her to call out, especially during a fine amnesty."

"She is made of good New England stock," Lindsey said. "I was surprised at how emotional she became. It really wasn't like her at all."

"Ms. Whitley touched a lot of lives," Sully said. "What book was it?"

"Salinger's *The Catcher in the Rye*."

"Huh." Sully frowned.

His bright blue eyes looked lost in thought and Lindsey wondered what he was thinking. She didn't ask, knowing that he would tell her when he was ready. Instead, she sipped her wine and waited.

"I had Ms. Whitley for English two years before she died," he said. "At the time, she seemed like such a grown-up to me, but looking back I realize she wasn't much older than any of her students. She was only in her midtwenties, so she had maybe ten years on us, if that."

"What was she like?"

"Smart, pretty, patient," Sully said. "I remember we had a guy in class, Joey Prentice, who was a menace. His entire academic career was spent seeing if he could make his teachers cry, including the male ones."

"I think I know the type," Lindsey said. "They're the ones who usually avoid the library at all costs, so my run-ins with them during my youth were few and far between."

"Yeah, I doubt if Joey even knew the school had a library, at least for most of his high school career," he said.

"Did Joey make Ms. Whitley cry?"

"He tried. He had it in for her from day one. He did every textbook rotten thing a student could do to a teacher. He put tacks on her seat, glued the pages of her dictionary together—"

Lindsey let out a gasp of alarm and he smiled.

"He stole knickknacks off her desk and held them for ransom, he moved the hands of her clock ahead so that she thought class ended ten minutes earlier than it did."

Sully was grinning and Lindsey gave him a chastising look. "It looks like he wasn't the only one who enjoyed the pranks."

"Oh, it was funny," he said. "But Ms. Whitley wasn't one to take that kind of behavior sitting down."

"Especially with tacks on her seat."

"Exactly. No, you don't need to feel bad about Joey picking on her. She got her revenge."

"How?" Lindsey asked. Her mind began to race. Had Ms. Whitley publicly shamed the prankster? Maybe Joey murdered her as payback in their prank war and no one had put it together until now.

"She taught him how to read," Sully said.

Lindsey blinked. Of all the answers she had expected that was not one of them, not even close.

"I know," he said. "Pretty amazing, right? Joey caused so much of a ruckus in her classroom that she had him stay after school just about every day. What he didn't realize is that she used the time to diagnose his dyslexia and teach him how to cope with it. It was an intensive one-on-one learning session that by the end of our school year had him passing English with a solid B+."

"That's incredible."

"That's the sort of teacher she was," Sully said. His voice was soft. "No one cried harder when she was killed than Joey."

Lindsey ran a finger down the side of her glass, following the drips of condensation. The loss of such a good teacher had to have been quite a blow to the small community.

"What happened to him?"

"He went on to college and became a teacher," Sully said. "Now he teaches history in New London."

"She made a lasting difference there," Lindsey said. "What more could she have done, how many other students could she have helped, if her life hadn't been cut short? I suppose we can only hope that the book offers some clues as to who murdered her so that justice is finally served."

Sully slowly lowered his beer and gave her a pained look. "I'm guessing you have more to tell me."

"Just a teeny bit," she said.

She held up her thumb and pointer finger so that they were just an inch apart. Then she told him about the rest of her day. He prepped the food while she told him about giving the book to Emma and about Herb's nervous visit to the library.

When Sully gestured for her to follow him outside, she

picked up her wine and followed him out onto the deck where he cooked and she talked until the steaks were sizzling and she was out of details to share.

Sully leaned against the railing on his back deck and stared past the sandy dunes and out into the bay.

"It's hard to believe that after all this time, her murderer would be so dumb as to return the book she had with her on the day she died," he said.

"It might not have been her murderer," Lindsey said. "It's just that the coincidence of her checking out the book on the same day that she died is . . . unsettling."

"I don't believe in coincidences generally. Besides, if it wasn't her murderer who took the book when he killed her then why wasn't it turned in years ago?" Sully asked.

"That is the question, isn't it?"

Lindsey moved to stand beside him and pressed her body into his, seeking comfort. Sully put an arm around her and they stared out at the bay together.

"You know who you might want to talk to about the book?" he said after a few minutes.

"Me? Talk to anyone about the book?" she asked. She gave him a surprised look that she knew he knew was bogus. "That sounds like you think I might meddle."

"Shocking thought, I know," he said with a chuckle. "I am just embracing what I know to be true."

"I like the embracing part," she said. She hugged him to her. He returned it by wrapping both his arms around her and holding her close. It was the most peaceful Lindsey had felt all day.

"I'm thinking you should talk to Chief Daniels—rather, former Chief Daniels," Sully said.

Lindsey pulled back to study his face. "Daniels? Who was

the chief before Emma? The one who thought I was a nosey parker and if I remember right was not exactly my number one fan?"

"That's the one," Sully said. "He was on the force at the time of Candice Whitley's death but wasn't chief yet. He might remember something about the book, if it was found at the scene or whatnot. It's worth a shot."

"Do you really think he'd talk to me?" she asked.

Sully shrugged. "You won't know until you try. Besides, I'm sure Emma will talk to him, too, so he'll probably be expecting you."

"Because I'm that big of a buttinsky?" Lindsey asked.

"Well, it does have to do with a library book, so you've got that connection going for you, but yes, your reputation for being inquisitive is well-known."

"I'm not sure that's a good thing," she said.

"I find it alarmingly charming," he assured her.

"That might be the nicest thing you've ever said to me," she teased.

He laughed. "I'm going to have to work on my material, then."

As if by unspoken mutual agreement, they didn't discuss Candice Whitley or the book during dinner. Lindsey was relieved. She felt as if the cold case had consumed her for most of the day and it was such a tragic story that it felt draining to keep thinking about it.

After the dishes were done, they decided to take a walk along the beach and let Heathcliff run himself to exhaustion. They held hands while they walked, laughing at Heathcliff as he tried to chase the waves that chased him back, making him bark at the water in a playful way.

Lindsey inhaled the salty sea air and let the cool ocean breeze swirl around her. Maybe it was because her day had been consumed with tragedy, but she realized that this was one of those perfect life moments.

She knew how lucky she was to have both Sully and Heathcliff in her life. To share dinner and companionship with her two men was a gift beyond measure. The urge to let Sully know how much she cared for him bubbled to the surface but she held her tongue. They were taking it slow; they hadn't even gone public yet, and she didn't want to bust out the "L" word before he was ready to hear it.

She supposed it was cowardly to hold it in, but she was aware that today had been an emotional roller coaster and she didn't want to be swept up in the moment and ruin the new relationship she and Sully were making by rushing things.

"What are you thinking?" Sully asked as he pulled her close and let go of her hand to put his arm around her waist, securing her to his side.

"I'm trying to decide if Heathcliff is going to need a bath tonight," she said.

Sully kissed her head. His voice was low when he whispered in her ear, "I'm happy to help, you know, if you two want to stay over."

Lindsey pulled away and looked up at him. "I don't know. Nancy and Charlie might notice if I don't come home tonight."

Sully didn't say anything. He simply watched her, waiting for her to work through it.

"I mean, we're still taking it slow, right?" she asked.

He nodded as he pulled her close so there was no space in between them. Lindsey was pretty sure she went cross-eyed at the body-to-body contact, but she pressed on.

"I mean, we don't want people to get the wrong idea," she said. "If we're just friends, then I probably shouldn't be spending the night."

"We're not just friends," Sully said. "And we haven't been for a while."

"Oh," she said. "Okay."

"If you spend the night tonight, we could actually just sleep," he said. "Although, I will try to convince you otherwise."

He kissed her right there in the middle of the beach with Heathcliff racing around their feet, barking his fool head off. When he pulled away, Lindsey had made her decision.

"Well, all right, then," she said. "A sleepover it is."

The smile Sully sent her was blinding and again she was tempted to tell him what she was feeling, but she kissed him instead, driving all thought of big emotional confessions right out of her head for the moment.

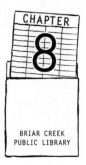

Lindsey stood on the Daniels' doorstep, knowing she was overstepping her boundaries and pushing the doorbell anyway. She supposed if she wanted to justify her reason for being here then she could claim that she was just following up on the overdue book, but really, that sort of defeated the whole point of an amnesty day, when people were allowed to return their long-overdue items without fear of retribution.

She heard the bell ring somewhere in the house. She waited, wondering what she was going to say when the door opened. Should she get right to it, make small talk, what?

The door clicked as it was unlocked from the inside, and for a nanosecond, she thought about fleeing the scene—because that was so mature. Before she could bolt, the door was pulled open and Chief Daniels stood there looking ten years younger than when he'd retired. She'd heard retirement did that for people, like turning back the clock, drinking out of the fountain of youth or finally just getting enough carefree sleep.

He looked slimmer than she remembered. He was wearing jeans and a long-sleeved T-shirt with a black apron over it that looked like a flak jacket from a SWAT team. Very clever.

"Lindsey Norris," he said. "What brings you here?"

"Murder," she said.

Daniels's eyebrows rose up on his forehead. From somewhere in the house a beeping sound started and he glanced over his shoulder and then back at her.

"That's my sauce," he said. "Come on in and you can explain while I cook."

Lindsey followed him into the raised ranch. They went up the stairs and through the living room to the kitchen. It was a big wide-open space full of granite and copper with double everything: ovens, sinks and dishwashers.

"You're like a regular Rachael Ray," she said.

Daniels laughed. "I'll take that as a compliment. I've been working on my barbecue recipes. I'm going to publish a cookbook one day."

Lindsey paused to sniff the air. "Is that what smells so good? I'll put in my order for a copy of the book now."

"I'm working on a honey pecan barbecue sauce," Daniels said as he hurried over to the stove to stir something in the pot.

Lindsey checked her chin for drool. Seriously, if it tasted as good as it smelled, he was definitely cooking up a winner.

He stirred the sauce with a large wooden spoon and adjusted the temperature of the stove by turning the dial. He then moved to the oven and opened the door. He grabbed two pot holders and pulled out a large baking dish, shutting the oven door with his foot.

"Do you mind getting the door?" he asked.

"Sure," Lindsey said.

She moved across the kitchen and opened the door that led outside to the deck. Daniels hustled the heavy dish out the door and Lindsey slid it closed behind her as she followed him. He set the glass dish down on the table and then opened the lid to one of three grills that filled the raised deck. He used big metal tongs to plop the ribs on the hot grill.

Lindsey opened her mouth to speak, but he gestured her to wait.

"One more second," he said.

He hurried back inside and grabbed the pot off of the stove. Then he dashed back outside and used a brush to coat the ribs with the amazing-smelling sauce. Lindsey wondered if she could make her questions last until lunchtime and wrangle an invitation to eat. Yes, it smelled that good.

Once the ribs were coated, Daniels closed the lid and turned back to Lindsey.

"Okay, what's this about murder, and why are you talking to me instead of Chief Plewicki?"

He gestured for her to take one of the two Adirondack chairs that sat on the far side of the deck away from the grills, and Lindsey sat in one while he took the other.

"Because you were there and Emma wasn't," Lindsey said.

Daniels frowned. "Are you talking about what happened to the book author a couple of years ago? I thought that case was dusted and done."

"No, this goes further back to when you were a uniformed officer," she said.

"Candice Whitley," he said. He turned away from her and stared out into the trees at the end of his yard. They were leafy and green and full of the promise of the new life of spring.

"How'd you guess?"

"I heard that a library book that had been loaned to her was returned," he said with a shrug. "Small town."

"Not only was it checked out to her," Lindsey said, "it was checked out to her on the day she died."

Daniels tried to suppress a shudder and failed. Lindsey knew he was feeling the exact same thing everyone else felt when they heard. Chilled to the bone, and not from the cool spring temperatures either.

"So, you're thinking it was returned by her murderer," he said.

"Maybe," Lindsey said. "Sully told me you were on the force during the original investigation, and I was wondering if you remembered anything that might seem significant in hindsight."

"Like whether she had a library book with her or not?" Daniels asked. Lindsey nodded.

Daniels glanced back at the woods while he thought about it. His eyes narrowed as if he were trying to look through the trees of the present and into the past. He rubbed his chin with the back of his hand. His voice sounded gruff when he spoke, as if traveling through his memories was a rough ride.

"It—rather, Candice—was my first dead body, not only professionally but in life," he said. "I'd never seen death before. To see it up close and personal like that on someone about the same age as myself, who by all accounts didn't have any enemies and was well liked, well, it was tough. I had nightmares for weeks."

Lindsey knew exactly how he felt. She'd brushed up against death more than she'd liked over the past few years.

She nodded at him in understanding, encouraging him to continue.

"I was the new guy on the force, the rookie, so I was the one on evening patrol when the call came in," he said. "An older couple was walking their dog around the high school when they found her."

Daniels released a long, slow breath as if steeling himself for the memory to come.

"Candice was under the high school football stadium bleachers. She was just lying there, with her arms crossed over her chest and her feet crossed at the ankles, looking perfectly peaceful—almost as if she was taking a nap."

"Oh," Lindsey said for lack of anything else to say. Since it was a murder she had just assumed it was grisly, but what Daniels described was even more unsettling, almost as if her killer felt the need to make her comfortable after snuffing the life out of her.

"It was odd. Her hair looked as if it had been carefully arranged about her shoulders, her bright blue sweater was buttoned all the way to her throat with tiny white pearl buttons, no visible snags or tears, her skirt was smoothed over her knees and her shoes weren't even scuffed."

Daniels glanced at Lindsey and his face looked uneasy.

"It was almost worse, finding her like that. Because she looked so peaceful, I actually thought she was napping for a moment. And then when I got close, I saw the ligature marks around her throat. They were red and raw and cut into her skin. When I realized she was dead, I had to go throw up in the bushes."

"I'm sorry," Lindsey said. She wasn't sure if she was sorry for the young officer who had thrown up in the bushes or for the man she was asking to relive such a horrible experience or for both. Probably, it was both.

"Thanks," he said. "Her purse was sitting right beside her as if someone had put it there just like they arranged everything else, but there was nothing else. We canvassed the area, looking for the murder weapon, but we never found what was used to strangle her and we never found a book. Sorry."

"No, don't be," Lindsey said. "I'm sorry I asked you to relive it. It must have been just awful."

"No, it's all right," he said. "I expect when she opens the case file Emma is going to do the same, so this was a good practice run for me."

"I heard that Benji Gunderson was a suspect," she said. "He was Candice's boyfriend at the time."

"He was a person of interest—the partners of the victim always are—but he had an airtight alibi. He was out of town at a conference, which was confirmed, when she was murdered," Daniels said. "Though that never stopped people from suspecting him. I felt bad for the guy, but statistically it usually is the boyfriend or husband who is the guilty party, and this was such a shocking murder case, the townspeople needed someone to blame."

Lindsey nodded. She had seen that fearful reaction from people a number of times.

"What was Candice Whitley like?" she asked. "Did you know her?"

"Not until I was investigating her murder," he said. "From what I learned she was a great teacher, very well liked by her students and colleagues. She worked hard, was passionate about teaching, loved books and reading and dabbled in writing a bit. As you know, she was dating Benji Gunderson and her best friend was her fellow teacher Judy Elrich."

Lindsey glanced at him in surprise and he nodded. "Yes, the same Judy Elrich that teaches at the high school now. If I remember right, she left town a few weeks after Candice's murder. She said it was too hard to be here, but her mother, Nora Elrich, stayed in town. Sadly, Nora became ill about a year ago and Judy came back to take care of her. She resumed her old teaching position at the high school, which must have been difficult."

"Judy comes into the library all the time to get audio books for her mother," Lindsey said. She knew Judy was a big science fiction and fantasy reader and always had her name down first for the latest Kevin Hearne novel.

"You could talk to her about what happened all those years ago," Daniels said. "But she took it extremely hard back then so you'd want to tread lightly."

"Understood," Lindsey said.

They were both silent for a while and then Daniels rose to check on his ribs and Lindsey figured she'd better go.

"Thanks for talking to me, Chief," Lindsey said.

"It's just Tim now," he said with a smile. "It was no trouble, but I have to ask: Why does a twenty-year-old murder interest you so much?"

"Honestly, I don't know. I just feel like if I can find out who returned that library book, I can figure out who murdered Candice Whitley," she said. "And I feel like she deserves that."

"And that matters to you why?" he asked. "You didn't know her. You didn't even live here back then."

"I guess because I'm a librarian and I have a deep-seated need for answers to questions," Lindsey said. "All questions."

Daniels nodded as if he understood, but Lindsey knew he didn't get it. How could she explain? It was as if it was stamped somewhere in her DNA that she must be able to find the answers to questions.

Being a librarian meant finding the solution—no matter the problem—by using the information and knowledge that the library housed to solve everything from how to build a microhouse to how to speak Tatar, or, in this case, to discover who wanted Candice Whitley dead and why. She would not rest, could not rest, until she got the answer.

CHAPTER

9

BRIAR CREEK
PUBLIC LIBRARY

**"T**here you are. I had almost given up hope," Robbie said as Lindsey strode past him into the library. "So, what were you about on your lunch hour? Snogging buoy boy?"

Lindsey paused to look at him. He was sprawled in one of the comfy reading chairs just inside the front door. He had a stack of gossip magazines beside him.

"Looking for articles about yourself?" she asked.

"Always," he said. "I particularly love it when they have me in a torrid relationship with an alien, you know, an outer-space alien. I have to read that rag to find out what's up with my extraterrestrial offspring. Apparently, one of them is an intergalactic superstar." He put a hand on his heart and looked choked up and said, "I'm so proud."

Lindsey laughed and shook her head. Only Robbie could find it funny to be so stalked and derided by the paparazzi. She continued walking toward her office and he followed as she suspected he would.

She did a visual scan of the library as she walked. The Internet computers were full. The reading area beside the magazines was cleared out as Mr. Tewkes and Mr. Johansen had their daily squabble over the sections of the *New York Times*. Lindsey knew them well enough to know that they could mediate the situation themselves so long as they were left alone.

In the far corner, the children's section had a line of strollers parked against one of the interior walls as Beth was doing her weekly baby time for the nursing, drooling and newly sitting-up crowd.

The circulation desk, while still buried in book trucks, now at least had a path carved through the carts, so that was progress.

Lindsey stored her purse in her office and was about to go out to the floor for a more thorough sweep when Robbie thrust a paper bag at her.

"What's this?" she asked.

"A gift for you," he said.

"I can't," she said. She gave him a somber look. "We've been over this. We're just friends."

"And friends give each other stuff all the time," he argued. "You should see the list I have started for my birthday. It will bankrupt you, seriously. Now don't be a spoilsport. Open it."

He sounded as excited and bossy as an eight-year-old at a birthday party. Curiosity won out and Lindsey opened the bag. A pattern of houndstooth wool stared back at her.

"What the . . . ?" She reached into the bag and pulled out a deerstalker cap just like the iconic one Sherlock Holmes always wore.

"Try it on!" Robbie insisted.

Lindsey put the bag down and put the hat on her head.

It was a tiny bit too big and the brim hung over her face. She had to tip her head back to see him.

"Is it me?" she asked. She tried not to grin but she felt so ridiculous that she failed miserably.

"Absolutely," he said. "If we cram your hair up in there, I'm sure it'll fit better."

Without waiting for her consent, Robbie lifted the hat off of her head. Then he gathered her long blond curls and wound them into a bulky sort of bun that he jabbed two short pencils into to hold it in place. He placed the hat back on her head and, sure enough, it fit much better.

"Okay, Sherlock," he said. "Now you're ready to do some sleuthing, and naturally I will be assisting you as I am playing the part of your dear Dr. Watson."

"My who?" Lindsey asked. She glanced at her reflection in the window of her office. She looked like a pointy mushroom. She went to take the hat off but he grabbed her hand and held it.

"I'm your Dr. Watson," he said. "We can be crime busters together and we'll start by solving the case of the overdue library book."

"Oh, boy," Lindsey said. Then she narrowed her eyes at him and pulled her hand out of his as she planted her fists on her hips. "Are you making fun of me?"

"Not at all. Quite the contrary, in fact," he said. "I just know your love of solving mysteries and I figured this would be a way for me to win your affections."

Lindsey dropped her hands. "Oh, Robbie, that's really very sweet, but it won't work."

"Of course it will," he said. He sat on the edge of her desk and stretched out his legs, crossing them at the ankles as if he were an unbudgeable piece of desk statuary. "I mean, we're bound to get into a life-threatening situation, and then, well, sparks will fly and you'll forsake the manly manatee for me."

"Robbie, my affection is spoken for—" she began, but he interrupted.

"At the moment," he said. "But I'm counting on the boat captain to sink his ship again."

Lindsey pinched the bridge of her nose between her fingers while she dug deep into her reserve of patience.

"Even if Sully wasn't the issue, you still can't be my Dr. Watson," she said. "You have to actually care about finding the truth when you involve yourself in an investigation like this."

"I do care," Robbie said. "In fact, I spent all last evening reading all of the newspaper articles from back in the day about the Whitley murder."

"Really?"

"Yes, really. Go ahead, ask me anything."

"Where was her body found?" she asked. She crossed her arms over her chest in an exasperated stance. She knew this question was an easy one but she had to start somewhere. Besides, if he didn't know the answer then she'd know he was just trying to work an angle.

"Under the football stadium seats," he said. He mimicked her, standing up and facing her with his arms crossed over his chest.

"How did she die?"

"Strangled, although no weapon was ever found."

"Who was the prime suspect?"

"Benji Gunderson."

"Who found her body?"

"An older couple while out walking their dog. Actually, the dog found her," he said.

Lindsey stared at him for a moment. Truthfully, she'd

read all the same articles and there wasn't much more to be learned. She supposed he could have gotten all of that from town gossip but somehow she doubted it.

She decided to go for one more just to see how committed he was. "Who was her best friend?"

"That wasn't in the articles," Robbie said. "But I happened to chat up our boy Milton and he said that her best mate was a woman named Judy, who happens to teach at the high school."

That did it. Lindsey knew she had to reassess Robbie's desire to help her out. Maybe he was a chronic buttinsky like her or maybe he really thought this would bring them closer together. Either way, he was a terrific study of people and Lindsey knew that ability would come in very handy.

"You're serious," she said. "You really want to help find out if the person who returned the library book is Candice Whitley's killer."

"Yes," he said. "And I have some theories."

"Do tell," she said.

"The boyfriend," he said. "It had to be. It's always the boyfriend. Probably, she was cheating on him and he found out and then strangled her in a violent rage."

"He had an airtight alibi," Lindsey said. "He was out of town."

"All right, then the boyfriend was cheating on her and his lover killed Candice in a jealous rage so they could be together," he said.

"And this theory is substantiated on what?" Lindsey asked.

"Wild speculation," he said. "Oh, and I saw it in a movie."

Lindsey laughed. She couldn't help it. Robbie looked so pleased with himself.

"Sherlock Holmes does not approve," she said. She took off the hat and dropped it on his head. "You need to have facts, Watson, not guesses and movie plot lines."

Robbie pushed the brim of the hat up off of his face and peered at her from beneath it. "Fine. Let's hear your theory."

"I don't have one yet. I'm still gathering the facts," she said. She glanced through her office window to the library beyond and saw a familiar figure headed their way. "But I do have a few more leads to follow up on."

"Excellent!" Robbie looked interested. "Care to share?"

"Share what exactly?" Sully appeared in the doorway, making Robbie start and Lindsey smile.

Robbie put his hand to his chest. "Don't sneak up on a man like that; you're likely to scare him to death."

"Not seeing the downside," Sully said. He frowned. "What's with the lid?"

Robbie took the hat off and dropped it onto Lindsey's desk. "A gift for a friend since we're going to be partners in this whole investigating thing."

"What?" Sully looked at Lindsey with one eyebrow lowered in concern.

"Robbie has offered to be the Dr. Watson to my Sherlock," she said.

"You're encouraging her?" Sully asked Robbie. "Why would you . . . Oh, I get it."

"Get what?" Robbie asked. He looked innocent—too innocent.

"You're thinking if you can be her investigating sidekick, it'll give you an in with her and you can romance her into more than friendship. Am I right?"

"Maybe," Robbie said.

"It won't work," Sully said.

"Says you," Robbie retorted.

"Yes, says me, because firstly, she's with me and secondly, oh yeah, she's with me," he said.

"She is not *with* you," Robbie said. "I've been watching you two and it's downright painful. It's sort of like watching two tortoises run at each other. Maddening."

"And you would be what, then?" Sully asked. "The bird of prey who swoops in and snatches one of the tortoises?"

"I fancied myself as more of the speedy hare, who sadly dozes off in the middle of the race but then makes up for lost time," Robbie said.

"Sorry, jackrabbit, but you aren't going to be making any time here." Sully grabbed Robbie by the elbow and led him to the door. "No hard feelings, *mate*, but I actually have information for Lindsey that I'm not sharing with you."

With that he pushed the Englishman out the door and shut it in Robbie's face before turning back around to face Lindsey.

"Rude!" Robbie shouted through the door.

"Did I say he was growing on me like a fungus? Because now I'm not so sure," Sully said. "Now he feels more like a bloodsucking tick."

"You did say that," she said. "But I think you've just established some very clear boundaries."

She glanced at the clock on her wall. "I hate to say it, but I only have five more minutes until my lunch hour is over and then I really can't be socializing."

"Five minutes? I can work with that." Sully reached out and took her hand and led her into the only corner of her office not visible through any of the windows. Then he kissed her.

It wasn't a long kiss. It was a swift decisive press of his mouth against hers; no less potent for its brevity as it was clearly a stamp of possession. Lindsey was utterly appalled at the fluttery feminine part of her that kind of dug it.

"Feel better?" she asked when he released her.

"Almost," he said. He took the pencils out of her hair and let it fall about her shoulders. Then he cupped her face and kissed her one more time, less swiftly and much more thoroughly. When he leaned back, his blues eyes sparkled at her. "Now I'm good."

Lindsey was glad she could read lips, because with all of the blood rushing to her head in an overheated reaction to Sully's nearness, she couldn't hear a word he said.

Since they had rekindled their relationship, Sully had been much more forthcoming in his actions and words, minus the whole "L" word thing. Although they were keeping their relationship on the down low, Lindsey was never in any doubt that he was as attracted to her as she was to him. It was pretty intoxicating.

She glanced at the clock. Lunch hour was over. Pity.

"Okay, then, right, back to business. What library-related thing were we talking about?" she asked.

She sidestepped away from him and moved behind her desk. She was at work, for crying out loud. She needed to get a grip. She had to at least try and appear professional and not throw herself at him even though she wanted to, right?

Sully grinned as if he understood her need to keep a healthy boundary between them and why. "We were talking about me having a name for you as to who might have returned that overdue book."

"We were?" she asked.

"We were about to," he clarified.

"What's the name?"

"Matthew Mercer."

Lindsey frowned. She had spent her morning reading every article she could find about the case. She hadn't seen that name mentioned, not once.

"That's a new one," she said.

"He was one of her students."

"So he was a minor at the time of the murder," she said. That explained why he hadn't been mentioned.

"Does he still live in the area?" she asked.

"No," Sully said. "But his parents do."

"Why would he have had the book?" she asked. She gestured for him to sit down as she sat behind her desk.

"He was a star student of Ms. Whitley's," Sully said. "A real reader; he always had his nose in a book. He was in my sister Mary's class, so I had to check in with her to make sure I remembered him right, but she confirmed that Matthew followed Ms. Whitley everywhere. She was always loaning him books and they would have big discussions about the literary merits of the works."

"It sounds as if they were close," Lindsey said. "Inappropriately close?"

"Mary said she didn't get that feeling but she was only fifteen at the time, so who knows for sure," Sully said.

"What happened to Matthew?" Lindsey asked.

Sully blew out a breath. "Although there was no evidence that he had any connection to the murder, the townspeople seemed to think it was either him or Benji Gunderson. Mercer was bullied so badly, he had to drop out of school and ended up taking the GED and leaving for an out-of-state college a year early."

"That's awful. It must have been really rough," Lindsey said. "First he loses his favorite teacher, who may or may not have meant more to him, in a horrible way, and then he is accused of her murder without any evidence."

"His parents still live here but as far as I know, he's never been back," Sully said.

"Sounds like a similar story to Benji Gunderson's," Lindsey said. "How hard it must have been for them to be driven out of their hometown on just suspicion."

"Have you heard anything more from Herb?"

"No. I get the feeling he just wants it to all go away, but these things never do that, do they?"

"Not in my experience, no, but especially not if someone returned the book in an effort to reopen the case," Sully said.

"But why after all these years would someone do that?" she asked.

"I don't suppose we'll know the answer to that until we know who returned the book."

"It's maddening."

"Agreed," he said.

Sully was looking over her shoulder out the window that looked into the library, and Lindsey got the feeling he wasn't talking about the case anymore.

She turned and followed the line of his gaze and saw Robbie pacing back and forth in front of the window, pausing every now and again to look up from the book he was holding to peer into her office.

When he did it again, both Sully and Lindsey waved at him. Robbie started and then frowned and stomped away.

"I'm thinking the next time that Peeping Tom comes by I'm going to give him his money's worth," he said.

"Really?" Lindsey asked with a laugh. "And how are you going to do that?"

Sully turned to face her and the look in his blue eyes scorched.

"Oh, oh my," Lindsey said. It came out breathier than she intended and he grinned.

A knock on her office door stopped whatever else she might have said, which was probably a good thing since she was pretty sure she was seconds away from taking him up on his unspoken offer.

"Lindsey, can I talk to you for a sec?" Ann Marie asked as she opened the door just enough to poke her head in. "Oh, hi, Sully."

"Hi, Ann Marie," he said. "How are those boys of yours?"

"Serving a week's detention for switching the signs on the boys' and girls' bathrooms at school," she said.

Sully burst out laughing until he saw the look on Ann Marie's face. Then he sobered up immediately.

"You have to admit that as pranks go that's clever," he said.

"Yeah, other people have a college fund for their kids, I have a bail fund. Hmmm," she grumbled, sounding an awful lot like Marge Simpson.

"They're just rambunctious," Lindsey said. "They'll outgrow it."

"Yes, I'm sure I'll look back and find their shenanigans amusing, you know, after the principal takes me off his speed dial," Ann Marie said.

"What can I help you with?" Lindsey asked.

"Well, speaking of the boys, I need to chaperone a school field trip next week and I was wondering if I could take that day off?" she asked. "I think it's in the best interest of everyone that I go."

"No problem," Lindsey said. "We'll make it work. Shoot me an email with the date and I'll adjust your schedule."

"Thanks," Ann Marie said. She paused and glanced between them. "I wasn't interrupting anything, was I?"

"No!" Lindsey said at the same time Sully said, "Maybe."

Lindsey gave him an outraged look and Ann Marie laughed.

"I'll just be going, then," Ann Marie said. She went to close the door but Lindsey rose from her seat and grabbed the handle.

"Sully was just leaving, too," she said.

He rose from his seat and headed toward the door. He paused beside Lindsey and leaned close. She felt her heart stutter to a stop as she waited to hear what he had to say.

"Call you later?"

"Please," she said.

He looked like he wanted to say more—heck, he looked like he wanted to do more, a lot more—but he didn't. Instead, he stepped forward and kissed her forehead in a gesture that meant no more than friends, and then he was gone.

"I love my husband," Ann Marie said. "I really do, but that man just packs a wallop to your girl parts, doesn't he?"

Lindsey watched as Sully strode out of the library and forced herself not to chase after him.

"Yup," she said.

"And there's really nothing going on between you two?" she asked. She looked at Lindsey with pity in her eyes. Lindsey hated lying to her, but she just wasn't ready to have the whole town in on their relationship yet.

"Nope." At the moment, it was about as coherent as she could get.

"Explain to me again why we're doing this," Paula said as she and Lindsey strode through the front doors of the high school.

They were moving against the tide of students who had just been released. As it was Friday, Lindsey realized they were lucky they didn't get knocked down and curb-stomped for going in what was clearly the wrong direction.

"It's a cooperative project between the public library and the high school library to get every freshman a library card to encourage their summer reading," Lindsey shouted over the voices of the student body pouring out around them.

As two teens on skateboards came barreling at them, Lindsey grabbed Paula and dove to the side.

"I think we'd better hug the wall until the horde passes," Paula said.

"Cool hair!" a teen girl said to Paula as she jammed earbuds into her ears. She didn't wait for Paula's response.

"And that's why you're here," Lindsey said.

Paula glanced down at her thick purple braid. "You think they'll relate to me because of the tats and the hair?"

"Wouldn't you back in the day?"

Paula appeared to consider it and then nodded. "I was a bit of a rebel back then. I would have dug me."

"So unless you really don't want to be the liaison to the high school, I figured I'd put you in charge of the library card project," Lindsey said.

"Cool," Paula said. "Thanks."

"You're welcome."

Lindsey liked seeing her newest employee embrace the opportunity to do something all her own, and she did believe that Paula's appearance was going to help her build a rapport with the teens. Of course, it was a bit of a no-brainer given the choice between Paula and Ms. Cole as to who would work with the teens more effectively. It was Paula all the way.

Once the mob had cleared the entrance to the building, Lindsey led Paula up the steps and through the glass doors into the main lobby. Lindsey had only been in the high school twice before, so she had to stop by the office to sign in and get directions to the library.

Michelle Maynard, who ran the office, was pleasant but distracted as she had several teens underfoot all demanding her attention *right now* in the overly dramatic the-world-is-ending way that only teens can manage.

Lindsey glanced at a map on the wall and saw that the library was located on the upper floor next to the English department. Given that she had hoped to do some teacher recon, how fortuitous was that? She and Paula put on visitor nametags and headed upstairs.

The occasional slam of a locker accompanied by running feet and random shouts was the only noise that echoed off of the cement walls.

Lindsey had called ahead to make sure it was a good time to meet with the librarian, Hannah Carson. The double doors that led into the library were propped open and she and Paula walked in, pausing to take in the colorful room.

Short stacks of books lined the perimeter, angled so that anyone in between the shelves could be seen from the front. Tables and chairs filled the space in between while student artwork and projects were on display all around the large room.

Lindsey had toured the library before and remembered how much she liked the space for its natural light and bright colors. The school library where she had grown up had been dark and quiet with a pencils-only policy, and the librarian had been a fleshy lipped, gray-haired old man with a mean squint who minced when he walked like he was trying to keep a stick firmly lodged up his butt.

Dressed in a literary T-shirt featuring the cover art from *The Great Gatsby* and a pair of jeans with black Converse high tops, Hannah Carson greeted them looking nothing like the crotchety old man of Lindsey's adolescent nightmares. In fact, with her two-tone shoulder-length hair dyed blond on the top and dark brown beneath, she looked like she'd be more at home in the school's art department or possibly auto shop.

"Lindsey, over here!"

Hannah waved them over to the large table in the corner of the room where she stood. There was a pack of students gathered around the table, all talking at once. Lindsey had no idea how anyone could hear themselves think much less catch what anyone else was saying.

Hannah turned to the teacher beside her and said something, and then met Lindsey and Paula when they were halfway across the room.

"Welcome to the chaos," Hannah said. She shook Lindsey's hand and then extended her hand to Paula. "You must be Ms. Turner, the library's new hire."

"Please call me Paula," she said as she shook Hannah's hand.

"Cool. Call me Hannah."

Just then a raucous cry erupted from the table. Lindsey saw one of the students hold up what looked like a mechanical octopus with a big blue glowing head. The student was pumping his fist and roaring. Hannah looked at the group with an indulgent smile.

"That's our robotics team. They're practicing for the state tournament. They're very committed to winning."

Another burst of shouts and cheers came from the table.

"We might be better able to hear one another in my office," Hannah shouted.

She gestured for them to follow her and they headed around the circulation desk into a glassed-in room, which housed several desks and a worktable.

Hannah sat down at the table and Lindsey and Paula did the same.

"Can I get you anything? Water or coffee?" she asked.

"No, thank you," Lindsey and Paula both declined.

Another cheer sounded from outside.

"I've got to tell you, my school library was never this cool," Paula said.

Hannah smiled. "We're evolving and turning into more of a maker space. We do robotics, gaming, cooking, filmmaking, song recording, you name it. If the students can think it, I tell them we can do it here."

"We've been toying with the idea of converting one of our meeting rooms into a maker space," Lindsey said. "Of course, I have to get the library board to approve it."

"They will," Hannah said. "It's one of the many ways libraries are changing. Your library would be perfect. You're open more hours than I am and I'm betting many of the students would love to have access on the weekends. Even better, I bet you'd bring in a lot of the parents."

"So, an all-ages space, then?" Paula asked.

"I get a lot of adults asking me if they can come in here and use the equipment. The interest is there." She gestured out toward the robotics club. "The arms on that thing came from our 3D printer, and we've only begun to utilize its potential."

"You have a 3D printer?" Paula asked.

"Grant funded," Hannah said.

"I want, I want, I want," Paula wailed. She winked so Lindsey knew she was kidding, but there was an underlying lust for the printer in her eye that Lindsey completely understood. She wanted one, too.

"What software are you using?"

"AutoMaker."

"Dual nozzle?"

"Of course. That way you can use two filament spools for more color options."

"Wicked," Paula said.

"Wow, it's kind of like you're speaking English, but you're not," Lindsey said.

"Sorry," Hannah said. "I geeked on you."

"Me, too, boss," Paula said. "We really have to get one of those."

Hannah laughed. "Well, you're welcome to come here and use it anytime you want."

"Yes!" Paula pumped her fist.

Lindsey glanced between the two women. There was obviously a great gadget lovefest happening between them. Which was excellent because now she could excuse herself to take a call while Paula ironed out the details of issuing the cards to the freshmen with Hannah.

"So, how do we want to get these freshmen signed up for library cards?" Hannah asked. "Brilliant to get it done before summer, by the way."

"Paula, do you mind telling her our different ideas?" Lindsey asked. She pulled her phone out of her purse and stared at it as if she'd just gotten a message. "So sorry; I need to take this." She rose from her seat and said, "I'll be right back."

"Sure, take your time. I got this," Paula said. She pulled a notebook out of her purse, where she had jotted down the basic outline of their plan. "So, we were thinking . . ."

Lindsey ducked out of the office and into the hallway. She shoved her phone into her pocket and hurried to the right. Most of the classroom doors were shut and locked, but in the second one she saw a teacher in his room. He was sitting at his desk with a red pen in hand and he looked weary.

Lindsey had seen that look on both of her parents, who were college professors, during exam time. She often thought that teachers deserved hazard pay, for educating their students even when the students didn't care to be educated. It took a special person to devote their life to the learning and advancement of others. From what she had heard, Candice Whitley was that sort of special person.

Lindsey didn't see anything to indicate which room was Judy Elrich's, so she turned around and went back the way she came. She took her phone out of her pocket and put it to her ear in case Paula or Hannah saw her and thought she was lost or daft or whatever. She felt a little bit bad for deceiving them but her quest for information made her shake it off.

She went by two classrooms and was about to turn around when she saw Judy standing by the window of her classroom. She wore her light brown hair in a knot at the back of her head. She was dressed in a denim skirt and a loose-fitting jersey top. Her shoes were sensible. Her entire demeanor seemed to be one of a person who didn't want to be noticed.

Why had Lindsey never noticed that about her before? When she saw Judy in the library, she was still quiet in dress and manner, but here it seemed more pronounced. It struck Lindsey that Judy had the posture of a person who had been beaten down by life and had surrendered.

Lindsey pushed the thought aside. Because she knew of Judy's friendship with Candice, she was reading too much into the situation when the woman was probably just thinking about a student who wasn't doing as well as she'd expected, or about a parent who was too busy telling her how to do her job to properly parent their own kid. Lindsey knew the type.

Or maybe it was a personal issue. Daniels had said she'd moved home to take care of her mother. Maybe her mother had taken a turn for the worse and she was trying to decide what to do. Then again, possibly it was something deeper and darker than that. Perhaps Judy had heard about the returned library book and she was thinking about her friend and why she had killed her.

Lindsey blinked. That had escalated quickly. Now to see if any of it was true.

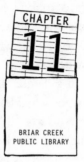

CHAPTER

11

BRIAR CREEK
PUBLIC LIBRARY

Lindsey knocked on the doorframe and Judy turned around with a prepared look, as if she was used to being interrupted. When she saw Lindsey she looked surprised and then frowned.

"Hi, Judy. It's Lindsey from the library," she said. "I know I'm out of context here."

Judy blinked as if trying to place her and then she smiled. "Hi, Lindsey, you're right. Sorry I didn't recognize you away from the books."

"I bet you get that from your students when they see you at the grocery store," Lindsey said.

Judy nodded. "I think it is a bit of a shock for them to realize that I do eat food. I'm sure a few of them think I snack on rats and snakes and whatever else falls into my cauldron."

Lindsey smiled. She liked the self-deprecating teacher humor. She did get a similar response from the younger kids she ran into outside of the library, although not the cauldron part of it, thank goodness. Still, the little ones did seem to think the "Library Lady" actually lived in the library.

"Are you that tough of a teacher?" she asked.

"I don't think so," Judy said. "But I do keep my expectations high. I think students will generally rise to the challenge if you give them enough support."

"People, too," Lindsey said, thinking of some of the people in her life who had surprised her.

"Were you looking for me?" Judy asked. "Is there something I can help you with?"

"No, I mean, I just happened by and saw you and thought I'd say hello," Lindsey said. "I'm actually meeting with Hannah Carson about a joint project."

Judy nodded as if that made sense. An awkward silence fell between them and Lindsey knew she only had a few minutes to broach the subject without things being weird. Okay, they were already weird, but she could live with that.

"It's been an interesting week at the library," she said.

She moved to stand beside Judy at the window, which looked out over the school's track and football field, the same football field where Candice's body had been found under the bleachers so many years ago.

Newly resolved, Lindsey drew a deep breath and said, "We had a fine amnesty day. It was fascinating the amount of overdue materials that came back."

"I'll bet," Judy said. "I hope I don't have any overdue materials. I know my mother enjoys her audio books, but I think I've gotten them all back."

Lindsey nodded. "You'd be getting love letters from Ms. Cole if you didn't. One of the books that was returned was checked out over twenty years ago."

"Really?" Judy asked. "Twenty years? What sort of shape was it in?"

"Almost perfect condition," Lindsey said. She turned and studied Judy with a direct stare. "I'm going to tell you this so that you hear it from me and not through the town gossip. The book was checked out by Candice Whitley on the day she died."

Judy gasped. She staggered back and her face went a deathly shade of white. Lindsey figured it was safe to assume that the stories had not reached Judy as yet.

"What?" she asked. "That can't be. How could you possibly know that?"

"One of the librarians is very thorough with her record keeping," Lindsey said. "When the book came back, we looked it up. It was a disturbing discovery."

Judy glanced out the window at the football field then moved back to her desk as if she needed to get away from the sight of the place where her friend had died.

"Do you know who returned it?" Judy asked. Her voice was soft, breathless with a tremor of fear in it. Lindsey felt bad for causing her distress, but, at the same time, if it was the murderer who had returned the book then Judy had better steel herself for the possibility that even worse things could be happening.

"No," Lindsey said. "We were mobbed all day."

Judy nodded. She glanced back toward the window.

"Judy, I know that Candice was your friend," Lindsey said. "And I am so sorry for your loss, but do you know anyone who wanted to harm her?"

"No," Judy said. There was no hesitation in her answer. "Don't you think if I'd known that someone wanted to kill her, I would have told the police all those years ago?"

Lindsey grimaced. She could understand Judy's anger.

"I was thinking it might have come to you later," she said. It sounded lame even to her.

"No, there's no one," she said. "Candice was an inherently good person. She loved her students, her community, her family, and everyone felt the same way about her in return. She was the sort of person who gave three hundred percent of herself and she managed to make others do the same."

Lindsey said nothing. She could see Judy was struggling with having the painful past dragged into her present.

"Candice always brought out the best in everyone," she said. "Even in me. She was my best friend. After she was killed, I just couldn't . . . I couldn't live here anymore. It broke my heart to walk the same streets, eat at the same places. The memory of her was everywhere and it hurt like a perpetual stab in my chest. I had to go."

Lindsey thought about what her life would be like if Beth was ripped out of it so violently. She couldn't imagine facing the day without Beth in her silly story time costumes, her exuberance for children and children's books gone from the library. Yeah, she imagined she'd have to quit, as it would be too painful to stay.

She'd probably return to an academic job like the one she'd had before she came to Briar Creek. The thought of Briar Creek without Beth was that horrible. She couldn't imagine how Beth's boyfriend, Aidan, would take it. He was completely besotted with her. Was that how Benji Gunderson took Candice's death?

"How was Benji Gunderson after she died?" she asked.

"He was a wreck," Judy said. Her eyes grew distant as if she were reexamining her memories to see if there was something she had missed. "He didn't kill her if that's what you're thinking. I know he was a suspect, mostly because they didn't have any others, but he was destroyed by her death. She was his everything."

Lindsey felt her heart clutch in her chest. Is that how she would feel if anything ever happened to Sully? She couldn't process it. The thought of never seeing him again left her breathless in the most painful way, as if her insides were collapsing in on themselves, trying to curl up into a protective ball to withstand the hurt. Was that what Benji had felt? She couldn't even imagine.

She shook her head. She couldn't get sidetracked by unsubstantiated accounts of how people felt. Despite his alibi, Benji could have been involved in her murder. Robbie, for all of his wild speculation, could be right. It could be that Benji had cheated on her and his lover had strangled her to get him all to herself. Yes, it was a dramatic version—no surprise there given that it came from Robbie—but stranger situations had happened.

"What about her student Matthew Mercer?" Lindsey asked.

Judy shot her a startled glance. "What do you mean?"

"I heard that he was quite attached to her," she said. "Was that true?"

"Why do you care?" she asked. "Candice was nothing to you. You didn't even live here back then."

"No, I didn't," Lindsey said.

"So, why dig it all up now?" Judy asked. "What's the point? It won't bring Candice back."

Her voice trembled and a tear spilled out of the corner of her eye. Lindsey felt terrible for poking at her friend's death and bringing her grief up to the surface.

"No, it won't, but if it was her murderer who returned the book . . ."

"It wasn't," Judy said. She snatched a tissue out of the holder on her desk and dabbed her eyes and blew her nose.

"How can you be so sure?"

"It's been twenty years," Judy said. "That book has probably been passed around from house to house with no one knowing it was checked out to Candice, and then your amnesty day came along and someone just happened to return it."

"I hope you're right."

"I am," Judy said.

"Do you know that for certain or do you really just want to believe it?" Lindsey asked.

Judy opened her mouth, looking like she'd argue, but then she didn't.

"Matthew was just a boy," she said. "He was smart, gifted, a talented writer. Both Candice and I saw that. I refuse to believe that he would have hurt her."

"Then who would have?" Lindsey asked.

"I don't know," Judy said. Her voice broke and she lowered her head. "I can't tell you how many sleepless nights I have spent trying to figure out who might have wanted to do such a horrible thing to her, but I just don't know."

The cloak of defeat draped around her like a shroud and Lindsey wished she knew Judy better. She wished she had the sort of familiarity that would allow her to give Judy a bolstering hug, but Lindsey was a little reserved by nature and Judy didn't give off a vibe that said she welcomed hugs. Lindsey settled for patting Judy's arm.

"I just hate to think that it was either Benji or Matthew," Judy said. "Candice was in love with Benji and she was so

proud of Matthew. He was her prize student. But . . . maybe
I've been wrong all these years."

She buried her face in her hands and began to cry. Now
Lindsey really felt awful.

"I am so sorry," she said. "It was never my intention to
upset you."

Judy sucked in a breath and lifted her head. She struggled
to get it together and rubbed her face with her hands as if
she could just wipe it all away.

"No, it's not your fault," she said. "I've been on edge ever
since my house was broken into."

"Oh, that's awful," Lindsey said. "I heard there was a series
of break-ins. I'm so sorry you were one of them."

"They didn't take anything of any value," she said. "Just
silly odds and ends, really, but it's the feeling of being violated,
of knowing that someone went through your things. It's un-
nerving."

She shivered and Lindsey almost did, too, knowing exactly
how it felt to have your home broken into, given that her
apartment had been broken into the year before.

"It is disconcerting," she said. "To say the least."

Judy looked at her. "You've been robbed?"

"More like vandalized," she said. "But it did give me the
heebie-jeebies for several days."

"And I live with my mother, who is getting on in years
and not well," Judy said. "She was fine, actually slept through
the whole experience, but the thought that she could have
been harmed. It's terrifying."

"I can imagine," Lindsey said. "If there's anything I can
do . . ."

"Thanks, but I'm fine," Judy said. She looked anything but.

Lindsey turned and went toward the door.

"I hope you're wrong," Judy said.

Lindsey turned back and gave her a questioning look.

"About the murderer being the one to return Candice's book," Judy said. "I really hope that it was just a happenstance, you know, someone finding it and returning it, having no idea that it was her book."

"It could be that," Lindsey said. "But if it wasn't, if it was the killer, I think it's best that we prepare for the worst."

"Meaning?"

"Her killer is still out there."

CHAPTER

12

BRIAR CREEK
PUBLIC LIBRARY

**"I** was seriously thinking I might need to send the robotics club on a search-and-rescue mission to find you," Paula said.

She and Lindsey were walking back to the library. The midafternoon sun was warm and the briny breeze blew in from the bay, tugging at their hair and clothes as if inviting them to come and play.

"Sorry about that," Lindsey said. "I ran into Judy Elrich and we started talking and I lost track of the time."

"She's one of the English teachers?" Paula asked.

"She is. In fact, she worked at the high school twenty years ago and then moved away, but recently came back to take care of her elderly mother," Lindsey said.

"Twenty years ago," Paula said. She turned to look at Lindsey and tossed her thick purple braid over her shoulder. "What an amazing coincidence that you just happened to run into her on our visit to the high school."

"I know, right?" Lindsey asked. She grinned at Paula, knowing full well that the other woman had figured out her ploy.

"Ms. Cole warned me about this," Paula said.

"About me?" Lindsey asked.

"Not so much you as your inclination for sleuthing," Paula said. "A little too much time spent in the mystery section of the library? Maybe you need to mix it up a little and tap a romance or a fantasy novel, or maybe a YA book."

"Why do I get the feeling you're making fun of me?" Lindsey said.

"No, I'm not," Paula protested. "Okay, maybe just a little."

"I've been told I have buttinsky issues," Lindsey said. "I thought about trying to change but then figured I should just embrace my character flaw and try to make the best of it."

"Well, if it helps track down a murderer, I don't see how I can really argue with it," Paula said.

They stepped onto the mat that led into the library at the same time. The building seemed quiet in the late afternoon, and Lindsey was relieved. She really wasn't up for a stopped-up toilet or an argument between patrons.

Paula stopped in the office to put away her purse before joining Ms. Cole on the desk. Lindsey went right out to the reference desk to give Ann Marie a much-needed break. For the next few hours it was business as usual.

When the library was finally quiet as people left to go home for dinner, Lindsey thought about her talk with Judy. She hadn't seemed to think that either Matthew or Benji could be responsible for what happened to Candice, but it definitely didn't seem like it could have been a random act of violence either—not with the way her body had been so carefully arranged after death.

Lindsey spent a grisly half hour reading up on the motives for strangulation by ligature. The information was alarming. According to the articles referenced in the book *Criminal Profiling: International Theory, Research, and Practice*, it takes five to fifteen seconds for the victim to be rendered unconscious, seventy-five percent of the victims are women, and the motives are usually rape, sexual jealousy or personal rivalry.

No one had mentioned whether Candice had been sexually assaulted. Judging by the lack of mention in the news articles, Lindsey assumed that she had not been. Could it be that Candice's attacker was driven off before he could abuse her? Maybe he hadn't meant to kill her, just subdue her, and he went too far. Lindsey shivered. She hated this. She hated everything about this. Mostly she hated that this poor woman had been dead for twenty years and her killer had gotten away with it.

She remembered that Daniels had said that Candice looked as if she was sleeping and that at first he had thought she was. That wasn't consistent with an attack where the perpetrator ran off in a hurry. Whoever had killed her, sex was not the driving motivator. So what was? Would they ever know?

Lindsey wondered if Judy was right. Maybe this whole thing was just a wild-goose chase. Perhaps the book had been passed from reader to reader and was found on someone's bookshelf and they returned it during the amnesty because they could, never knowing that it had been checked out to Candice on the day she died.

But there was that element of coincidence that was just too random. Why was the book still in Briar Creek? If it had been loaned about for twenty years, wouldn't it have ended up in another town or state? Lindsey wasn't one to believe in coincidence. Then again, why now? Why twenty years after the fact did the book suddenly reappear at the library?

"You look like you're brooding about something," Robbie said as he took the empty seat next to Lindsey's reference desk.

"*Brooding*; good word," Lindsey said.

"What have you uncovered about the death of Candice Whitley?" Robbie asked. "I know you must have figured out something because you look troubled and not in an I'm-in-love-with-a-divine-British-actor-and-don't-know-what-to-do-about-it sort of way."

"Actually, I am beginning to doubt myself. I think I may just be looking for trouble. I keep telling myself that I don't believe in coincidences but maybe that's all it is. Maybe the book being returned isn't a sign that the killer is back. Maybe it just found its way home."

Robbie shook his head back and forth as though he couldn't believe what she was saying.

"Lindsey, I am shocked. Shocked."

She looked at him with wide eyes.

"I did not think you were one to get discouraged so easily," he said.

"I just think . . ." she began, but he interrupted.

"That's the problem!" he cried.

He was so loud, several heads snapped in their direction. Lindsey was forced to bust out her shusher, which she generally avoided using unless the situation was extreme.

"Shhh," she said. She even did the finger to the lips, which made him smile.

"There's my librarian," he said.

Lindsey rolled her eyes.

"This is serious," she said.

"I know *shhh* in a library is a very big deal," he said.

Lindsey pressed her lips together to keep from smiling at his goofy face and encouraging his shenanigans any further.

"You know I'm not talking about that," she said. She propped her elbow on her desk and rested her chin in her hand. "A young woman was murdered, and by making a big deal out of a book she checked out being returned, I think I've upset some people."

"Ah," Robbie said. "You're feeling guilty." His green eyes were filled with understanding.

"No . . . Yes . . . A little."

He leaned forward, resting his arms on her desk while he studied her face.

"It's unfortunate that people have suffered because of the tragic events from twenty years ago, but no one suffered more than Candice Whitley. She lost her life. Doesn't justice outweigh the hurt feelings of a few people?"

"Of course it does, but there's no evidence that the book was turned in by the murderer," she said. "It's just speculation on my part."

"I love speculation," he cried with a wide smile.

"I know," she said. She tried to give him a discouraging look, but he wasn't having any of it.

"If you weren't so busy second-guessing yourself, what would be your next move?" he asked.

"I don't know. It was pointed out to me that the book was likely returned by someone in the community who just happened to have it on their bookshelf."

"That could be," he said. "But let's play this out. Here; get up."

"What?" Lindsey gave him a flabbergasted look as he rose

from his seat and then grabbed her arm and pulled her up to her feet.

"We're going to act it out," he said.

"No, we're not," she said.

"Come on, it'll help," he said. "You'll see."

Lindsey frowned at him but he ignored her.

He grabbed a book off of the short reference shelf behind her desk and handed it to her. It was the *World Almanac.* Lindsey took it and looked from him to the book.

"What am I supposed to do with this?" she asked.

"Carry it like it's the library book you just checked out," he said. "Now, it was a weekday that she was attacked, which means she must have gone to the library after teaching at the school, right?"

"According to the interviews in the paper, she was at school that day and by all accounts no one noticed that she was upset or agitated about anything," Lindsey said. "So, if it was just a normal day, she would have left school about four in the afternoon. Her body was found a little after six."

"So, we have to assume that between four and six, she came to the library and checked out the book."

"You know what they say about assuming," Lindsey said.

"Right, right," he said. He moved her away from the desk and out into a more open space. "Ass. U. Me. Got it."

Lindsey lowered her head so he didn't see her smile.

"Now, you're Candice and you're walking past the football field," he said. He moved Lindsey so that she had her back to him. "I'm going to strangle you."

"Really?" she asked. She was not down with that.

"No, not really," he said. He shook his head. "Firstly, I don't have anything to strangle you with and secondly, I would never hurt you."

"I'd feel better if you reversed the order of those two things," she said.

He made an impatient gesture with his hand. "I didn't list by order of importance. Now turn around."

She did and he said, "Okay, you're walking and all of a sudden someone grabs you from behind and they're choking you. What do you do?"

He stepped close to her back and put his hands gently around her throat. Lindsey dropped the book she was carrying and shot her elbow back into his ribs. He released her with an *oomph* of air and stepped away from her.

"Oh, sorry. Did I hurt you?" she asked. She turned around, shaking her hands in a helpless gesture.

Robbie sucked in a breath and clutched his middle.

"Lindsey, you didn't tell me we were allowed to beat up the patrons," Ann Marie said as she joined them. "I know a few Internet users who could use a beatdown or four."

"I'm fine, truly," he said. He straightened up with a small grimace. "But look, what was your first response when I grabbed you? It was to drop the book."

Lindsey bent over and picked up the thick paperback. She considered it and then Robbie.

"So, you're thinking that since she had to have been at the library right before her murder then she likely had the book with her, which she probably dropped the second she was grabbed, so the murderer must have taken it," Lindsey said.

Ann Marie looked between them. Her face was grim when she said, "It makes sense."

"It does, doesn't it?" Robbie asked. "That's why you can't get discouraged just because people get upset when you ask questions. Something happened that night. You found a key:

you found the book she checked out, and it arrived here for a reason. You have to follow up on it. It's a moral imperative."

"I did follow up," Lindsey said. "I gave the book to Chief Plewicki."

"Who is busy trying to figure out who is committing all of the break-ins that have happened over the past few weeks," he said. "She doesn't have time for a cold case."

"You're just trying to get me to stick my nose in this thing so you can help," she said.

"Is that so wrong?" he asked. He spread his arms wide. "I have become very attached to this community, and I care about the people who live here. If there is a murderer among us, I want to do my part to help catch him."

"He is right about the police being busy," Ann Marie said. "I heard Toby Sherwood telling Dean Gilroy at the grocery store that there have been four break-ins now with no leads."

"Four?" Lindsey asked. "That is a lot. Poor Emma must be working around the clock to cover the town with her small staff."

"See? We have to step up and take care of the other matter," Robbie said. "Now what would you do next?"

Lindsey thought it spoke well of her that she didn't laugh right in his face but rather turned to the side and chuckled. The man was as transparent as glass.

"All right, I'd probably start talking to the family members of the people who were closest to Candice and see if they knew of any tension in any of her relationships," she said.

"Excellent," Robbie said.

She turned to Ann Marie and asked, "Are you here now?"

"For the rest of the evening."

Lindsey glanced at the clock on the computer. It was the first Friday of the month, which meant the library as well as all of the other city offices and local businesses would stay open until nine o'clock to participate in the monthly art show called First Friday that took over the center of town every month. It was a fun family-friendly art tour about the town, which, while being fairly new to Briar Creek, had proven to be quite successful.

The library, in conjunction with the elementary school, put on a display in one of the back rooms. This month the children from Mrs. Kelly's third-grade class had their work on display.

Beth was in charge of it, and Lindsey knew she would be working the room in her painter's smock and a beret, pimping the children's books on drawing, painting and sculpting while she offered the families fruit punch and cookies. The event really drove up the circulation numbers on their art books, and not just the children's books either.

Lindsey had some paperwork that she had to give to Herb Gunderson for some upcoming programs. Knowing that he would still be at the town hall, which also hosted an art show on First Friday, she figured now was as good a time to catch him as any.

She and Beth were asking for a boost to their summer reading program budget as they wanted to give away books as the final reading prize for the kids who participated. Beth had a couple of children's book publishers interested in discounting books to the library, but Lindsey wanted to get the go-ahead from the mayor's office before she spent the money.

"All right," she said. "I have to run over to the town hall and drop off some paperwork. I'll have my cell phone with me. Call me if you need any help with reference or crowd control."

"Roger that," Ann Marie said.

She took her seat at the desk and opened up the latest issue of *Library Journal*. Ann Marie was compiling a list of books to buy as the fiscal year started in July and Lindsey always liked to put in a big order on the off chance that disaster struck and her budget got frozen in the upcoming year.

"Great. Who are we going to see?" Robbie asked as he fell into step beside Lindsey.

"You're not going to see anyone," she said. She walked to her office and took a manila folder off the top of her inbox.

"Aw, come on," he protested. "How can I be the Watson to your Sherlock if you don't let me tag along?"

"This is official town business," she said. "You can't come with me."

"Fine," he said. He continued tailing her like a shadow as she left the library.

"What are you doing?" she asked.

"Nothing," he said. "Just taking a walk."

"And does your walk just happen to be headed in the direction of Herb Gunderson's office?"

"Maybe." He shrugged.

"You. Are. Impossible."

CHAPTER

13

BRIAR CREEK
PUBLIC LIBRARY

66 That's true, but my charming personality more than
makes up for it," he said.

"Fine," she said. "You can walk with me, but you're not
coming into the office. You will wait in the hallway."

Robbie gave her a salute that she was pretty sure was
mocking, but she didn't call him on it.

The center of town for Briar Creek consisted of one road
that ran right past the library, the police station, the small
grocery store and bakery and then split into two roads, one
of which ran along the shoreline and the other of which
turned inland toward several churches, the community theater and the town hall.

Lindsey walked to the town hall a couple of times per
week, usually to attend department meetings but also to turn
in paperwork and sometimes to help herself to office supplies
when the library was running low, although she tried to keep
that on the sly.

The town hall was housed in an old redbrick-style Federal building with public offices like the water department, tax assessor and recreation on the first floor, while the mayor and his minions were housed on the second floor. Lindsey always figured the mayor liked to keep a layer of bureaucracy between him and the public, but in a town as small as Briar Creek, it really wasn't much of a front line.

The offices on the first floor had closed at five, but the building was still open for First Friday and would be until nine o'clock when Trevor Watson, the maintenance man, ushered everyone out—usually by grabbing a sweeper broom and literally brushing them in the direction of the exit, after which he closed and locked the building for the evening.

Lindsey led the way up the stairs and past the mayor's office. She saw Sally Kilbridge, his secretary, sitting at her desk and waved. Sally waved back but when she recognized Robbie Vine, she made a *squee* noise and then hid under her desk.

"Nice to know I've still got it," he said. Lindsey gave him a side eye and he said, "That is how most women react to me."

"And it never gets old," she said.

"Never," he agreed.

Herb's office was next. The door was open. He didn't have a secretary, so Lindsey peeked around the corner, knocking on the doorframe to get his attention.

He glanced up and then looked concerned, cautious and even a bit leery. "Hi, Lindsey and, er, Mr. Vine."

"Call me Robbie."

"All right, Robbie." Herb extended his hand. "I'm Herb."

"Pleasure," Robbie said and shook his hand.

To Herb's credit, he didn't *squee* and hide under his desk, for which Lindsey was ever so grateful.

"What can I help you with?" he asked.

"Summer reading, actually," Lindsey said. She handed him the manila folder.

"Oh, well, fantastic," Herb said.

He looked vastly relieved as he gestured for them to sit and he resumed his seat behind the desk. Lindsey realized he had probably thought she was coming here to question him about his brother. Well, she was still going to do that, but at least he'd have a few minutes of normalcy before she ruined his day.

He reviewed the numbers for spending for the summer reading program. He was very enthusiastic about books for prizes and seemed to think they could squeeze any extra money they might need out of the budget. He promised to talk to the accounting department and get back to Lindsey within the week.

"Excellent," Lindsey replied.

She noticed that Herb's gaze kept straying from her to Robbie and she wondered if he was trying to figure out their relationship. She felt like she needed to explain Robbie's presence in that she didn't want Herb to get the wrong idea. They were not a couple. They would never be a couple.

Herb hooked a finger in his collar as if to loosen his tie. He looked distinctly uncomfortable and shifted in his seat. This was not the look of a man worried about her relationship; this was the look of a man who found himself in an unexpected hot seat.

Lindsey turned and glanced at Robbie. He was studying Herb through one narrowed eye as if trying to get his measure. He had his elbows on the armrests of his chair with his hands in front of his chest with fingertips meeting like he was holding an invisible grapefruit or something. Lindsey had seen this considering gesture before, usually from a bank officer or the like right before he stamped DENIED on a loan application.

Robbie glanced quickly at her and Lindsey shook her head ever so slightly to indicate that he should let her handle this. Robbie shook her off like a pitcher shaking off a catcher's signal. Why, oh why, had she allowed him to come with her?

She figured she'd better move quickly before this whole thing unraveled on her.

"So, you think the budget will be okay even after all of the revenue we lost because of amnesty day?" she asked. She was hoping to segue into the discussion of amnesty day returns.

"As you pointed out when you asked to have an amnesty day, I think our gain in returned items far outweighed any revenue we might have lost and it's encouraged people to return to the library," Herb said.

Lindsey noticed that his words looked rehearsed, as if he'd been practicing them for just this sort of conversation. She had planned to coyly ask him if he had returned any overdue items but Robbie beat her to the punch.

"How about you there, Herb?" Robbie growled. He leaned forward in his seat and glared.

"I'm sorry," Herb said. He looked at Robbie like he had no idea what he was talking about. Lindsey could tell it wasn't an act; even suspecting Robbie's purpose, she wasn't clear on what he was trying to achieve.

"Admit it." Robbie slapped his hand down on the desk, making them all jump, and then pointed at Herb. "You had overdue books to return!"

"What? No!" Herb protested. He looked at Lindsey in shock. "I didn't. I wouldn't. I never!"

Lindsey raised both of her hands in a calming gesture. "Let's all just calm down."

Then she leaned close to Robbie and hissed, "What are you doing, auditioning for *True Detective*? Knock it off."

"I'm just trying to get answers," Robbie said. "He'll crack, you'll see."

"No, I won't because you're stopping this right now," Lindsey protested, but it was too late. Robbie rose from his seat and stalked around Herb's office like a caged panther. He rubbed his jaw with the back of his hand and circled Herb's desk, even walking behind it once before he spoke.

"Tell us the truth," he said in a menacing voice as he leaned over Herb, blocking the poor man in with one hand on the back of his chair and one hand on the desk. "Whitley's book came from your house, didn't it?"

"No, I swear!" Herb protested.

"You returned it for your brother, didn't you?" Robbie continued.

"No, I didn't return anything on amnesty day," he said. "Nothing. I'm a very good borrower."

"How long have you waited to get rid of that book? How long did you know that your brother stole the book from a dead woman, a woman he murdered, and hid it at your house? How long?" Robbie was practically frothing at the mouth, but Lindsey saw Herb's face go pale then grow flushed. He looked like he was on the brink of an episode and Lindsey did not want to be a part of the fallout.

"Robbie, that's enough—" she began, but Herb interrupted.

He rose from his seat. He shoved Robbie back, sending the man staggering, then he loomed over him and yelled in his face.

"My brother is innocent!" he yelled. "He loved Candice. He was going to ask her to marry him. He never got over losing her, never. So don't you dare accuse him of harming her. He didn't do it and he's lived his life banished from his hometown and forced to start over, all for a crime he didn't commit. I would stake my life, my reputation, my everything on it."

Herb stood with his fists clenched and his chest heaving, looking like he wanted to smash something, probably Robbie's face. Lindsey had known Herb for a couple of years now and even when the town had been shut down by a blizzard, he had never lost his cool. To her, it proved more than anything that his brother was innocent, or at least that Herb was sure his brother was innocent—especially if he was willing to put his reputation on the line. Herb's reputation was everything to him.

"Okay, well, we're really sorry to have disturbed you," Lindsey said.

She rose from her seat and grabbed Robbie's arm. While he tried to continue his stare down with Herb, she yanked him across the room and then got behind him and pushed him out the door.

"You'll let me know when you talk to accounting, then?" she asked.

Herb blinked, looking confused.

"About the book prizes," she said.

"Oh, yeah, absolutely," he said.

Lindsey gestured to the door where Robbie lurked. "Sorry about that."

"No, no," Herb said. His shoulders slumped as if all the fight had gone out of him. "He just said what everyone is thinking. I know they are. All these years of working to put the past behind us, hoping we could salvage my brother's reputation, and for what? A book shows up at the library checked out to Candice on the day she died and all the old suspicions come roaring back to haunt us."

"I'm sorry," Lindsey said. She saw Robbie step forward as if he was going to come back into the office and she waved him away. "It was never my intention when I brought the book to Emma to stir up bad memories for you or your family. I really felt I had no choice."

"I know," Herb said. He sat on the edge of the desk and ran a hand over his precisely cut hair. "It was the right thing to do and I would have done the same. It's just . . . It's been a bit of a shock to have it all come back."

"I imagine it has," Lindsey said. "Have you been in touch with your brother? Does he know?"

Herb gave her a searching look.

"I'm sorry," she said. "I was just wondering out loud. It's none of my business."

"No, it's fine. I have spoken to him, in fact," Herb said. "He lives in a small town up in Maine. He hasn't been down here in years. He seemed to think it was a good thing that the book was returned. He actually sounded optimistic about what it might mean."

"He did?"

"Yes, he thinks the case is overdue for being solved," Herb said. "But I just can't get swept up in it all again. It was agonizing for my parents the first time and now they're older and they're tired. They have enough to deal with since their house was robbed."

"Oh, no!" Lindsey said. "Recently?"

"Yes, they are one of the rash of burglaries that have happened," he said. "Which is why I wasn't eager to have Emma's attention be taken up by an overdue library book. We really need to get a handle on these burglaries."

"I agree," Lindsey said. She felt a prickly feeling at the base of her neck. First she learned Judy's house was one of the ones that was robbed and now Herb's parents. If she were Spider-Man, she'd say her Spider-Sense was tingling.

"Thank you," Herb said. "I appreciate the support since the overdue book is really more your issue. I can see where you think it might take precedence."

"No, I think you're right. The burglaries are important, even more than I realized." Lindsey turned and strode to the door. She didn't slow down as she called over her shoulder, "Thanks for your time, Herb."

CHAPTER

14

BRIAR CREEK
PUBLIC LIBRARY

**"W**here to next?" Robbie asked.

"For you? Home," Lindsey said.

"Oh, come on. We're clearly a great team," Robbie said. "I'm the bad cop and you're the good cop. Look at how we got that bloke singing like a bloody canary."

Lindsey looked at him as if he was cracked. "He didn't confess to returning the book or anything. How do you figure he was singing like a canary?"

"He talked about his brother," Robbie said. "That was significant. His little brother was definitely the prime suspect back in the day and getting him to talk about him was key."

"Maybe."

"What do you mean, maybe?"

Lindsey kept striding forward. She was on a mission now.

"Hold up there, librarian," Robbie said. He caught her by the elbow and forced her to stop. "What's going on in that head of yours?" he asked. "Don't deny it. I can hear the gears grinding and I'm pretty sure I smell smoke."

Lindsey thought about not telling him, but she knew he'd just badger her and badger her until she relented.

"Four burglaries have happened in the past few weeks," she said. "One was at Herb's parents' house and one was at Judy Elrich's mother's house. What do these people have in common?"

"No idea."

"They are the parents of people who were very close, the closest actually, to Candice Whitley. Benji was her boyfriend and Judy was her best friend. I need to know who else was robbed and whether or not they have any connection to Candice Whitley."

"Oh, this is good," Robbie said. "So, where are we going?"

"The police station to talk to Emma," Lindsey said. "Do not under any circumstances try your bad-cop routine on her. Am I clear?"

"As the water in the Thames," he said.

He strode forward and Lindsey followed, frowning. She was pretty the water in the River Thames was not clear, not at all.

Lindsey tried to catch up to him but his stride was longer and he was moving at a clip. When they got to the front door, only his ingrained manners to hold the door open for her allowed her the advantage of getting inside ahead of him.

Officer Kirkland was manning the front desk and he glanced up when Lindsey entered with Robbie on her heels.

"Evening, ma'am," he said. He glanced past her and added, "Sir."

"Hi, is Chief Plewicki here?"

"She was in her office a little bit ago," he said. "I'll check."

"Thanks."

Kirkland ducked through the door that led to the back office. Lindsey took the opportunity to tell Robbie one more time to behave himself.

He raised his right hand as if swearing on it, but Lindsey would have felt better if there was a judge present, or a minister, or Robbie's mother—basically, anyone with some power over the charming actor.

Kirkland reappeared and opened the half door that led to the back. "Come on in."

Lindsey gave Robbie one more warning look before she led the way through the door. He grinned at her, and she got a very bad feeling about it.

He didn't wait for Lindsey to enter Emma's office first but rather strode into the space like he owned it. Emma glanced up from her computer with a smile that quickly morphed into a frown as Robbie sat in one of the two guest chairs facing her desk and propped his feet on the corner of her desk.

Lindsey went to take her seat, shoving Robbie's feet off as she went. She glowered. He looked unrepentant.

"Lindsey, Robbie, what's up?" Emma asked. She glanced at them in turn as if trying to figure out what would have brought the two of them to her office.

"Murder," Robbie said.

He was using his dramatic actor voice and Lindsey had to fight the urge to roll her eyes. Emma did not suppress the urge, but instead rolled her eyes and huffed out an impatient breath, as if she were a teenage girl being told to go back to her room and change her outfit.

"You think that's annoying?" Robbie asked. "Really? A

woman is dead and you're not interested in what we've discovered."

Emma narrowed her eyes at him and turned to Lindsey. "Is this a new murder or the cold case?"

"Cold case."

"You discovered something?" Emma asked.

"Maybe," she said.

"*We* have been working the case and found a connection between the burglaries and the dead girl," Robbie said.

Emma frowned at him. "Why are you here?"

"Helping," he said.

"Oh, is that what you call it?" she asked.

Lindsey glanced back and forth between them, watching the verbal sparring match. She had thought Emma and Robbie were friends, especially since they had worked together before to thwart a would-be murderer, but maybe she'd been wrong. Maybe there was no love lost between the officer and the actor.

"Yes, that's what I call it," he said. He leaned forward in his seat and glared at her. "What do you call it?"

"Hindering an investigation," she said. "Or in your case, being a nosey parker."

Robbie gasped and sat back in his seat as if she'd slapped him. "You cut me to the quick."

"Not yet," she said. "But if you push me, I might shoot you."

"Are you threatening me?" Robbie asked.

Now he rose from his seat, planted his hands on Emma's desk and stared her down. Bad move. Lindsey could have told him that but she doubted he would have listened. Just as she expected, Emma rose up from her seat and met him halfway across the desk until they were nose to nose.

"I was thinking it was more of a warning, but you can call it whatever you like," she said. "You are a civilian—a celebrity civilian, which is the absolute *worst* kind—and you need to steer clear of anything happening with the police. We have a hard enough job without you bringing the paparazzi to our front door and making our lives a misery."

"You're discriminating against me because I'm famous!"

"No, I'm not," she argued. "I just don't want you anywhere near this case, stirring up all sorts of trouble." She pointed to Lindsey. "She does enough of that!"

"Hey, I'm not in this!" Lindsey protested.

"But with my status, I can protect you," Robbie said. "You know, make sure the media reports it the right way and puts you and your people in the most positive light. And if things get dangerous, I can watch your back and save you if you get into a jam."

"Save me?" Emma shook her head as if she must have heard him wrong, then she patted the gun strapped to her side. "I think I've got all of the protection I need."

"Well, that's subtle," Robbie said.

"Listen, I'm not going to argue with you," Emma said. "This case is none of your business and you need to butt out."

She pushed back from her desk, putting some distance between them. He took the opportunity to sit on the corner of her desk and cross his arms over his chest. He did not look happy.

"Well, then I guess you don't want to hear what we have to say," he said.

"No, I'll be happy to hear what she has to say after you leave," Emma said.

"What?!" Robbie looked insulted.

"She is a town employee and as such I can tap her research

resources for help with my cases, but you, you're noth—"
Emma broke off, clearly thinking better of her word choice.
It was too late. The damage was done.

"*Nothing?*" Robbie asked. He sounded outraged. "I'm
nothing?"

"That came out harsher than I meant," Emma said. "But
in regards to your relationship with this office, yes, you are
nothing but a regular citizen who we promise to protect and
serve, and that is all."

"Well, I guess there is *nothing* more to be said." Robbie stood
and strode out of the office, slamming the door behind him.

"That went well," Emma said. She sank back into her
chair and pressed her fingers to her temples.

"He's butt-hurt now, but he'll get over it. He always does,"
Lindsey said. "I'm sorry. I didn't really think about the position I was putting you in when I let him tag along."

"It's okay," Emma said. "He just brings a level of global
scrutiny with him that I can live without right now."

"Understood," Lindsey said. "Okay, I won't take up more
of your time. I just have a question."

Emma raised her eyebrows. Lindsey took this is as a go-
ahead-but-I-may-not-answer-you sort of look.

"Two of the houses that were robbed belonged to the
Elrichs and the Gundersons," Lindsey said. She watched
Emma's face to see if she made the connection. Emma looked
confused. So, that was a no. "Who were the other houses?"

"Why?"

"Because Judy Elrich was Candice Whitley's best friend
and Benji Gunderson was her boyfriend," Lindsey said.
"That's two families who had people close to Candice that
were robbed. Who were the others? Do they have the same
connection?"

Emma blew out a breath. She had the look of someone who had just found the last piece in a five-hundred-piece jigsaw puzzle.

"The Mercers and the Larsens," Emma said.

"Oh, wow," Lindsey said. "The parents of the student who worshipped her." She frowned. "But I don't know the Larsens."

"Sure you do," Emma said. "James and Karen Larsen. He's the principal of the high school."

"How long has he been principal?"

"For as long as I can remember," Emma said.

"Then he could have been the principal when Candice taught there, which would mean he was her boss," Lindsey said. "And there's our connection."

"Not only a connection," Emma said. Her eyes glittered. "Now we have a suspect list."

CHAPTER

15

BRIAR CREEK
PUBLIC LIBRARY

Lindsey left the chief's office after receiving a stern warning from Emma to stay away from the case. Yeah, right. She wondered if the chief even heard herself when she talked. How could Lindsey possibly ignore what Nancy Drew would certainly call *The Case of the Overdue Library Book*?

She pushed out the front door and found Robbie waiting on the front steps for her. He was picking the leaves off of the mountain laurel bush beside him and shredding them between his fingers. His hair was mussed as if he'd run his hands through it repeatedly, obviously before moving on to thrashing the shrubbery.

"You okay?" Lindsey asked as she sat down beside him.

"She dismissed me," he said. "I thought we were friends, comrades in arms, crime busters. Obviously I was mistaken."

"Well, you are, as she said, a celebrity civilian."

"That didn't hurt as much as being called nothing," he said.

"I don't think she meant it that way," she said. "She was referring to your relationship with the police department."

"How do you as a librarian outrank me?" Robbie asked. "I am an international star of the stage and screen. And you're just . . ."

"Nothing?" Lindsey asked with a small smile.

Robbie shook his head. "I would never call you that."

Lindsey blew out a breath. He was clearly still hurt. She wondered if there was anything she could say to make it better. Probably not, but she had to try.

"Listen, I do research for Emma, and I'm employed by the town as well. It gives us a cooperative relationship," she said. "Whereas you as an actor—"

"Oh, please, save the spin on this pep talk where you give yourself investigative credentials. I know you, love. You are an avid reader of a mystery series about a bunch of Arizona cupcake bakers who solve crimes—as if that's even possible," he snapped.

Lindsey was out of patience. He could pick on a lot of things but not her choice of reading material.

"Do you want to know what she said or not?" she asked.

"Of course I do," he said.

"Fine. Then curb your attitude," she said.

"Sorry," he said. "I'm just not used to being dismissed. It's a bit of a shock to my ego."

"I thought one of the things you liked about me is that I am immune to your fame," Lindsey said. "Isn't that true about Emma as well?"

"I do like that about her, about both of you," he said. "But whereas you're easy and pleasant to be with, she irks me and winds me up."

"Is that a bad thing?" Lindsey asked. "It sounds like she challenges you."

"But that's what is weird," he said. "No one ever challenges me. I pretty much always get my way."

"Well, get over it, Watson, because Emma is never going to cater to you," she said.

Robbie looked thoughtful, as if he wasn't sure what to make of this new development.

"Of course, you'll have to adjust if you're still planning to help me," she said. "If you want to sit and pout, well, I can't help you with that."

Lindsey rose from the step and started walking back to the library, leaving Robbie no choice but to follow if he was still interested in helping her.

"You mean it?" he asked. "You'll still let me help even though the dragon has cut me loose?"

"Why not?" she said. "With that celebrity status of yours, you might be able to get people to talk to you who won't talk to me."

"Such as?" he asked.

Lindsey told him about the other burglary victims. Robbie was suitably impressed by the fact that their theory was correct and all four burglary victims had a relationship with Candice Whitley.

"I think I could manage that," he said as they entered the library. "So, what's our next move?"

"I'm not sure yet," she said. "Let me think on it tonight and I'll be in touch."

"So, that's what you're doing tonight? Thinking?"

"Not entirely. I'll also be eating dinner with the crafternoon gals," she said.

"Just girls?" Robbie asked. Then he frowned. "No water boy joining you? What exactly is going on with you two? Are you or aren't you a couple?"

"Good-bye, Robbie," Lindsey said. She opened the door to her office just enough to squeeze through and then quickly closed it.

"If you learn anything good, I want a full report," he said through the door. "No matter how late!"

Lindsey shook her head. After witnessing the back and forth between Robbie and Emma at the police station, she was intrigued by their response to each other. Emma was usually blunt but with Robbie she was even more so, and Lindsey got the feeling it was so she could keep him at a distance. Hmm.

There was more going on there than either one of them realized, Lindsey was sure of it. She had no doubt that having Robbie help her with this case was going to prove very interesting.

The Blue Anchor looked like it was hemorrhaging people as the outside patio overflowed with customers wanting to enjoy the cool evening air and the half-priced drinks during the extended hours of the First Friday happy hour.

This was when being crafternoon buddies with the owner came in handy, Lindsey observed as Mary had two busboys drag a table from inside out onto the pier for Lindsey and her group.

Violet and Nancy arrived just after Lindsey. Nancy brought Heathcliff on his leash. Once he caught Lindsey's scent, he almost strangled himself in his effort to get to her. When she was close enough, Nancy let him go so he could charge his person. Lindsey bent down and hugged him close, which was no small feat as he wriggled and wiggled with excitement.

Ian popped out of the back door of the restaurant with a big chewy bone for Heathcliff. After Heathcliff licked his chin, Ian gave him the treat and Heathcliff settled himself at Lindsey's feet, as all was perfect in his world now.

It was agreed that a large bottle of wine was in order and Violet was generous with her pours as she filled their glasses. Since Mary was working and Charlene was anchoring the late-night news in New Haven neither of them could join the group, but Beth was due to arrive as soon as she changed out of her artist's outfit and locked up the library.

"Lindsey, I heard you and Robbie were at the town hall this evening and then the police station," Nancy said. "So, what gives?"

"Spending time with my friend Robbie?" Violet asked. "Do tell."

"There's nothing to tell," Lindsey said. She paused to take a healthy sip of her wine. "He fancies himself the Dr. Watson to my Sherlock and we were following up on some leads about the library book."

"The one Candice checked out on the day she was murdered," Nancy said. "I really don't think you should get involved in that."

Violet looked at her with one eyebrow raised. "You do know you're talking to Lindsey, right?"

Nancy sighed.

"You don't need to worry," Lindsey said. "Emma has already warned me away from the case."

"Because you're known for taking orders so well," Violet said.

"What does Sully have to say about this?" Nancy asked. "You know, about the case and your spending time with Robbie?"

"They're not dating," Violet said. "Sully has no say in who she spends her time with, right, Lindsey?"

"Yeah, sure," Lindsey lied.

Now she felt bad. As much as she liked keeping her private life private, she took no pleasure in lying to her friends, even if they were just lies of omission. She glanced toward the entrance to the patio to see if Beth was anywhere in the vicinity to help her out.

Instead, she saw Sully striding through the crowd headed straight for them. She felt her heart hammer in her chest at the sight of him and she had the sudden urge to flee the scene like a criminal. What if he said or did something that gave them away? Then her friends would know she'd been fibbing.

As if he sensed her panic, Sully caught her gaze and grinned. He didn't slow down or change course. He just kept striding toward her with that look. It was a look that said they were a whole hell of a lot more than friends.

Suddenly, Heathcliff sensed Sully's presence and, with a happy bark, he picked up his chewy and ran at him.

Lindsey had never loved her dog more. Not that she wasn't thrilled to see Sully—she was—but she feared that, caught off guard, her feelings for him would be clear for everyone to see, even him, and she wasn't sure she was ready for that yet.

While Sully stopped to lean down and give his buddy Heathcliff some love, Lindsey took the moment to take a breath, regain her composure and suck down a big gulp of wine.

"Easy, girl," Violet said. Her dark brown eyes were twinkling and Lindsey got the feeling that she knew Lindsey was flustered.

"Hi, Sully," Nancy called with a wave. "What brings you here, other than the food?"

She looked pointedly at Lindsey and just like that Lindsey's newly won calm fled into the night like a thief with the family jewels.

Sully stood up and Heathcliff resumed his spot at Lindsey's feet. Sully looked right at Lindsey and said, "I came to see my girl."

He gave her one heartbeat to deny it, but she didn't. Instead she felt a grin burst out of her from within and she tilted her head up to meet his gaze. Then he leaned down and kissed her in front of everyone.

"Well, it's about damn time," Nancy said.

"Amen," Violet said.

When Sully stepped back, Lindsey was dizzy and her ears were ringing. How did he do that?

He pulled up a vacant chair and sat next her, sliding his fingers in between hers.

Both Nancy and Violet looked unsurprised and Lindsey frowned.

"Wait," she said. "Did you two know?"

"Oh, honey," Nancy said. "Did you really think you had anyone in town fooled?"

"Honestly," Violet said. "You light up like a firefly whenever he's within a hundred yards."

"Plus, those sleepovers fooled no one," Mary said as she stopped by the table with a basket of bread and butter. She snorted. "The morning I saw him driving you home and you actually ducked down below the dash. Hiiiiilarious."

Lindsey drained her wineglass. Well, at least she didn't have to feel guilty anymore.

"Hey, boss." Charlie Peyton, Nancy's nephew and Lindsey's downstairs neighbor, stopped by their table. "Ladies."

"Hi, Charlie," Lindsey said. She could have kissed him she was so happy for the diversion. "Did your band play tonight?"

"Over at the bakery," he said. "Now we're doing a set here. You should come in after you eat."

"Will do," Lindsey said.

She went to raise her hand to knuckle bump him, forgetting that she was still holding hands with Sully. Charlie's gaze caught sight of their entwined fingers and he went wide-eyed.

"Are you two . . . Are you a . . . Are you two dating again?" he asked.

Sully let go of Lindsey's hand and put his arm around the back of her chair before he answered. He looked at Lindsey as if gauging her consent. She nodded, and he said, "Yes."

"Well, all right, all right, all right!" Charlie pumped a fist. "I knew you two were made for each other." His gaze was caught by someone at the far end of the patio and he added, "Just like those two."

They all turned to see who Charlie was looking at. Lindsey blinked.

"Is that . . . ?" Violet's voice trailed off.

"Beth and Aidan?" Nancy asked.

"I believe at the moment they are Princess Zelda and Link," Lindsey said. The only reason she knew this was because Beth was wearing her purple vest over a white dress. Also, she seemed to have pointy ears on, as did Aidan, who was dressed in a green tunic over green pants and brown suede boots.

"And they look like elves, because . . . ?" Sully asked.

"They are planning to host a gamers' prom," Lindsey said. "I bet they are giving their costumes a test drive."

"They look . . . nice," Charlie said as if he was struggling to come up with an appropriate adjective.

"Nice?" Mary asked. She clasped her hands over her chest. "Look at them. They're adorable."

Then she started to cry. Not little happy tears, or delicate little sniffles—oh, no, these were great big watery, shoulder-shaking sobs.

Sully stood and put his arm around her and pulled her close. He looked at Charlie and jerked his head in the direction of the restaurant, clearly indicating that Charlie should go and get Mary's husband, Ian.

"Oh, hey, don't cry," Aidan said as they joined the table. He snatched his green Robin Hood hat off. "See, it's just me." He glanced at Beth and whispered, "Usually, I only scare the real little kids who think I'm the Jolly Green Giant and I'm going to make them eat their vegetables."

"Mary, are you all right?" Beth asked. She patted Aidan's arm to reassure him that it wasn't him.

"I'm f-f-fine." Mary sobbed.

"No, you're not," Sully said. He shook his head at her. "But you will be in about six months, give or take."

Mary gasped. "How did you . . ." She whirled on Lindsey. "You told him!"

"I didn't, I swear," she said.

"You knew?" Sully asked Lindsey.

"I guessed," she said. "A while ago, actually."

He grinned at her like he expected no less, which made Lindsey warm from the inside out. He wasn't even mad that she hadn't told him.

"Guessed what? What's going on?" Beth asked, confused.

"She's going to have a baby," Aidan whispered.

"You know, too?" Mary cried. She started sobbing again and Sully pulled her closer and let her sob all over his shirtfront.

"I figured," Aidan said. "My sister got wound up like this a lot when she was pregnant."

"I am not wound up!" Mary protested.

"Oh, please, you're clearly hormonal," Sully said. "I knew it the day you got on the radio when Ian was out on the water taxi and you demanded that he bring home pierogis and fudge sauce. I didn't say it then but I'm saying it now— gross."

"What's wrong? What's the matter? Are you okay, Mary?" Ian came tearing out of the restaurant.

"She's fine," Sully said. "Just hormonal. Congratulations, by the way."

"She told you," he said. "Thank God. I didn't think I was going to be able to keep it in much longer." He cupped his wife's face and looked into her eyes. "Are you all right, darling?"

She smiled at him through watery tears. "Yes, they were just so cute. They hit me right in the feels."

She pointed at Aidan and Beth. Ian glanced at them and grinned.

"They are that," he agreed. "Now I have to steal the lime-light before I explode."

He pulled out a chair and climbed up on it. Sully handed him a water glass and a spoon, which Ian tapped repeatedly to get the crowd's attention. As people turned in their direction, their voices dropped in volume as they speculated about what was happening. Ian shouted over the whispers.

"Ladies and gents, boys and girls, I have an announcement," he said. He grabbed Mary's hand and kissed her fingers. "Me and the missus are having a baby!"

The entire restaurant broke out in happy cheers and applause. Lindsey saw Violet and Nancy exchange a look and she frowned at them.

"You knew about it, too?"

"We saw how much she was eating," Violet said.

"We were thinking it might be twins," Nancy said.

They exchanged a laugh. Then Violet rose from her seat and pulled Mary away from Ian and gave her a big hug.

"Congratulations," she said.

"We're having a baby!" Nancy cried as she took her turn to squeeze Mary tight.

Lindsey and Beth joined the group hug and Mary's tears slowly turned into laughter. After many congratulations, Mary and Ian went back into their restaurant to get a handle on the chaos, and the diners all resumed their conversations.

"I can't believe I'm the only one who didn't know," Beth said. She looked at Lindsey. "Even you knew!"

"Sorry. I didn't think it was my news to tell," Lindsey said.

"I felt the same way," Sully said, then glanced out at the islands and smiled. "My parents are going to go berserk."

"If they're anything like my parents, you'd better get used to the sound of *beep-beep-beep* as the delivery truck backs up to the house and vomits toys all over the front yard," Aidan chimed in.

"Noted," Sully said, and the two men exchanged a look of understanding.

"So, what do you think of our outfits?" Beth asked. "Aidan brought them by the library and we just had to try them on."

"You make an excellent ruler of Hyrule," Sully said. Both

Aidan and Beth looked at him in surprise. "What? Who hasn't played *The Legend of Zelda*?"

Aidan looked at Beth and said, "I knew I liked him."

Beth grinned and then she looked at Lindsey and noticed Sully's arm around the back of her chair. "You're not the only one."

Lindsey winked at her and Beth giggled. Beth's lack of surprise clued her in to the fact that Beth had probably figured out what was going on between her and Sully as well. Ah, well, so much for her covert op.

The group enjoyed their meal until the hour grew late and Nancy and Violet declared it was time for them to call it a night. They left, with Nancy taking Heathcliff home with her.

Beth and Aidan followed shortly after them, leaving Sully and Lindsey to linger over coffee while she told him about the robberies all being connected somehow to Candice Whitley. Sully listened closely. He didn't offer any questions until after she was done.

"The only one that doesn't really fit is the Larsens," he said. "Unless they had a personal connection outside of the school."

"That's what I was thinking, too," Lindsey said. "Of course, I'm sure Emma is already on it."

"Hey, why do you two look so pensive?" Mary asked as she stopped by their table with the coffeepot. "It's not because of me, is it?" She turned to her brother. "I asked Lindsey not to say anything to anyone."

"No, we're fine," Sully said. He grabbed his sister's free hand and gave it a squeeze. "I'm glad you and Lindsey are close enough that you can confide in her and she'll be there for you."

He gazed at Lindsey with a look of pride that made her get the warm fuzzies inside. He was pleased that she and his sister were close. She knew it was because he was feeling very optimistic about their do-over. She smiled back. She was feeling the same way.

"Oh, good. I would have felt terrible if you two were at odds over my own silliness," Mary said. "It took me a while to settle into the idea of a baby, you know? I already have that big one in there." She pointed toward the inside of the restaurant and Lindsey knew she meant her husband, Ian.

"Don't you worry," Sully said. "We'll help you burp and diaper the two of them."

Mary snorted a laugh and said, "Careful, I may take you up on that, especially the big one."

"Mary, Sully told me that Matthew Mercer was in your class," Lindsey said. "What did you think of him?"

"Is this about that overdue library book?" Mary asked. "Sully told me that you brought it to Chief Plewicki. Is she really opening up the case on Candice Whitley?"

Lindsey didn't want to say too much, so she shrugged.

"All right, I see how it is," Mary said. "You're not going to say anything in case I blab."

"No, that's not it," Lindsey said. She was afraid Mary might feel hurt and start crying again.

As if reading her mind, Mary said, "Don't worry. I have pregnancy brain. I wouldn't trust me with any information either. You know yesterday I forgot to put the car in park and then couldn't figure out why I couldn't get the key out of the ignition. I sat there like an idiot for ten minutes, thinking the car was broken. I swear this peanut is sucking the brain juice right out of me."

Lindsey smiled, mostly because Mary looked so pleased to have her brains being siphoned off by a peanut.

The restaurant had quieted down, so Mary took a seat at their table. She looked nervous. "Listen, I do have some information about the situation that I think you might find valuable, but you have to promise you won't judge me too harshly."

CHAPTER

16

BRIAR CREEK
PUBLIC LIBRARY

**"M**ore than you told me before?" Sully asked.

"Yeah," she said. She hung her head, looking ashamed. "I remember Matthew was very quiet."

"Quiet like thinking-about-ways-to-stalk-and-kill-people quiet?" Lindsey asked.

"No." Mary shook her head. "More like old-soul quiet. Matt always seemed years ahead of the rest of us, not just in smarts but in overall maturity."

"So, he didn't fit in?" Sully asked.

"Yes, but I don't think he was angry or bitter about it. He wasn't anti-social, he was more just tolerant of the rest of us, like he was an older sibling forced to sit at the kids' table. I always got the feeling that he was patiently awaiting his freedom."

"If he was that mature, did you sense he was interested in Ms. Whitley as more than a teacher?" Lindsey asked.

"No, she was with Benji Gunderson, and he came by the

school quite a bit," Mary said. "I'd see the three of them talking often. There never seemed to be any hostility."

Lindsey looked at Sully. "Having Matthew be a deranged teen stalker would have been too easy of an answer, I suppose."

"He was a poet," Mary said. "He read one of his poems to the class once. It was full of literary references I didn't understand but it also captured the angst of adolescence. I remember one image about standing on the knife's edge between childhood and adulthood and hoping not to get sliced in half. It spoke so clearly of the pain of those years. I'm sure I'm not getting it exactly right, but I thought he was so much smarter than the rest of us. He seemed to have a level of understanding about life and literature that the rest of us were missing."

"That doesn't sound like a teen who is swept up in unrequited love angst," Lindsey said.

"No," Mary said. "And after Ms. Whitley was killed, he was so angry. I remember hearing him berating the principal for not doing more to find Ms. Whitley's killer. I don't think Matthew had a very supportive home life. Ms. Whitley was probably the only person who fostered his brilliance. It must have been devastating for him to lose her in such a brutal way and to then be considered a suspect. I never blamed him for leaving town and never coming back."

"What about Benji?" Lindsey asked. "You said he came by the school. Did you ever see anything suspicious about him?"

"No," Mary said. "He was funny and goofy when he came by the classroom. He always made Ms. Whitley laugh. When she was killed he seemed, I don't know, *broken* would be the word, I guess. It was as if everything he had known to be true was suddenly proven wrong and he didn't know what to do or think. Looking back, I can see how devastated he must have been, but at the time . . ."

Mary paused and looked away. Lindsey knew her well enough to know she was embarrassed about something. Sully knew it, too, because he reached across the table and took her hand in his.

"Hey, it's okay," he said. "You can tell us anything."

Mary hung her head. "This is awful. I've never told anyone this before, mostly because I pushed it so far away, I never even thought about it until all this talk about Ms. Whitley and her murder started up."

Lindsey and Sully exchanged concerned looks.

"I did not have the best sort of friends back in high school," she said. "Michelle Moskowitz and Audrey Tapp were my besties at the time."

Lindsey glanced at Sully and noted he made a face like he'd tasted something bad.

"I know, I know," Mary said. "You didn't like them."

"They were horrible," he said.

"You think that because you know they only became friends with me so that they could get close to you," she said.

Now Lindsey made a face like she tasted something bad. Her brother, Jack, had been quite the high school heartthrob; she knew all about being befriended by mean girls so they could get close to her brother. "Using you to get to your brother; that's the worst."

"It's okay. It was a good life lesson for me in how to choose my friends more wisely—you know, after I cried buckets when they cut me loose because Sully left for college and I was of no use to them anymore."

"That's awful," Lindsey said. She wished she'd known

these girls so she could do some damage to them for harming her friend.

"Not everyone is as true as the crafternooners," Mary said. She put both of her hands on her belly as if to find comfort in the life taking shape inside. "Besides, I deserved it."

"No, you didn't," Sully said. "You were a bit of a princess during your adolescence but you weren't mean."

"Yes, I was," Mary said. Her voice was soft and low and Lindsey had to lean forward to hear her. "I was so caught up in being part of the in crowd that I didn't care what it cost or who got hurt."

Sully frowned. "What are you saying?"

"Do you remember the rumors surrounding Benji at the time of Ms. Whitley's death?" Mary asked.

"A few of them," he said.

"They were mostly about how he was so possessive of Candice, how he had a terrible temper, how they fought all of the time because of it."

"I vaguely remember something like that," Sully said. "But even then I knew it wasn't true. Benji was as mild mannered as they come."

"Well, there was another rumor that he hit on the girl students in Candice's class and that the two of them had fought about it."

"I don't think I ever heard that one," Sully said. "It wasn't true, was it? He never hit on you, did he?"

"No." Mary shook her head. "He never hit on anyone. Not only that, but he wasn't at all possessive nor did he have a temper. It was all lies; horrible, horrible lies told by vicious girls because they wanted to bring attention to themselves and be the poor victims of the madman."

Sully blew out a breath and looked out over the water.

"Those lies ruined his life. The whole town turned against him. He was fired from his job. No one would even talk to him."

"I know," Mary said. Her voice was shaky and she pressed her lips together as if to keep from crying. "And it's my fault because I knew who was telling the lies and I never did anything to stop them."

"Michelle and Audrey?" Lindsey guessed.

Mary nodded.

"Where are they now?" she asked.

"Michelle is on her third husband. I heard he's in his seventies and keeps the purse strings pretty tight. She's been in and out of rehab for the past ten years. Audrey is bitter since she lost everything when her billionaire divorced her since she was the one who was caught cheating and they had a solid prenup. Now she lives in a rundown apartment in New Haven and is scouting for a new sugar daddy, but I think she might be past her prime for that."

"Karma can be a bitch," Sully said.

"Indeed," Mary said. "Which is why I wonder, what does it have in store for me?"

"You didn't tell any lies about him," Sully protested. "You're not to blame."

"Aren't I?" Mary asked. "If you know the truth and you don't say anything, aren't you just as bad as the person telling the lie?"

"No," Lindsey said. She didn't want to see Mary beat herself up over a decision made when she was just a teenager. "You made a bad decision at the most vulnerable time in your life. That doesn't make you a bad person."

"I have to disagree," Mary said. "But that's why I'm going to visit Emma tomorrow. I'm going to tell her everything I know about Benji and the lies that were told about him so that this time when the murder is investigated his name doesn't get ruined again."

"I know Herb will appreciate that," Lindsey said. "He's been upset that they were going to have to live through this all over again."

"But if what Mary is saying is true—and I believe that it is—then who killed Candice Whitley?" Sully asked. He paused and gave his sister a side eye as if to check and make sure he didn't make her cry.

Mary didn't look teary now so much as determined. Lindsey had a feeling that by deciding to right the wrongs of the past she was on a mission, and everyone knows there is no room for tears on a mission.

"I don't know," Lindsey said. "But someone returned the book and, as far as I can tell given the short time between Candice checking the book out and her murder, I think it must have been taken by the murderer. So it stands to reason that they are the one who returned it."

Mary shivered and both Lindsey and Sully patted her arms.

"Sorry," she said. "I just never thought . . . I mean . . . I guess . . ."

She stammered to a stop and Sully gave her a rueful look.

"You thought her murderer left town," he said.

"Even knowing that they weren't the killing type, we were all quick to assume it was either Matthew or Benji. When they both left town . . ." Mary's voice trailed off.

"It was easy to believe the killer was gone," Lindsey said. "I can see that."

She leaned back in her chair and a yawn snuck up on her.

She covered her mouth with her hand but it was too late. Both Sully and Mary yawned, too.

"Stop that," Mary said. "I have to make it to closing."

"Sorry." Lindsey shook her head as if she could shake off the sleepy. Another yawn tried to creep out but she clamped her jaw together, refusing to let it.

"Come on, sleepy librarian," Sully said. "Let's get you home."

I t was a quiet ride in Sully's truck back to her apartment. With the windows down, the cool night air blew into the window, ruffling her hair and bringing in the sound of crickets chirping. Lindsey wondered if Candice had heard the crickets right before she was murdered.

"Hey, why the frown?" Sully asked. He reached across the seat and took her hand in his. "Thinking dark thoughts?"

"You know me so well," she said. She squeezed his hand. "I was thinking about Candice on her last night and what might have been going through her mind."

"Even darker than I suspected," he said. "I don't suppose we'll ever know the answer to that, but I'm hoping for her sake that it was quick."

Lindsey gave him a sad look.

"Yeah, I know," he said. "It's highly unlikely that strangulation would lend itself to quick and painless, but I still hope."

He pulled into the driveway in front of Nancy Peyton's house, where Lindsey rented the third-floor apartment. Sully walked her to the door, where they were greeted by an exuberant black ball of fuzz.

Heathcliff jumped back and forth between them, demanding love and making Lindsey laugh as he wagged his tail and barked at them as if he was trying to say hello. She bent over and scratched his ears.

"He was dead asleep until he heard the truck turn the corner onto our street, and then he bolted for the door," Nancy said from the open door of her first-floor apartment.

"Thanks for watching him," Lindsey said. "He was okay? No chewing?"

"He would never," Nancy said.

Lindsey just looked at her. "I know you love him, but if he's been naughty, you can tell me. I know he chewed up two of your throw pillows."

Nancy bent down and rubbed Heathcliff's head. "I was planning to replace those old things anyway. He was doing me a favor. See? He is a perfect dog."

Lindsey looked down at Heathcliff, who sat on her foot and gazed up at her from under his hairy black eyebrows. "You are so spoiled."

He thumped his tail on the ground as if in agreement.

"And how about Mary's news?" Nancy asked. She hugged Sully tight. "You're going to be an uncle."

"Crazy, isn't it?" he asked. His grin was huge and Lindsey could tell he was happy about the news. "I can't decide if I want Ian to get a wild boy like himself or a girl just like Mary. I'm thinking either way the baby is going to give them a wonderfully terrible time and I have a front-row seat."

"So how soon will you buy the baby a drum set?" Nancy asked.

"I don't know. How old are they when they can sit up?" he asked.

Nancy chuckled and Lindsey shook her head at him. She gave Nancy a quick hug.

"Sorry to run, but I am beat," she said. "As always, thank you so much for dog-sitting."

"My pleasure," Nancy said. She waved to them and disappeared into her apartment.

Sully didn't spend the night since he had an early-morning pickup in the water taxi, and then he was headed out to Bell Island for the rest of the weekend as Mary and Ian had decided to share their news with their parents and they wanted Sully to be there, too.

Sully asked Lindsey if she'd like to join them, but Lindsey didn't want their being back together to take away from Mary and Ian's news. She liked the slow pace at which they were moving and felt like they could wait awhile before they told their parents that they were back together. Maybe she was superstitious, but she didn't want to jinx anything and she'd just feel better when they got the whole "L" word thing out in the open.

After a long lingering kiss at her door and the promise of a dinner date on Monday night, he ruffled Heathcliff's ears and headed home. Lindsey went inside and locked her door. Being a solitary sort of person, she usually felt a sweet sense of relief when she was home alone.

She could eat what she wanted when she wanted and how much she wanted, she had control of the TV remote, she could lounge in her comfortable not-for-company pajamas, she didn't need to make conversation and she could fall into a book and not have anyone trying to talk to her while she read.

Yes, technically she could still do all of these things when Sully was around, but it was different when you shared a space with someone else. There was a constant compromise in cohabiting that she did not miss. Until tonight.

When Sully had disappeared from view, she had felt weirdly bereft. The thought of not having him beside her on the couch watching TV, putzing in the kitchen making his signature hot cocoa or on the other side of the bed while she slept made her feel alone in a way she hadn't ever felt before. It was alarming.

She went through her nightly routine with Heathcliff at her heels. Thank goodness for him or she feared she'd be flat-out lonely. She checked the lock on her door and closed the blinds on the picture window in her living room that looked out over the bay.

As she twisted the rod that closed the blinds, she felt as if someone was watching her. It was a creepy, prickly feeling on the back of her neck that made her shiver. Lindsey snapped the blinds shut and stepped back from the window.

Thinking about Candice was obviously making her imagination run wild. Unable to help herself, she pushed aside the edge of the blinds and stared down at the yard. It was empty. No one was there. Unless they were hiding in the shadow of the trees, which would explain why she had the same spooky feeling that someone was watching her.

Lindsey dropped the blinds and stepped back and noticed her hand was shaking.

CHAPTER

17

BRIAR CREEK
PUBLIC LIBRARY

Sleep was elusive, leaving Lindsey feeling like she'd been trying to catch a moonbeam in a pickle jar. Just when her body would relax and she was sure she was drifting to sleep, she'd snap awake at a sound and stare into the darkness with her heartbeat hammering in her ears.

When Saturday dawned, she was relieved that she had two days off from work because she was going to need it to recover from the sleep she'd missed the night before. She had some paperwork to do over the weekend, but otherwise, she was determined to run her errands, do her laundry, enjoy her time with Heathcliff and forget all about the overdue library book, Candice Whitley and whoever might have killed her.

She did great right up until Monday morning, when she awoke hours earlier than she needed to and couldn't get back to sleep no matter how hard she tried. Knowing she was going back to work today, she just couldn't stop thinking about what had happened to Candice Whitley twenty years ago.

She rode her bike into work despite the steel gray clouds at the horizon promising incoming rain. She stopped at the small grocery in the center of town to buy the necessary fortifications to stave off exhaustion from the bakery counter. While standing in line, she felt the hair on the back of her neck tingle. Oh, no; not again.

She whipped her head from side to side, checking to see if anyone was watching her. There was no one. Other than Mr. Kelvey in line in front of her, the bakery area was empty.

"Hi, Ms. Norris. What can I get for you today?" Robin, the young woman who worked the bakery counter, greeted her.

Lindsey turned back toward the counter to see Mr. Kelvey shuffling out the door with his newspaper tucked under his arm while he held his coffee in one hand and his pastry bag in the other.

Robin had been working at the bakery for a couple of years now. When Lindsey had first met her she was in high school, but now she was a college student, commuting into New Haven for her classes. Despite the course load, she still managed to pop into the library for the free downloadable books.

"Hi, Robin," Lindsey said. The young woman looked as tired as she felt, which was verified when Robin covered her mouth with her hand to hide her yawn. "Did you stay up late studying last night?"

"I wish," Robin said. "I was up reading Lev Grossman's *The Magicians*. I knew I shouldn't start it right before bed. I think I need to design an app for my e-reader that closes the book for me and locks it at a designated time."

Lindsey smiled. "You could be onto something there. It would surely cure OMC syndrome."

"OMC?" Robin asked.

"One More Chapter."

"Ha! With my luck it would switch off right at a cliff-hanger and I wouldn't get any sleep anyway," Robin said. "So, what's your excuse for looking like death warmed over? What author are you cursing this morning?"

"Oh, thanks for that," she teased. "I didn't think I looked that bad."

Robin grinned and Lindsey was pleased that the young woman knew she was just teasing. Truly, she had a mirror; she knew how rough she looked today.

"I wish it was a book. Unfortunately, I was up uselessly fretting," she said.

"You should have read a book," Robin said.

Lindsey laughed. "You're right; what was I thinking?"

"Largest coffee available, then?"

"Yes, with a blueberry muffin on the side."

"Done."

Robin went to fill her order and Lindsey took a moment to decide if she had the heebie-jeebies because she was over-tired or if she still felt as if someone was watching her. She stood very still and then casually glanced around the corner of the shop.

The Gilmores, a newly retired couple who had bought a cottage near Beth's, were walking toward her, but they were deep in conversation and not paying her any mind. She realized the feeling of being watched was gone and she wondered for the umpteenth time if she had imagined the whole thing.

"Here you go, Ms. Norris," Robin said.

"Call me Lindsey," she said. She paid for her coffee and muffin and left a tip in the jar.

Robin smiled at her. "Thanks, Lindsey."

Outside, Lindsey sat down at one of the picnic tables in front of the grocery. She supposed she could have eaten on the deck out back but she wanted to watch the world go by a bit and get her bearings. A thick coat of dew covered the bench in the shade so she moved to the sun-dried bench and enjoyed her first restorative sip of coffee.

Life might be worth living after all. She broke off pieces of her muffin and alternated between eating and sipping her coffee. She could see the town was just beginning to wake up; traffic was picking up on the lane headed out of town as people commuted to work. CLOSED signs were flipped to OPEN in some of the smaller shops on the street.

She listened to the birds' morning chatter and felt the breeze coming in from the water tug at the hem of her skirt and the ends of her hair. The sun was warm on her back and she felt at peace for the first time in days. She must have been imagining things on Friday night; undoubtedly, thinking about Candice's murder had her on edge.

But then, she felt it again. The hyperaware feeling that she was being observed. The blueberry muffin lodged in her throat when she tried to swallow, so she took a sip of the hot coffee, trying to dislodge it while appearing calm when what she really felt like doing was standing up and screaming, *"What?"*

"Lindsey, hey, glad I caught you."

She jumped. Thankfully, the lid on her coffee prevented her from spilling it all over her lap. She whipped her head around in the direction of the person who had spoken and found Brian Kelly standing behind her. Relieved, she put her hand on her chest and blew out a breath.

"I'm sorry." He cringed. "I scared you, didn't I? I'm such a clod."

"No, it's fine," she said. She slid over and gestured to the bench. "Did you want to sit?"

"For a minute, sure," he said. "I'm meeting Milton Duffy here."

"Oh, are you interested in the historical society?"

"No, I'm joining him for his early-morning yoga on the beach," Brian said. He pushed his black-framed glasses up his nose. "I hear he's quite good."

"He is. I frequently find him in the most curious postures," Lindsey said. "It seems yoga really is a part of his everyday life."

"It can be very helpful in clearing the mind," Brian said. "You look as if something is weighing on your mind. Maybe you should join us."

"Thanks, but I'm not really dressed for it," she said. She glanced down at her flouncy skirt and then back at him. "You are the second person today to point out that I am not at my best. Is it really that bad?"

He looked pained. "Wow, I'm really imploding at the conversational arts today, aren't I?"

"It's all right," she said. "I am aware that I look a bit sleep deprived. The truth is I've been preoccupied by a . . . well . . . a murder."

Brian's eyes went wide. "Okay, I didn't see that coming."

"Don't worry," she said. "It wasn't recent. It was the murder of a local teacher twenty years ago."

"So, why are you thinking about it now?" He sipped the large cup of coffee he held and watched Lindsey over the rim.

"It was never solved," she said. "Then we had our amnesty day and a book was returned that had been checked out twenty years ago. When we looked up the record just to see what the fines would have been we discovered it was checked out to the teacher on the day she died—murdered by strangulation, in fact."

Brian shivered. "I think a ghost just walked over my grave."

"I know, it's awful," she said. "The thing is there doesn't seem to be a motive to kill her."

"No husband?"

"She wasn't married." Lindsey paused to sip her coffee. "There was a boyfriend, but he doesn't seem to have a motive, and she did have a student that she seemed close to but from what I've heard there doesn't seem to have been anything inappropriate going on. It seems that she was a very well-liked, hardworking, nice person with no enemies."

"Random killing by a drifter?" he suggested.

"You've noticed how small this town is?" Lindsey asked. "It's the sort of place where everyone seems to know everyone else's business."

Brian gave her a pointed look.

Lindsey smiled. "Yes, including me."

"I was thinking particularly you," he said.

His eyes were teasing. She studied him while he drank his coffee. He seemed very at ease. She didn't get the feeling that he was being critical or judgmental about her nosiness— just accepting.

"Yes, it's the librarian need for answers in me, and this situation is bugging me. I want to find out what happened to Candice Whitley," she confessed.

"Why?"

"Because it's important."

"Why?"

"How old are you?" she asked. She felt as if she was talking to one of Beth's four-year-old story timers.

"Just trying to help you work through it, but if you must know, I am thirty-six," he said.

"Sorry, I shouldn't have been sharp with you," she said. "I'm just frustrated."

"Well, start at the beginning. Who do you think returned the book?" he asked.

Lindsey was quiet for a moment. Then she turned and met his gaze and said, "Her murderer."

"Whoa."

"I know it sounds crazy," she said. "But I just can't help feeling like that book being returned wasn't an accident."

Brian's face was serious and he nodded as he considered her words. "I think you're right."

"Good morning, Brian, Lindsey," Milton greeted them as he strode toward the bench. He was in his usual tracksuit—Lindsey was sure he had one in every color—and his bald head was shining in the sun.

Lindsey and Brian both greeted him and Milton frowned at them.

"You both sound gloomy," he said. "Is everything all right?"

"It's fine," Lindsey lied.

"It's horrible," Brian said.

They looked at each other and Lindsey shook her head at Brian to signal for him not to say anything. He raised his eyebrows in question but nodded in understanding.

"What I meant, of course, was that horrible loss the Red Sox took last night to the Yankees," Brian said.

Milton beamed. "Really? I rather thought that was a spectacular game."

"You're a Yankees fan?" Brian asked. He sounded betrayed. "I thought everyone in Connecticut was a member of Red Sox nation."

"When you live in Newyorkachusetts, you come to accept

that you are a state divided," Lindsey said. "But I'm with you on the game. Wait, aren't you from Oregon? How is it that you root for the Red Sox?"

"I have family ties in the Boston area," he said. "Besides, much like Connecticut, we don't have a national baseball team in Oregon."

"Lindsey, I don't want to be negative, but you look anything but fine," Milton said.

Lindsey finished her coffee, hoping for a jolt of wakefulness. There was nothing.

"I'm a little overtired," she said.

"Thinking about the returned book?" Milton guessed.

"Maybe a little," she said.

Milton rocked on his heels as if considering what he wanted to say. "Maybe this time you need to let Emma do her job and steer clear of the situation."

Lindsey dropped her head to her chest. It occurred to her that she had been wondering how long it would be until someone offered her this advice. The problem was she had no interest in taking it.

She glanced at Milton and gave him a small smile. "I'll think about it."

"Which means you plan to completely disregard me," he said. Then he returned her smile, letting her know there were no hard feelings. "You know as the town historian, I feel the need to point out that not much changes in Briar Creek."

"Meaning?" she asked.

"In the twenty years since Candice was murdered, trees have grown, paint colors have changed on the buildings, but the residents by and large remain the same," he said. "Whoever killed her is likely still here, living among us."

"Oh," Lindsey said. Her voice sounded faint and she cleared her throat.

"For what it's worth," Brian said, "I think you need to be true to yourself, follow your heart, as they say."

Lindsey considered him for a moment and then nodded. As a fellow newcomer to the town, she knew he saw things with the same fresh perspective that she did.

"And now we're off to do some yoga by the sea," Milton said to Lindsey. "Care to join us?"

"Thanks, but I've got a staff meeting," she said.

They both grimaced.

"Nice empathy there, really," she said.

"Sorry," Brian muttered while Milton winked at her to let her know he was sorry.

She watched as they crossed the street toward the small beach beyond the town park, then she rose from her seat and dumped her refuse into a nearby trash can.

Town staff meetings were probably her top most-dreaded activity as an employee of the town of Briar Creek. It wasn't that she didn't like the other department heads, it was mostly that Herb Gunderson, who ran the meetings, was the most—there was no nice way to say it—boring person to run a meeting ever.

The only thing that made it bearable was that there was usually food, but today after her large muffin, she wasn't even hungry. This was going to be the longest hour of her life. Lindsey walked toward the town hall feeling as if her shoes were fashioned out of lead.

She walked to the meeting room on the second floor just down the hall from the mayor's office. Sally Kilbridge was at her desk busily clacking away at the keyboard. Today she returned Lindsey's wave without having to hide under her desk because there was no Robbie, although Lindsey noticed that Sally craned her neck, looking around Lindsey in a hopeful way.

Lindsey wondered if it ever bothered Robbie that people saw him as something special because he acted on stage and screen. He was talented, there was no question about that, but he was just an actor. He wasn't curing cancer or feeding starving people.

Lindsey wondered what it said about them as a society that a man who could memorize someone else's words and spit them back out in a convincing performance was paid more than the teachers and caregivers who educated and looked after their children. It was one of the many observations about human nature that left Lindsey boggled.

The door to the meeting room was ajar and as she approached she heard raised voices. This never happened in one of Herb's staff meetings. She hurried toward the room, wondering what catastrophe might have hit that required yelling.

When she got to the door, she froze on the threshold with her mouth agape. Herb Gunderson had Tim McIntyre jacked up against the wall with his hands fisted in Tim's shirtfront while holding him a foot and a half above the ground. Herb's whole head was a vivid shade of apple red while Tim looked bug-eyed and pasty.

"Herb, what the hell are you doing?" Lindsey cried.

Herb never lost his cool. Never. What had happened in here that he had Tim, the head of human resources, dangling in the air as if Herb was the school bully trying to shake lunch money out of the weaker kid?

Herb snapped his head in her direction. Veins throbbed in his neck and his eyes were full of rage. For a moment Lindsey wondered if he was going to come after her next.

"Herb! Drop him!" she said. She used her misbehaving-patron voice, which was more of a sharp bark but it usually got the point across.

Herb let go of Tim's shirt and stepped back. Tim fell to the ground and began to choke and cough. He put a hand at his throat and glared at Herb.

"He tried to kill me," Tim accused. He pointed one stubby finger at Herb and turned to Lindsey. "You're my witness."

Lindsey crossed her arms over her chest and studied Tim. She didn't like him. She had never liked him. He was a sawed-off little spark plug of a man, who derived a sense of power from his position by denying people's requests instead of facilitating them. She had gone more than a few rounds with him over vacations, extended leaves and overtime for her staff. He had been particularly vicious about her newest hire, Paula Turner, when she didn't come with the required three references. Lindsey had to go over his head to the mayor to argue for Paula.

"I have no idea what you're talking about," she said. "The next time you boys want to act out whatever big play was on *SportsCenter* last night could you kindly not do it before a staff meeting? It's incredibly unprofessional."

Herb opened his mouth to say something. Lindsey knew he was going to be honest about what had happened and Tim would use it to get him fired and then Tim would go for the job he'd always wanted: Herb's. The thought of having to work more closely and under the direct supervision of Tim struck terror into her heart. Not an exaggeration.

"That's not—" Tim sputtered, but she didn't listen.

"Herb, I need you," Lindsey said.

She grabbed Herb by the arm and yanked him out of the meeting room before he could cause irreparable damage to his career. Thankfully, no one else had arrived yet and she could get this situation under control before the whole thing got out of hand, so to speak.

She pulled Herb down the hall, noting that his face color receded from crazy mad red to a slightly overheated pink as they went.

They passed Jason Meeger, the head of sanitation, on his way down the hall. He gave them a curious look—everyone knew that Herb never missed a meeting, nor was he ever late for a meeting, and it was now three minutes after the hour and he was headed in the wrong direction.

"I just need to borrow him for a sec," Lindsey said. "Library stuff, we'll be back in five."

Jason looked as if he'd been handed a reprieve and Lindsey knew he'd been dreading the meeting as much as she had, which was ironic given that Jason mostly slept through them. She would have thought he'd miss the nap time.

She shoved Herb into his office and shut the door behind them. She said nothing while he paced back and forth, obviously trying to get ahold of himself. Finally, he stopped and turned to face her. He looked distraught.

"What happened back there?" she asked.

"I lost my temper," he said. "I haven't done that since . . . Well, in a very long time. Thank you for trying to make it less than it was."

"That's my story and I'm sticking to it," Lindsey said. "I'm assuming you two were being knuckleheads and that's that."

"I have to go talk to the mayor," he said.

"I don't think that's a good idea. Maybe you should just take a minute, go apologize to Tim and see if he'll accept that."

"He won't," Herb said. He gave her a rueful look. "It's not in his nature, especially since his career advancement depends upon me losing my job, which is probably why he slandered . . . Well, it doesn't matter."

"He said something about Benji, didn't he?"

It was a guess, but Lindsey had a feeling Tim knew Herb's weak spot and had been only too happy to show up to the meeting early so he could pick at it. That was his nature as well.

"It doesn't matter what he said. I crossed a line and I have to report it," Herb said. He tugged on the cuffs of his jacket and straightened his tie. "Can I ask a favor?"

"Sure."

"Tell everyone the meeting has been canceled," Herb said. "I'll be in touch with a new date and time, assuming I'm still employed here."

"You really don't have to do this," Lindsey said. "It's his word against yours."

Herb put his hand on her shoulder and squeezed it. It was a rare gesture of affection from him.

"Yes, I do," he said. "I'm not built any other way."

"Good luck," Lindsey said. She patted his hand and followed him out of the office.

He went one way and she went the other. Several times she thought about tackling him to the ground and stopping him from committing career suicide, but Herb was a by-the-book sort of guy and she knew he was right. He wouldn't be able to live with anything less than full disclosure.

When she got to the meeting room, the rest of the department heads were there but Tim was conspicuously absent. She had a feeling as soon as she'd gotten Herb to his office, Tim had scurried to the mayor's office like the little cockroach that he was to tattle on Herb without mentioning how he provoked him. Damn it.

"Meeting is canceled," she said. "Something suddenly came up."

The group, which had all looked bleary-eyed and pasty a second before, now looked bright-eyed and ready to face their days. They also bolted for the door like kids released for recess who were afraid the teacher might change her mind. Lindsey dove to the side to keep from being trampled.

Jason Meeger was the last one to leave. He paused beside

Lindsey and asked, "What happened? In all of the years I've been here, Herb has never canceled a meeting."

"Emergency convo with the mayor," she said.

Jason tipped his head to the side. "Something I should know about?"

She shrugged. "I really don't—"

"Because Tim McIntyre left just as I got here and he looked like someone had just handed him the winning Powerball ticket."

Lindsey stared at Jason. She didn't know him well, except that he was a Creeker, meaning he had been born and raised in Briar Creek. He had been the star of the football team back in his day but his muscle had gone to paunch as he trudged toward middle age.

Now he coached flag football in his free time because he loved the sport. But he was far from a big, dumb jock; Lindsey had helped him the day he'd brought his ten-year-old daughter into the library to check out knitting books. When Lindsey had found a local class, he had taken his daughter to it and had sat there and tried to learn how to knit with her and two of her friends. He was a good guy.

"Tim and Herb might have had a little dustup before you got here," she said.

"I knew it," Jason said. He punched his fist into his palm. "Tim has wanted Herb's job forever and now he'll use this to get it. How bad was it?"

Lindsey closed her eyes and groaned. "I've never seen Herb lose his temper before, so maybe it was just alarming to me because it was so out of character."

"That bad, huh?" Jason whistled between his teeth.

"You don't seem surprised. Is Herb known for having a temper?" she asked.

"Not in the past several years, but he did put a guy in the hospital once," Jason said.

"Herb? Our Herb?" Lindsey could not have been more shocked if Jason had told her that Herb had a secret passion for women's lingerie and stiletto heels.

"Yeah, but it was back when we were young, and his family—" Jason stopped speaking.

Lindsey waited but he didn't finish his sentence. Finally, she asked, "What about his family, Jason?"

"I can't," he said. "It doesn't feel right to talk about that time."

"What time?" Lindsey asked. She curled her fingers into her palms, trying to keep calm. She was a librarian. There was nothing more maddening to her than information being withheld.

"Herb was a DE on our football team," Jason said.

"Huh?" Lindsey looked at him like he was speaking Greek; actually, Greek might have made more sense.

"DE, or defensive end, is a very aggressive position," Jason said. "You get a guy who's big and fast like Herb and he can sack a QB in a blink. QB is a—"

"Quarterback, I got that," Lindsey said. "I'm just not following what this has to do with his temper or 'that time.'"

"Herb had a pretty vicious temper and when he got out on the field, well, it was a thing of beauty to watch him take down the opposing team."

"Still not following."

"His temper was not so awesome off the field. Herb didn't handle it well when Benji's girlfriend was murdered and people were looking at Benji as the killer. Herb got into a few fistfights defending his brother, and then someone pointed out that with Herb's temper he could easily have killed Candice Whitley himself."

"Oh, no," Lindsey gasped.

"Yeah, it was bad," Jason said. "Doug Renner got himself beat to a pulp for that one and if Benji and I hadn't pulled Herb off of him, he might have killed him. Herb went right into therapy after that. He was damn lucky Doug didn't press charges or he likely would have done jail time."

Lindsey shook her head. "I can't even picture Herb like that."

Except she could. She had seen the rage in his eyes when he'd held Tim McIntyre up against the wall. It had been fearsome and he had frightened her.

She couldn't help but wonder what Herb's relationship had been with Candice Whitley. Had they been close? How close? Had something happened between them that ignited his temper? Could the man she knew as mild-mannered Herb Gunderson be the one to have killed her?

CHAPTER

19

BRIAR CREEK
PUBLIC LIBRARY

When Lindsey arrived back at the library earlier than usual, Ms. Cole was already at the circulation desk. She glanced at Lindsey over the top of her reading glasses with surprise.

"Morning," Lindsey said. "Staff meeting was canceled due to unforeseen circumstances."

"Anything to be worried about?" Ms. Cole asked.

Lindsey knew this was a blanket question that included surprise firings, budget issues or any other conundrum that was likely to sneak up on a public servant and slam them in the back of the knees.

"No, nothing to be concerned about," Lindsey said. Unless, of course, she mentioned the possibility that the mayor's right-hand man was a murderer, but she wasn't going there. Not yet, anyway.

Lindsey scanned the library; all the usual suspects were in attendance. Ann Marie was at the reference desk; Beth was in the children's area with several moms and little ones; Peter

Schwartz, a crotchety older gentleman who enjoyed reading the paper, was in his customary cushy seat by the window; and several patrons were browsing the new-book rack.

She recognized Gina Rubinski, who was married to Dr. Rubinski, the local veterinarian. Gina was petite with short-cropped brown hair and a ready smile. Since her husband, Tom, was close friends with Sully, Lindsey had spent several evenings with the couple back when she and Sully had first dated, and she had grown very fond of them. She realized that now that she and Sully were being open about their coupleness again, it was likely that they'd get to double-date with the Rubinskis again.

"Gina, how are you?" she said as she joined her by the display.

Gina grinned at her and showed her the basket of books on her arm. "Optimistic."

"That's a lot of books to try and read in three weeks."

"I imagine I'll quit on some of them," Gina said. "I give them fifty pages, but if the author hasn't hooked me by then I have to break up with them."

"That's a good rule," Lindsey said.

Gina studied her closely, then she leaned in close so that Brigit Hardaway on the other side of the bookcase couldn't hear her. "You look tired. Is everything all right? I heard a rumor about . . . Well, if it's true . . ."

"The point, Gina," Lindsey said gently.

"You and Sully didn't break up again, did you? Because I heard you were back together but you don't look like a girl caught up in the back-together glow. You look like someone who didn't sleep at all last night, and not in a good way," she said. Then she looked horrified. "Did I just say too much? I did, didn't I?"

"No, you're fine." Lindsey shook her head. "Sully and I did not break up. In fact we're doing great. Really. I just have some stuff on my mind."

"Oh, good," she said. "The four of us should get together for a game night. I don't think Tom has any impending puppy deliveries."

"Make it Scrabble and I'm in," Lindsey said. "Gina, you grew up in Briar Creek, right?"

Gina nodded.

"This is rude of me to ask, so please forgive me, but are you old enough to have had Ms. Whitley as an English teacher?"

"It's not rude at all mostly because I'm not old enough," Gina said. "She was killed when I was still in middle school, but I remember how freaked out everyone was afterward. Because they never found the killer, we lived in a constant state of alert for the next year or so. No girl ever went anywhere alone just in case there was a serial-killer thing happening."

"That must have been awful," Lindsey said.

"It was," Gina said. Her cell phone chimed and she glanced at it. "Sorry, it's Tom calling from the office. I have to take it."

"No problem," Lindsey said. "We'll talk soon."

"I'd like that," Gina said. She walked to the circulation desk with her basket while answering her phone.

Lindsey scanned the new books. There was a new one all about barbecue. Well, wasn't that convenient? As a good librarian, she always tried to keep an eye out for books she knew her patrons might be interested in, and since former police chief Daniels was interested in barbecue, she was just being a good librarian by calling him and letting him know they had a new book he might want to check out. Yes, that was her story and she was sticking to it.

She went into her office and called the Daniels' house. He picked up on the fourth ring.

"Daniels' residence, can I help you?" he asked.

"Hi, this is Lindsey at the library," she said. "I think I have a book you might be interested in."

"Is that so?"

"It's about barbecue, Tennessee style," she said. "Did you want me to put it aside for you?"

"That's thoughtful of you," he said. "Thanks."

"That's what I'm here for," Lindsey said. She grabbed a pen out of the holder on her desk and tapped it on a pad of Post-it notes. "We'll hold it under your name at the front desk for three days."

"Excellent. Now go ahead," he said.

"Go ahead, what?" Lindsey asked.

"Go ahead and tell me why you really called," he said. "This has to do with the Whitley murder, doesn't it?"

"Well . . ." Lindsey drew out the word as she answered in an effort to buy time. In hindsight, she probably should have prepped a bit more before she made this call. Daniels had caught her off guard. "Okay, you got me. What do you know about Herb Gunderson's temper?"

"Ah, so that little gem turned up again," Daniels said. "Who mentioned it?"

"Actually, I saw it," she said.

"Oh." He sounded intrigued.

"And I was wondering if anyone ever looked into his relationship with Candice or his whereabouts during the killing."

"We did, because there was an altercation that caused us to look at him more closely. He was cleared as a person of interest," Daniels said. "He wasn't in Briar Creek at the time of the murder, which we verified."

"Then why did Doug Renner make such horrible accusations?" Lindsey asked.

"Because Doug was jealous of Benji's relationship with Candice and he knew he could provoke Herb," Daniels said. "Or, more accurately, because when it comes to women men are stupid."

"Speaking from experience there?" Lindsey asked.

"My wife might think so," he conceded.

They were both silent for a moment. Lindsey had one other question for him but she wasn't sure how to phrase it. She tapped the pen on the pad again and decided just to go for it.

"Since we're talking about Candice Whitley in a purely conversational and not at all inquisitive way, I was wondering one other thing," she said.

She thought she heard amusement in his voice when he said, "Go ahead."

"What was the Larsens' relationship with Candice?" she asked.

"As in Principal James Larsen and his wife, Karen?" Daniels asked.

"Yes."

"He was Candice's boss, so naturally we interviewed him," he said. "I was in uniform back then so I wasn't as in on the details as the powers that be."

"Any idea what was said?"

"The chief back then was mostly concerned with any personal issues Larsen might know of in regards to his employee," he said. "If she had a rival at work, what her relationship with her students was, that sort of thing."

"Did anything turn up?" she asked.

"There was one thing," Daniels began, but then hesitated. "Let me ask a question before I say anything more."

"All right," she said.

"What brought the Larsens to your attention?"

"Well, as you said, he was her boss," she said. "You are aware of the robberies in town?"

"Yes, Chief Plewicki and I have talked about them," he said.

"Did she tell you that each person who was robbed had a connection to Candice Whitley?"

"She did," he said. "She also said that you were the one who figured it out—well, you and that Englishman."

"So, that's why I'm interested in the Larsens," she said. "Which you probably already knew if Emma told you about our discovery."

"I did, but I was curious to see if you'd be square with me. Thanks for that," he said. "I'll tell you what I told Emma. James Larsen was rumored to be having an affair with Ms. Whitley, but he denied having anything to do with her in that regard. We couldn't substantiate any relationship between them other than a purely professional one. If they had an affair, they were incredibly discreet about it, so he was never really a person of interest as he was at a school board meeting at the time of the murder. The rumors were considered to be just local gossip in the aftermath of a horrible crime."

"I can see that," she said. "He and his wife have been together for a long time."

"They had been married for a couple of years at the time of the murder, so it's most definitely a long marriage," Daniels said. "Which makes it seem even less likely that Larsen cheated on his wife. If he was a cheater, wouldn't there have been some gossip about him cheating again over the past twenty years? But there's been nothing."

"True, but their house was robbed just like the others," she said. "So someone has an issue with him."

"But until we know who that person is, you really need to let the police handle this," Daniels said. "I understand that you started the investigation with the book, but, Lindsey, the murderer is still out there. You need to be very careful."

"I'm always careful," she said. She knew she sounded contrary and possibly a little defensive so she added, "I promise."

Daniels heaved a deep sigh.

"Really, I will," she said. "Thanks for the information."

"No problem," he said. "Of course when I talk to Chief Plewicki, I will be mentioning our conversation to her."

"Do you have to?" she asked.

"Yes," he said.

"Even if I fast-track all the new barbecue books that come in to go to you first?"

"Is that a bribe?"

"I was thinking of it as more of an incentive program."

"Listen, I only told you what I did because anyone from twenty years ago could have told you the same, but also because I know what it's like to be invested in discovering the truth," he said. "It gnaws at you relentlessly."

"Like a dog with a bone," she agreed.

"Be careful, Lindsey," he said. "This dog has a nasty bite."

Lindsey hung up her phone and leaned back in her seat. She couldn't shake the feeling that she was missing something. She was sure of it.

Then again, maybe the book wasn't the clue that she thought it was. Maybe it had just turned up on someone's shelf after traveling through a long line of readers and that person had decided to do the right thing and return it.

But that was one of the things that bugged Lindsey about the whole situation. She used to be an archivist. She was up close and personally familiar with books that had aged poorly. If Candice's book had been well traveled, it would have been well-worn. If the book had been neglected, it would have been dusty, moldy, dried out, any of those scenarios. But it wasn't.

In the time she'd had the book, she had observed that other than some yellowing of the pages, the book was in excellent condition. According to the old-style library pocket on the inside of the book, it hadn't been checked out more than a half dozen times. Whoever had had the book for the past twenty years had taken impeccable care of it.

That brought her right back to the murderer. She watched the ID channel. She knew how killers felt about mementos from their victims. Like a kid getting a participation award in soccer, Candice's book could have been a trophy for her killer, something he held on to relive the murder again and again. So what would make a killer give up his trophy?

CHAPTER

20

BRIAR CREEK
PUBLIC LIBRARY

**"G**ood morning, Sherlock!"

Lindsey glanced up at the door of her office to see Robbie Vine standing there. He was wearing jeans and a collared shirt, both of which looked to be a bit dusty, and he had a stack of books in his arms.

"Back atcha, Watson," she said. "What do you have there?"

"Old high school yearbooks," he said.

She tipped her head to the side and studied him. "Any particular reason?"

"I'm so glad you asked." He strode into the room and set the books on the edge of her desk. "Dylan and I were going through his yearbook last night, I like to point out the girls I think he should ask out, you know, give him some lines to try out on them—"

"Seriously?"

Robbie raised one eyebrow at her. "I never joke about schmoozing the ladies."

"Which is one more reason why you and I never dated," she said.

He frowned. "Anyway, it occurred to me that insight into the unfortunate Ms. Whitley might be found within the pages of the yearbooks from her teaching days."

"That's brilliant!" Lindsey said. "Huh, why didn't I think of that?"

"You're not the only one with the gift of deductive reasoning," he said.

"Where'd you get the yearbooks?"

"Milton loaned me some duplicate copies from the historical society's storage area," he said. "I had to go up into the attic to retrieve them. I should get extra points for that. Dreadful place."

Lindsey took one of the books and cracked it open, turning away when a plume of dust rose up in her face. The book was heavy with faux leather binding with the school emblem embossed on the cover.

She glanced at the candid pics of the seniors that filled the first page and smiled. Even though Lindsey had been just a kid in the early nineties, she remembered the fashion well.

"Oh, wow, chunky boots, overalls, and Nordic sweaters. Did we know how to dress back then or what?" she asked.

"Obviously the fashion police were on hiatus during that decade," Robbie said. He opened a book and began to peruse the pages. He paused to wipe the years of accumulated grime off his fingers onto his pants. "Ew."

Lindsey smiled. She whipped through the pages of students until she came to the events pages. She had seen the headshot the newspapers had run with the announcement of Candice's death, but she was curious as to what other photos there might be of the well-liked teacher.

Candice Whitley had been an English teacher and also the drama coach, so the pages devoted to the school plays and musicals included several pictures of her. In the first one Lindsey found she was painting a piece of set onstage and she had her head back and was laughing at the person taking the picture. Two other adults were with her and they were laughing, too. Lindsey read the caption, hoping to get more names of people to talk to about Candice. The names listed were Candice Whitley, Judy Elrich and Benji Gunderson.

Lindsey opened the top drawer of her desk. She pulled out a large square magnifying glass she kept in there and held it over the page.

"Find something?" Robbie asked.

"Benji Gunderson," she said.

"The boyfriend?"

"Yep," Lindsey said.

"Let's see, then," he said.

She handed him the book and the magnifying glass. Robbie studied it. "Not a bad-looking chap."

"Thanks, I appreciate that."

Lindsey and Robbie turned to the door to find Sully standing there, leaning against the doorjamb with his arms crossed over his chest.

"Don't tell me he's managed to make himself useful?" Sully gestured at Robbie with a doubtful look.

"He has. He brought me the Briar Creek High School yearbooks," she said. Then she looked at him and narrowed her eyes. "In fact, I bet you're in some of these."

"Oh, no, don't," he said. He waved his hands at her like he was signaling that the bridge was out.

"Oh ho, yes, do," Robbie chortled. "Let's see what the water rat looked like back in his prime."

Sully dropped his head to his chest as Lindsey snapped open the book from his graduation year.

"Let's see . . . *S* . . . Schultz . . . Slauson . . . Sullivan . . . There you are. Oh, my."

"Let me see!" Robbie leapt out of his chair and circled the desk. He took the book from Lindsey and stared at the picture. When he glanced up he was grinning. "Good God, man, were you wearing flannel?"

Sully shrugged and held his hands out wide. "I wasn't the fashion plate back then that I am now."

"And your hair—did you not own a comb?" Robbie asked. He was thoroughly enjoying this.

Lindsey glanced at her boyfriend in the doorway. With his square jaw, thick chestnut curls and bright blue eyes, he would be handsome even if he chose to wear nineteen-seventies' disco fashion.

She grinned at him, and said, "I think the picture is very sexy."

Two deep dimples bracketed his mouth when he returned her smile. "We're definitely going to discuss that later and in greater detail."

"People, please, I was so looking forward to lunch today," Robbie said. "Now I'm feeling positively ill."

Their smiles deepened as Robbie threw himself back into his chair and picked up another book, obviously ignoring them.

"What brings you by?" she asked Sully.

"I just got back from running Lisa Dutton to her island," he said. "She told me that Herb Gunderson has been suspended without pay. I thought you'd want to know, if you didn't already."

"I didn't," she said. She put the book aside and leaned back in her chair, crossing her arms over her chest.

"And yet you don't seem surprised," he said.

She glanced up to find both Sully and Robbie watching her speculatively.

"I'm not," she said. She gestured for Sully to come in and close the door. She liked Herb. She would tell Sully and Robbie what she knew but she didn't want anyone else to overhear what she'd learned about a man she considered a solid coworker.

She glanced at the clock on her computer. She knew she had to be on the reference desk shortly, so she gave them a brief accounting of what had happened at the morning's staff meeting.

Robbie looked shocked. "Herb Gunderson? I never would have guessed it. He's as mild mannered as a hamster."

Sully did not look as shocked. "I remember a few episodes from our youth. Herb was a hothead, no question, but he wasn't a bully. The only time he ever scuffled was if someone messed with him or his."

"Well, I think Tim must have said something to make him snap today," Lindsey said. "I don't think the mayor had a choice but to suspend Herb."

"Any idea what was said?" Robbie asked.

"No. Tim's a spineless weasel so I bet he'll deny baiting Herb, which was quite clearly what he was doing."

"Hopefully, Herb will come clean with his accounting of the situation," Sully said. "I know he's not the most exciting soul in Briar Creek, but he does a great job of dotting all the *i*'s and crossing all the *t*'s. I don't know what Mayor Hensen is going to do without him."

"Hopefully, we won't have to find out," Lindsey said. She frowned at her phone. "I'm surprised the mayor hasn't called me. Since I broke up the altercation I was sure Tim would use me to corroborate his story."

As if her words beckoned the summons, her phone rang. The number on the display was the mayor's.

"Sorry, boys, but it looks like I spoke too soon. I have to take this," she said.

They both gave her looks of sympathy. It was never comfortable to receive a call from the boss when they wanted information on the bad behavior of a coworker.

Robbie left the office first and Sully took the opportunity to plant a quick kiss on her lips.

"It'll be okay," he said.

Lindsey nodded and reached for the phone as he shut the door behind him.

"Hello, Mayor Hensen," she said. "What can I do for you?"

CHAPTER

21

BRIAR CREEK
PUBLIC LIBRARY

It was an uncomfortable call. Lindsey liked Herb. She did not particularly care for Tim, so it was very difficult to give an unbiased account of what had occurred, but she did her best.

Afterward she logged a few hours on the reference desk, which was unusually quiet. A surprise afternoon rainstorm seemed to have dampened anyone's interest in coming to the library. Lindsey couldn't blame them. If she wasn't working, she'd be sitting at home with a pot of tea and a good book, curled up in an afghan with Heathcliff by her side.

Instead, she spent the next hour working on the schedule and checking over payroll. When both tasks were done, she turned back to the yearbooks Robbie had left in her office. She picked up the one from the year before Candice's death.

She flipped through the pages, looking at the young faces of the students. How many of them were affected by having their teacher murdered on campus? How many of them left their childhood behind that day? She suspected it was a turning point in many of their lives, and not a good one.

She flipped through the pages, looking for Sully. Yes, she had already seen his senior picture but now she wanted to see what he looked like when he was younger.

Why was she so interested in what he had looked like as a teen? She didn't need to ask herself the question. She already knew. She loved him. More than that, she was *in* love with him. The mere sight of him made her heart clutch in her chest. He was the yin to her yang, her other half, her soul mate. She had pretty much known it from the moment they met, and he had known it, too, but it had taken him a bit longer to trust it. Trust her.

Like all great romantic heroes, Sully had needed to do a significant bit of growing before they could be together, but if the past few months were any indication, the boy had finally gotten it.

She found his picture. He was a sophomore in this one, but he still had the same two dimples that bracketed his mouth, and his blue eyes twinkled at her from the picture. Lindsey sighed. There was no question. When it came to this man, she was a goner.

She glanced out the window toward the pier where Sully spent his days. She knew she was a hopeless believer in happy endings but she really thought they'd find theirs.

A few months ago Robbie had divorced his manager wife and made it very clear that he wanted to date Lindsey. For a nanosecond, she seriously considered accepting his offer. For while Sully and Robbie shared many fine qualities such as being kind, smart, funny and not hard on the eyes, Robbie was always much more emotionally available than Sully. It was so tempting to date a man whose emotional compass was so easy to read.

Sully was the original strong, silent type. In many ways this was not a bad thing. Unlike Robbie, he didn't talk her to death, but when it came to knowing how he felt about her or them, she was always uncertain. When they first dated, it made for feelings of insecurity that she didn't enjoy, and then he broke up with her out of the blue—leaving her even more bewildered and confused—because he was afraid that she was having a change of heart. He'd never bothered to ask her; he just dumped her. When she thought about it, she still felt a little irritated.

During their breakup, which was miserable for both of them, they reestablished their friendship. Sully made a real effort to talk to her and share his feelings and the past hurts that he'd kept buried. He gave her hope that maybe they could find their way back together again.

But when Robbie arrived back in town, divorced and announcing his intention to pursue Lindsey, everything changed. It was like the kick in the pants both Lindsey and Sully needed. Not wanting to embarrass him, Lindsey told Robbie in private that she couldn't date him, but he refused to listen and vowed that he would win her over. Lindsey had been amused, knowing Robbie was always full of bluster and that, while she cared for him, her heart belonged to Sully and it always would.

The gossip about Robbie's intentions, however, moved through town like a flame licking up gasoline and left about as much destruction in its wake, as there were many single women with their eyes on Robbie. When the story reached Sully mere hours later, the tale had warped and twisted into one of Robbie and Lindsey eloping that very night.

Lindsey had been in her apartment, wearing her favorite plaid flannel pajama pants with a matching blue thermal shirt when there was a knock on her door so fierce and so loud she was sure it would wake everyone in the house.

Heathcliff barked himself into a frenzy until she opened the door and found Sully. She stared at him with her toothbrush still clenched between her teeth while holding Heathcliff by the collar to keep him from knocking Sully down.

"Me," Sully said. "You're dating me."

Lindsey released Heathcliff, who jumped on Sully in an enthusiastic greeting, and pulled the toothbrush out of her mouth.

"Are you asking me or telling me?" She tried to ignore how hard her heart was hammering in her chest.

"Telling you," he said.

She raised her eyebrows in surprise. She refused to acknowledge the ridiculous female part of her that was having an Austen-worthy fit of the vapors, in a good way, at his macho declaration. This was not the nineteenth century. She would not swoon even though she thought she might.

"Is that so?" she asked. She was pleased her voice sounded so calm, but she suspected it was shock. She was seeing more emotion pour out of him than she was used to.

He shoved his hand through his hair, clearly exasperated. "No, it's not. I'd like to tell you you're dating me, period, but I suppose that's not civilized."

"Much like banging on someone's door at . . ." She turned and glanced at the clock, and said, "Eleven thirty at night."

Sully's face turned a hot shade of red but then he smiled and locked his gaze on hers. He leaned in close and took her hand in his and tugged her toward him until she was just inches away from him.

"I can't help it," he said. "You do not bring out the most civilized version of me. I've tried, really, I have. I've taken it slow, I've tried to be just friends so that we can rebuild what was lost between us due to my bungling, but here's the thing. I don't want to be friends."

"No?"

"No."

He pulled her closer so there were just the smallest of air particles between them.

"You once said to me that you were not going to chase me, that if I wanted to ask you out, I needed to strap on a pair and get it done," he said.

"I remember," she said. Her voice wasn't much more than a whisper. She was having a hard time thinking. He was so close she felt engulfed in his body heat, and the smell of the sea that seemed to be so much a part of him swamped her senses and fritzed her brain.

"So, I guess we're there again," he said. "I'm asking: Will you go out with me?"

"Yes," she answered.

She felt Heathcliff sit on her foot as he wedged himself in between their legs, as if determined to be a part of the moment. She was sure Sully was going to kiss her now, but he didn't.

Instead, he cupped her face with one hand and said, "At the risk of sounding proprietary, and not really caring if I do, I need to be clear that you're dating just me, no one else—particularly, no Englishmen."

"You're not a good sharer, huh?" she asked.

"Not when it comes to you," he said.

He looked vulnerable making the declaration, letting her know how much she mattered to him, and it melted Lindsey's heart just that much more. She threw her toothbrush over her shoulder and wrapped her arms around him and pulled him close.

"That's all right. When it comes to you, I, too, am not a good sharer. I'm sorry, but you're not allowed to date any Englishmen either."

The grin he sent her was blinding. Then he kissed her. It was the sort of kiss that staked a claim and made promises about forever, and while she loved to revisit the memory, as it still made her toes curl, she tried not to overthink it.

They'd been dating for the past few months and Lindsey could not remember a time when she'd been this happy. Because it was so fragile and new, they had kept it quiet, seeing each other on the sly and never in public, and Lindsey was glad.

She had wanted to keep it just between them for as long as possible before other people's opinions started to shape and color what they had. But now, now they were out there again, back in the public eye. She took a moment to savor that. It felt right and she was happy. She loved him. She wasn't ready to tell him just yet, but she was getting really, really close.

She glanced back down at the yearbook in her lap. Teenage Sully grinned at her and she couldn't help but grin back. Suddenly everything seemed possible.

She shook her head and flipped through the pages of the book, studying the candid shots for glimpses of Candice Whitley. She went through the other books as well. In several of them, Benji Gunderson was helping his girlfriend. Lindsey studied his face and the expression in his eyes when he looked at Candice. He looked like a young man in love.

Lastly, she found Matthew Mercer's portraits. His hair

was a thick thatch of black and he seemed to be looking past the photographer at something behind him. It made for an eerie portrait, but there was a deep sadness in his eyes that gave him more the look of a lost puppy than a look of menace. Lindsey could understand why a teacher would feel compelled to look out for him.

She glanced at the small description beside Matthew's picture. It was a few lines of poetry that she suspected were his own.

It read: *Love from afar is an unopened letter, to leave the contents unknown makes nothing better . . .*

Lindsey knew that poetry was open to interpretation, but this one seemed most definitely to be about the anguish of unrequited love. She took the book to the copier and ran off a copy. She had a feeling Emma would want to see this. No, it didn't prove anything, but Lindsey couldn't help but think that it gave some insight into the emotional state of Matthew Mercer.

"Boss, I'm heading over to the high school to show the librarian how to sign the students up for library cards," Paula said as she approached the reference desk. "I was thinking I'd give her a stack of flyers for our summer programs, too."

"Great idea," Lindsey said. She glanced at the clock. Ann Marie was due back in five minutes. "If you can wait a couple of minutes, I'll come with you."

Paula squinted at her. "You think I need help?"

"No, nothing like that," she said.

Paula studied her for a second and then shook her head as if she had just figured out that Lindsey had another agenda entirely and she knew better than to ask.

"It'll take me a few minutes to get my things together," Paula said. "Meet you by the back door."

"Sounds good," Lindsey said. She carried the yearbooks back to her office and locked them in her desk. She wasn't sure why, but since they were the property of the historical society and not the library she felt the need to be extra cautious with them. As she tucked the key to her desk back in the side pocket of her purse, she felt the hair on the back of her neck prickle.

There it was again, the feeling that she was being watched. She glanced out the window of her office and saw Ann Marie walking toward her door. So that explained the feeling. Obviously, Ann Marie was looking for her. She blew out a breath in relief.

"Lindsey, so glad I caught you," Ann Marie said as she popped into her office. She gestured toward the window. "I caught sight of Beth through the shelves and thought she was you."

Lindsey glanced toward where she pointed and saw Beth walking through the stacks, wearing Lindsey's purple vest, the one that was supposed to be for her gamers' prom but now looked like it had gone into rotation in Beth's regular wardrobe. She shook her head. Borrowing clothes and both of them dating—it was like they were roommates all over again.

She wondered if that was the sort of relationship Judy Elrich and Candice Whitley had shared. Judging by the pictures in the yearbook, it was, and she felt a pang of sympathy for Judy. She couldn't imagine how she'd feel if anything happened to Beth. And to lose a friend in such a horrible way—Lindsey wasn't sure how a person ever got over that. She suspected Judy still hadn't.

Which made Lindsey wonder if Judy had heard the rumors about Candice having an affair with Principal Larsen.

Lindsey was sure she had, but she also figured that Judy must not believe them. After all, how could Judy work for him now if she believed or knew such an awful thing about him before?

Then again, someone believed the rumors. Why else had the Larsens been robbed? Lindsey was determined to find the connection.

"Lindsey, hello?" Ann Marie waved her hand in front of Lindsey's face.

"Oh, sorry, I missed what you said."

"Uh-huh, I got that." Ann Marie nodded. Then she smiled. "I just wanted to let you know I saw Herb Gunderson headed this way."

"If he asks for me, I'm at a meeting," Lindsey said, and she ducked out the back to meet Paula.

CHAPTER

22

BRIAR CREEK
PUBLIC LIBRARY

Hannah was waiting for them when they arrived. It was the end of her day; even the maker-space students had cleared out.

"Can I offer either of you a chai tea?" she asked. "I make it myself with fennel, cardamom, cloves and a bunch of other stuff, including Darjeeling tea."

"Yes, please," Paula said. "That is the perfect antidote for the post-rain dreariness out there."

She pointed her thumb at the window. The skies were still dark from the earlier rain but the clouds were moving swiftly and not lingering or dropping any more moisture.

"Sounds great," Lindsey agreed.

"Excellent," Hannah said. She gestured for them to follow her into the workroom, which housed a small kitchen. "Now, are you sure you trust me to sign these kids up? I'm pretty loosey goosey around here and just use their student IDs for book checkout."

"Sure we do," Lindsey said. "This town is small enough for us to hunt down an overdue teen."

"Okay, then," Hannah said. "I had nightmares about Ms. Cole coming after me for not following protocol, but if you're certain . . ."

"We are," Lindsey and Paula said together.

"Don't worry, I won't let her bully you," Paula said. "Especially since you've taken two of my four cats and are open to visitation by me and Momma cat."

Hannah smiled. "Always."

A few months ago, Paula, with the help of Lindsey's dog Heathcliff, had found a mother cat and three kittens in an abandoned fishing shack. Together they had rescued them before disaster struck. It was a bond and Lindsey knew how much Paula had come to love her small herd of cats.

Lindsey looked at Paula in surprise. "Hannah took two of the kittens?"

Paula nodded. "It was tough, but it was just too much. So I kept Momma and Sissy, the girl kitten, and she took the boys."

"Fred and George," Hannah said. "They've only destroyed four rolls of toilet paper, the back of my armchair, and two curtains so far so I think they're acclimating—you know, if shredding is indicative of kitten contentment."

When Hannah went to go get some extra mugs from her office, Lindsey looked at Paula and said, "You two seem to have this in hand, so I'm just going to—"

"Snoop," Paula interrupted her.

Lindsey gave her an affronted look. She wasn't annoyed, just surprised that in the few months she'd worked there Paula had gotten her number so easily.

"That obvious, huh?"

Paula nodded. "But it's all right; go do what you have to do. I'm happy here with Hannah."

Lindsey studied her clerk for a moment.

"So that's how it is?" she asked.

"Maybe," Paula said. Then she smiled and Lindsey patted her on the shoulder.

"Good for you," she said. "I'll be back shortly, but if you need me call my cell."

"Okay, boss," Paula said. Then she grabbed Lindsey's hand and added, "Be careful."

"Always."

Lindsey slipped out the door before Hannah returned, trusting Paula to make her excuses to the librarian.

The last time she'd been here she'd wanted to talk to Judy, but this time she was setting her sights higher. This time she wanted to talk to Principal Larsen.

She left the library and hurried downstairs to the front office. When they had arrived, the principal's office door was closed, so she hadn't been able to see if he was in, but she was hoping if she loitered in the office long enough she might be able to find out if he was available.

Lindsey pushed through the glass door with the enthusiasm of an adventure-story heroine starting out on a quest but stumbled to a halt as soon as the door shut behind her.

"Hello, Lindsey," Chief Plewicki said. She was standing at the front counter beside the sign-in sheet. "Imagine meeting you here."

"Uh . . ." Lindsey stalled. She glanced away from Emma's scrutiny and then back. She shook her head. She didn't need to feel guilty or be intimidated. She was here on library business. "Actually, given that I'm working with Hannah, the high school librarian, on a project, it's not really that surprising."

Emma gave her a flat stare. Michelle Maynard, the petite middle-aged woman who ran the school's front office, gave Lindsey an alarmed look that indicated she thought Lindsey was in deep trouble. Then she hurried back to her desk and hid behind her computer monitor, obviously not wanting to get in trouble by association.

Suddenly, Lindsey felt like she was fourteen and had been sent to the office for skipping class—which had never ever happened—and she found she had new sympathy for the school rule breakers.

She stiffened her spine. She was not going to be intimidated. "It's true. Hannah is helping us issue library cards to all of the freshmen to keep them reading this summer. You know, to improve the literacy rate in our community."

Emma pursed her lips. Lindsey knew she had her on the ropes. She reached into her purse, looking for one of the summer program flyers. Instead, she found Matthew Mercer's poem from the yearbook.

"What's that?" Emma asked.

Lindsey shoved it down in her purse and grabbed a flyer. She handed it to Emma. The chief looked from it to her.

"This looks good," she said. Lindsey felt herself relax. "But I was talking about the other thing. It looked like a page from a yearbook."

Lindsey huffed out a breath. What was it Daniels had said about being like a dog with a bone? Emma had them both beat. She was a boa constrictor squeezing the facts right out of her.

"It's just something I found in an old yearbook. I was actually planning on showing it to you later."

"I have time now," Emma said.

Lindsey opened her purse and pulled out the page. She handed it to Emma, who scanned it with interest.

"Matthew Mercer," she said. "Candice's prize student."

"I thought the poem was of particular interest," Lindsey said.

Emma read the words and then glanced at Lindsey. "Sounds like a case of unrequited love."

"By all accounts, Candice Whitley was the only person who took an interest in him," Lindsey said. "If this poem is about her, it could be that he was in love with her and she rebuffed him, and . . ."

"He killed her," Emma said. "I thought the same, but I've been over the case files and Mercer had a solid alibi. He was taking the PSAT exam at the time of her murder. I saw the paperwork, timed and date stamped. He's clear."

"Someone has to be lying," Lindsey said. "There is a reason the four houses that were broken into all have a connection to Candice's murder. Someone wants this case reopened."

"But who?" Emma asked. "And why?"

"To bring her killer to justice," Lindsey said.

Lindsey and Emma stared at each other. Lindsey could tell that Emma believed what she was saying but was frustrated because there were no leads to follow, no clear direction to take, no smoking gun to be found.

"I'm right about this," Lindsey said. "That book was not a coincidence."

"Maybe," Emma said. "I have been trying to find both Mercer and Gunderson. I want to know where they were on amnesty day. So far, I have not heard back from either of them, which is not a big surprise as any lawyer worth his six-minute billing cycle would advise them not to say anything unless it is forced out of them by a court of law. Still, I'll keep trying."

The door to the principal's office opened and James Larsen stepped out with his wife, Karen. He started at the sight of Emma, which Lindsey found to be an interesting reaction.

"Chief Plewicki." Karen Larsen strode forward. "I am so sorry. Have we kept you waiting?"

She was a petite, pretty woman and wore her thick brown hair in a half-up-and-down sort of hairdo that looked effortless. Her slender figure looked very modern housewife in a collared cotton blouse paired with skinny jeans and calf-hugging brown boots.

"No, actually, I just arrived," Emma said. "I was talking to Lindsey—you know, our town librarian—about her summer programming."

Lindsey gave Karen a small wave. Karen and James weren't regular library users but Lindsey had seen them about town enough to recognize them.

"Nice to see you," Karen said. She shook Lindsey's hand in a warm, firm grasp. Her husband stepped forward and did the same.

"Hannah tells us you're signing up all of our freshmen for library cards," he said. "Great idea."

"Thank you." She took a moment to study him.

James Larsen looked like a principal. In a dress shirt with the cuffs folded back, a tie in the school colors of red and blue, and charcoal gray trousers, he wore the uniform of a man who wielded authority comfortably. His close-cropped gray hair and kind brown eyes also made him appear wise and compassionate.

Lindsey had heard that the students liked him and she

could see why. He seemed like the sort of man you could trust to give sound advice and just discipline when it was deserved.

"What's the news?" Karen asked Emma.

Emma tipped her head to the side, clearly confused.

"About the robbery at our house," Karen said. "I do hope there's some news. I haven't been able to sleep a wink knowing that some stranger walked around in my house and touched my things. It's just so creepy."

"I'm sorry, Karen," Emma said. "I'm still waiting on the results of the partial print we got off your glass door, but as soon as I have news, I'll be in touch. I'm actually here for a different matter. I need to speak with you, James, about one of your teachers."

He looked at Emma in alarm. "Is someone on my staff in trouble?"

"No, it's about a former employee," Emma said. "I need to talk to you about Candice Whitley."

Lindsey did not think she imagined it when James's face went a few shades paler and he seemed to stagger on his feet a bit. She wondered if Emma caught it, too. If she did she didn't show it, and Lindsey made a mental note to never play poker with the chief of police.

"Oh, that poor woman," Karen said. "I remember her and that horrible, horrible night."

James put his hand on his wife's shoulder and gave it a gentle squeeze.

Karen turned to her husband with her brow furrowed in sadness. "She was such a good teacher and just a lovely person, inside and out. It was the worst sort of tragedy with no rhyme or reason, just devastation. Personally, I always felt like her boyfriend, Benji, was involved."

"But he wasn't in Briar Creek at the time," Lindsey said. "It would have been impossible."

"Maybe he wasn't working alone," Karen said. "Maybe he paid someone to kill her for him."

The group was silent. Lindsey watched Emma study everyone's face. She wondered what the police chief was thinking. Did she suspect the Larsens had something to do with Candice's murder or was she here to rule them out?

"Candice taught my cousin's kid Joey Prentice to read," Michelle, the secretary, said. "She was devoted to her students. Her death was a crushing blow to them."

"It was to us all," James agreed. His voice sounded gruff and Lindsey noted that he looked very uncomfortable.

Karen turned back to Emma. "I hope you have new information, something that will help catch her killer so that he can never do that to anyone ever again."

"Possibly, but I need to know as much as I can about her time here," Emma said. She gestured to the principal's office. "If you have a moment, James?"

"Now?" He glanced at her and then to the office, as if he was surprised she wanted to speak to him in private. "Well, okay." He kissed his wife's cheek. "I'll see you at home, dear."

"Take your time," she said. "You want to help in any way you can."

James and Emma disappeared into his office and shut the door behind them.

"I'm sorry to hear about your house," Lindsey said. "It seems there have been several robberies in town lately."

"I wish I could take comfort in the fact that others have suffered like us, but it just makes me even more anxious," Karen said. "I read a statistic online the other day that once a person is robbed they are likely to get robbed again as soon as they replace their things."

"Do you have a lot to replace?" Lindsey asked.

"No, actually, we aren't even certain of what they took, only that they smashed the window on the back door to get in," Karen said. "The police suspect they were interrupted before they could actually take anything."

"You're lucky you weren't home when it happened," Lindsey said. "That could have been terrible."

Karen nodded. She leaned against the counter. "James and I were both here. I'm a reading tutor here at the high school. I have been for years. The pay is lousy, but the boss is pretty cute."

She smiled in the direction of the office and Lindsey could see the affection in her eyes for her husband. She wondered if Karen had heard the gossip about James and Candice having an affair and if it had bothered her.

Lindsey knew that asking that question would raise her buttinsky tendency up to the level of out-and-out rudesby, but she had to know. Maybe she could make an informational end run.

"So, did you work with Candice, then?" she asked.

"Oh, yes, she was a lovely girl," Karen said. "We had common ground in that she was an English teacher and I was trying to increase the level of literacy, so we worked together quite closely. But personally, I'm afraid I didn't know her very well. It has always been difficult for me to establish close friendships with the rest of the staff, being the boss's wife and all."

She looked a bit chagrined by this but in a cheerful way so if she had heard the rumors, they didn't seem to bother

her. Lindsey didn't envy her the rock and a hard place her job put her in. She couldn't imagine having a husband under-foot while she was trying to run the library. Abruptly, an image of Sully working in the library flitted through her mind and she had to admit he looked good there. She vigor-ously shook her head. There was no need to be going there.

"Are you all right?" Karen asked her. She was giving Lind-sey a curious look.

"Yes, sorry, I thought I felt something buzz by my ear," she said. "I'd better get back to the library. I expect Hannah will wonder where I've gone."

"Nice to see you, Lindsey," Karen said.

"You, too."

Lindsey left the office feeling torn. On the one hand she hadn't gotten a chance to talk to the principal like she'd hoped, but on the other hand she did get Matthew's poem to Emma.

She supposed it was just as well. What could she have pos-sibly said to James Larsen that didn't sound like an accusation? And after meeting his wife, she really didn't want to accuse him of murder. The man had an alibi, after all. What could she really gain from asking him about Candice Whitley?

She was halfway down the hallway when it occurred to her that Emma was probably asking Principal Larsen some pretty personal questions. Lindsey wondered what James would answer, then she wondered if Emma would tell her what he said.

She almost laughed out loud at the thought of Emma's face if she demanded to know what she and Larsen talked about, except it wasn't funny. Emma would likely choke her out and lock her up.

Despite the Larsens' obvious affection for each other and

their appeal as a couple, James Larsen was hiding something. At the very least, he was ill at ease about something. Lindsey had wrangled with enough patrons on the status of their lost, stolen and missing library books to know when a person wasn't being completely forthcoming about something. She'd seen Larsen's face. He was definitely hiding something. But what?

CHAPTER

23

BRIAR CREEK
PUBLIC LIBRARY

When Lindsey arrived back at the school library, she found Paula and Hannah right where she left them in the small workroom. Paula had her shirtsleeve up and Hannah was examining her tattoo of flying books.

"That's beautiful," Hannah said as she traced the edge of a book with her finger. "It's like a painting."

Paula smiled at Hannah and they looked mutually charmed by each other. Lindsey wondered if she needed to do the requisite clearing-of-her-throat thing before this got awkward. Or would that make it more awkward?

She decided just to go for it and took two quick steps back and then strode into the room, pretending to just be arriving.

"Hey, there, you two," she said. "Don't tell me I missed the chai."

They both started at her abrupt arrival, but Lindsey

plopped down into her seat and busied herself with the mug in front of her.

"Not at all," Hannah said. "In fact, yours should be cool enough to drink now."

"Excellent. Thanks so much," Lindsey said. She took a sip. It was delicious; perfect for a rainy day. "Oh, this is really good. I'm going to need the recipe so I can make it for my crafternoon group."

"Crafternoon?" Hannah asked. "What's that?"

"A Thursday book club where we eat, discuss a book and do a craft," Lindsey said.

She glanced at the two women. Hannah was pretty isolated at the high school and Paula was new to town. It occurred to her that they both might be looking to expand their social circle.

"You know, you two should join us. It's a lot of fun and you're both book people. You'd fit right in," she said.

"I'm not very crafty," Hannah said. "In fact, unless it involves a soldering iron, I pretty much hate it."

Paula laughed. "Really? I love crafts. Lately I've been into beading."

"Well, maybe we can come up with a project that can incorporate beads and soldering," Lindsey said.

"I'd like that," Hannah said.

"Me, too," Paula agreed.

"Cool," Lindsey said. "I'll email the details to you."

While Lindsey finished her tea, Paula told her that Hannah was now up to speed on how to sign up the freshmen students using their online system. Hannah then discussed the possibility of making the high school a satellite library to the public library. Lindsey thought the idea had merit and promised to mention it to the library board at their next meeting.

"Hannah, what sort of archiving do you have here?" she asked.

"Meaning old books and such?"

"I was thinking more about old photographs, awards, newspaper clippings," Lindsey said. "From about twenty years ago."

Hannah nodded. She popped up from her seat and said, "Follow me."

Lindsey tried to contain her excitement. Hannah had the look of a librarian starting out on an information quest. This was always Lindsey's favorite part of the job: when someone asked for information that was hard to find and the librarian and patron were now engaged in a quest for the answer. Truly, there was no other high quite like it.

Hannah led them through the library to a closet door at the back of the room. It was painted bright blue and had a STAFF ONLY sign on it. Hannah typed a pass code number on the keypad next to the door and they heard the door unlock.

She turned the knob and pushed the door open. She reached up and pulled on a string that switched on the overhead light. The room was full of shelves of old overhead projectors, slide carousels, whiteboards, chalkboards and 8mm movie projectors.

"Wow," Paula said. "This is like the room where the last century in educational technology came to die."

Hannah covered her face with her hands. "Now you know my secret. I'm a hoarder."

Lindsey glanced around the room. It was neat and tidy with no dust and everything was clearly labeled.

"You're a saver not a hoarder," she said. "Trust me. I know the difference."

"Thank you. *Saver* sounds so much better. I keep thinking I should throw some of this out," Hannah said. "But then I think the kids can use the equipment for robot parts or for their inventions. You know reuse, recycle, renew."

Paula looked at the old filmstrip projector as if it were a relic in a museum. "They really made these things to last back then."

"Exactly," Hannah said. "This stuff is super sturdy for making battle bots."

"Awesome," Paula said.

"But what you're looking for is over here," Hannah said to Lindsey. She led the way to a large shelving unit that was filled with cardboard boxes. These were file boxes that came with lids and were clearly labeled.

"These are the high school archives. They go all the way back to the fifties. One of my many projects has been to digitize all of the files and make them accessible to former students and teachers. I've written a grant to buy a high-quality scanner but I haven't heard back yet."

Lindsey looked at the boxes. "That's an ambitious project," she said. "Have you thought about having the historical society do it for you?"

"I did," Hannah said. "I even had Milton Duffy come out here and take a look. He said his volunteers would love to do it for free but they'd have to take the boxes back to the historical society. Principal Larsen said no."

Lindsey frowned. "I don't understand."

"Neither did I, but he was quite adamant that none of the school's archives were to leave school premises," Hannah said. "Which is why I wrote the grant for the scanner. Milton thought he might be able to get his volunteers to work here. So now we're in the eternal holding pattern that is requisitions."

"You know if we did merge libraries you would have access to our equipment and we have a scanner," Lindsey said. "And our premises would be your premises and vice versa."

"I'm really liking this idea," Hannah said. She gestured to the boxes. "Is there something in particular you're looking for?"

"A picture of a person holding a copy of *The Catcher in the Rye* from October second, nineteen ninety-six," Paula said.

Lindsey ignored her. "May I?"

Hannah gestured for her to go for it. Lindsey stepped forward and started reading the labels. She worked her way back a few decades until she found the section of boxes labeled for the early- to mid-nineties. There were four of them. She grabbed the first one by the openings that acted as handles and pulled it off the shelf.

"Can we help?" Paula asked.

"Please," Lindsey said. "These four boxes cover the time period I'm interested in."

Hannah grabbed one and Paula grabbed the remaining two. Lindsey hugged her box to her side with one arm and pulled the door open. Hannah and Paula led the way out of the room. They all blinked against the brighter light of the library. Hannah put her box on the first table outside the storage room, and Lindsey and Paula did the same.

Lindsey lifted the lid off and glanced at the contents. More files and more labels all done in chronological order. Whoever had been the librarian back in the day had clearly had a rage for order.

She pulled out the first file and scanned the contents. It

was all about a Future Cities project. She moved on to the next one.

"What are we looking for?" Hannah asked as she opened her box.

"Any file that mentions Candice Whitley or Matthew Mercer," Lindsey said. "She was a teacher and he was her student."

"I know that name," Hannah said. "She was the teacher who was murdered twenty years ago."

Lindsey looked at Paula. "You want to tell her what you found on amnesty day?"

Paula did and Hannah's eyes went wide. "I just got chills. Do you really think it was the murderer who returned the book?"

"I don't know," Lindsey said. "It could be a random happenstance or a weird coincidence."

"But you don't believe in coincidences, do you?" Hannah asked.

"No," Lindsey said.

They all turned their attention back to the boxes. It took a lot of digging but Hannah was the one who found the first stash of pictures from one of the plays Candice and Judy had put on as the drama club coaches.

Lindsey had seen several of these photos in the yearbooks but one in the group Hannah found had a great closeup of Benji Gunderson. She put it aside. Paula found the next great picture. It was field day at the school and there was a picture of Matthew Mercer out in the sun, talking to Candice. Their conversation appeared to be intense and Lindsey noted the date on the picture. It was taken the day before Candice was murdered. She put that one aside, too.

By the time they finished looking at the contents, Lindsey had five pictures that showed close-ups of Benji and Matthew.

She knew it was a long shot, but her plan was to ask her staff if any of them had seen anyone who resembled either of these men on amnesty day.

"Hannah, can I make some copies of these pictures?"

"I don't see why not," Hannah said. "They aren't copyrighted and you're not taking the originals off the premises. I have a copier in my office. I'll go make them for you."

"Thanks," Lindsey said. "Oh, and, Hannah, you might not want to mention to anyone that you made copies of photos for me."

"What photos?" Hannah asked with a wink.

When Paula and Lindsey left the high school, Lindsey gave the office a side eye to see if Emma was still with James. His door was open and the room appeared vacant. Lindsey didn't know what to make of that and she didn't think calling Emma to discuss new books was going to work as well on her as it had on Daniels. Darn it.

They were halfway back to the library when Lindsey noticed that Paula kept glancing at her as if she wanted to say something but couldn't find the words.

"Spill it," Lindsey said.

"What?" Paula tossed her purple braid over her shoulder and looked toward the bay.

"Whatever is bothering you," Lindsey said. "Go ahead and ask me."

"Nothing is bothering me."

"Okay."

"Really, I'm fine."

"All right."

They walked in silence for a minute. And then Paula's words came out of her like a geyser that couldn't hold it in anymore.

"What do you know about Hannah? How well do you know her? Is there anything I should know before I ask her out? Oh my God, did I just say that out loud?"

"Yes, you did," Lindsey said. She couldn't help but grin. "I don't know much about Hannah except that she's always pleasant, she's very well-read, she does amazing things with her students, like robots, and I think she likes you, too."

"How can you tell?" Paula asked.

"There was definitely a vibe."

"Oh, good, I was worried it was just me."

They continued walking but Paula seemed less stressed. In fact, Lindsey was pretty sure she detected a spring in her clerk's step.

"Did you mean it, then?" Paula asked. "You're inviting us to join your crafternoon group?"

"Absolutely," Lindsey said. "It was never meant to be a closed group, but it sort of became that way. I suspect things are going to be changing, what with Mary expecting her first child, so I think it's time we got some new blood. I know how much you love reading and I've seen your beadwork. You're a perfect fit."

"Okay, then, what are we reading?"

"*The Catcher in the Rye*, ironically," Lindsey said. "When it caused such a stir upon its return Violet admitted that she'd never read it, so we decided to give it a go. This is my second go-round on it. I'm hoping I enjoy it more this time."

"You didn't love it?"

"No, but I didn't hate it either," Lindsey said. "I suppose I just didn't find Holden very relatable."

"I love that book," Paula said. "It's in my top twenty books of all time."

"I'm betting you own a copy," Lindsey said.

"Naturally," Paula said. "Doesn't everyone?"

"Excellent," Lindsey said. "I'll let the group know you'll be joining us and you can lead the discussion."

"Oh, I don't know about that," Paula said. Her spring vanished and now she looked alarmed.

"Look at it this way: it's your opportunity to get me to love it," Lindsey said.

"All right, challenge accepted."

CHAPTER

24

BRIAR CREEK
PUBLIC LIBRARY

Lindsey sat in her office with the pictures spread out on her desk. It was the longest of long shots given that the pictures were twenty years old, but she had asked each of her staff if they remembered anyone who resembled these two men on amnesty day.

In addition to the pictures being really old, the other problem was that amnesty day had been crazy busy with the amount of people in the building and the deluge of books that had poured in. She couldn't fault her staff for not recognizing either Matthew or Benji when she didn't recognize them either.

Of course there was always the possibility that it wasn't Benji or Matthew who had returned the book. Perhaps now, just like before, they were both innocent.

Lindsey would have felt better about that possibility if there was anyone else with a motive, but so far no name had popped up as having an issue with Candice Whitley. Her thoughts turned back to Principal Larsen. He had been at a school board meeting at the time of the murder. That was about as solid of an alibi as a person could get.

Lindsey frowned. The four people who had been robbed were all people who had a major role in Candice's life: her best friend, her boyfriend, her student, and her boss. One of them had to know something that would give a clue as to who murdered her. Matthew and Benji hadn't been in town in years, Judy had recently come back, and Principal Larsen had never left town. And yet, their families had all been robbed. Why?

The book! Lindsey did a face palm. How had she not thought of this before? It all fit. None of the people who were robbed had lost anything significant. Karen had said it herself—she wasn't even sure of what was missing, if anything.

It made perfect sense. The person who had robbed all four of the people who had a connection to Candice must have been looking for the book. Once they found it, they must have returned it during amnesty day. Again, Lindsey couldn't help but wonder why. What was their purpose?

They couldn't have known that the library would notice who had checked out the book and on what day or that Lindsey would bring the book to the chief of police. So was it someone who wanted attention to be drawn to Candice's murder, or was it the murderer hoping to unload a piece of incriminating evidence after all this time?

Lindsey felt her head start to throb. So many questions and no answers, the biggest question being who wanted Candice dead? She wondered if Detective Trimble with the state police had had any luck with the book. She decided to call Emma and see if she had anything to share.

Emma answered on the second ring.

"Chief Plewicki," she said. Her voice was clipped and Lindsey had the feeling she was not having a great day.

"Emma, it's Lindsey," she said.

"Oh, boy," Emma said. "Let me do a preemptive strike. I haven't heard anything from the state police about the book. It is not a high priority given that the only thing we know about it is that it was checked out to Candice on the day she was killed. There was no blood splatter or anything else to indicate that it was a part of the murder. Does that appease your curiosity?"

"Partly," Lindsey said. "What I was really calling about was the burglaries."

"What about them?"

"When was the last one?"

"Why?"

"Because if it is just those four families who are connected to Candice Whitley who have been robbed then that means the robberies stopped after the book was discovered on amnesty day, which might mean that the robberies were done to find the person who might have had the book. And if that's the case then the last house robbed is probably where the book was, meaning that the murderer was that person or the person belonging to that family. See where I'm going here?"

Emma was silent for so long that Lindsey thought their call might have been cut off.

"Hello, Emma, hello."

"I'm here," Emma said.

Lindsey heard the rustling of papers.

"Well, what do you think?"

"Other than the fact that you're way too involved in this case?" Emma asked.

"Yeah, besides that."

"I'm looking at the reports from the burglaries. Two of them happened on the same night with the other two happening two nights before that."

"That's no good," Lindsey said.

"No," Emma said. "If I go along with your theory—and that's a big *if*—then I'm still left with the Larsen and Elrich houses as the last robberies."

"So there's no way to tell which house was robbed last?"

"No, but even if there was we have no way of knowing if it was the book the perp was after," Emma said. "It's pure speculation. Good speculation, but still."

"There has to be a connection," Lindsey said. "I know it sounds crazy but I can just feel it."

"Not crazy but doggedly determined," Emma said. "I have to ask you: In all of your library school training, did it never occur to you to study criminal justice and become a cop?"

"No," Lindsey said. "But if you think about it, the occupations really aren't that different."

"How so?"

"You have to work with people, you have to mediate whatever situation you find yourself in and you have to discover the truth or the facts or the information that is needed, which is different on any given day," Lindsey said.

"It's the people aspect that always throws a wrench into things, isn't it?"

"So true," Lindsey agreed. "The facts are the facts but the human element always manages to twist and change things."

"Well, this human element has to brief her officers on the latest," Emma said. "I'll talk to you later."

"You say that as if you've accepted that it's so," Lindsey said.

"I'm picking my battles," Emma said. "I know it goes without saying, but I'll say it anyway: be careful. If the murderer is still out there, you really don't want to make yourself a target by asking too many questions."

"I promise."

"Don't go anywhere alone," Emma said. "Part of what bothers me about this case is that Candice was walking alone on the school grounds on the night of her murder. It was fall, it was getting darker earlier. If she had just been with someone . . ."

"I'd be willing to bet her best friend, Judy, thinks about that all the time," Lindsey said.

"If she wasn't the one who killed her, I'll bet you're right," Emma said.

"That's harsh to think of the best friend as a suspect," Lindsey said.

"Everyone's a suspect," Emma retorted. "Everyone who was here in nineteen ninety-six at any rate."

"I'll call you if I discover anything of note."

"Thanks."

Lindsey hung up the phone. From what Milton, the town historian had said, Briar Creek hadn't changed much over the years that had passed since Candice's death. As he'd put it, the trees were taller and there were new coats of paint on some of the buildings, but overall, it was the exact same town right down to its residents.

Staring at the pictures on her desk, she wondered why this case was bothering her so much. Was it because Candice had been a great teacher struck down in her prime? Was it because of the returned book? Did it just really bug her that the murderer could so blithely return a book that he had taken from the woman he killed? Was it because there was seemingly no motive? Was it just her librarian's need for answers in a chaotic world? Was that why she couldn't let it go?

Lindsey gathered the pictures and put them away. Clearly, if either Benji or Matthew had been in the library no one had recognized them. She would have to think of something else that might tie the book to the killer.

It occurred to her that she hadn't asked anyone if they'd seen Principal Larsen or Judy Elrich on the day of the amnesty. She popped out of her office and went out to the front.

"Ms. Cole, by any chance did you see Judy Elrich or Principal Larsen here on amnesty day?"

Ms. Cole turned away from the computer screen and lowered her reading glasses until they perched on the end of her nose like a little bird on a branch.

"Do you honestly expect me to remember every person who came in here on amnesty day?" she asked.

"Well, when you put it like that . . ."

"It sounds mental," Ms. Cole said.

Lindsey sighed. She wished she had a case for argument but she knew she didn't. She glanced out at the late-afternoon sky. It looked as if the storm that had dropped rain on them earlier was circling back to dump some more moisture on them.

"I'm going to bring the flags in," she said.

She hoped the fresh air would do her some good. Maybe it would clear her head or give her an epiphany of some sort. She stepped outside and noted that the breeze had picked up. The band of steel gray clouds was moving in from the water like an advancing army. Lindsey hurried down the steps. Chilly gusts of air pulled at her long curls and she quickly wound it into a knot at the back of her head to keep it from blocking her vision.

"Need a hand there?"

She turned to find Robbie headed her way. The collar on his jacket was up and he leaned forward as he walked, as if the breeze was pushing him away from her.

"Thanks," she cried. She untied the ropes and Robbie lowered the flags. She caught them before they touched the ground and led the way into the library foyer, where they could fold them out of the wind.

Lindsey glanced out at the pier to see if Sully's boat was out. She didn't like to think of him getting caught in this weather, although if anyone could handle it, it was Sully. His boat wasn't at the pier. She tried not to fret.

When she turned back around, she found Robbie watching her with a resigned sort of expression.

"Are you all right?" she asked.

He shrugged. Lindsey held one end of the flag out to him. They folded it silently. When she worked the triangular shape all the way to the end and took it from his hands, he stopped her. He moved his hands to her elbows and held her in place.

"Are you sure?" he asked.

"About?"

"Him," he said. He nodded his head in the direction of the pier and Lindsey knew he was talking about Sully.

"Yes," she said. She met his gaze steadily so that he would have no doubts about her sincerity.

"You're serious."

"I'm sorry, yes."

"Bloody hell!" Robbie cried. "This romance between you two has been like watching two slow-moving sloths galumphing at each other. Honestly, it's downright depressing."

"I think sloths are adorable," she said.

"Well, that's it, then."

"It's been it for a while. You just haven't been listening."

"Of course I haven't. You can't blame me for hoping that the knuckle-dragging barnacle would sink his own boat on this one," Robbie said. "His record to date has been spotty at best."

"That's not very nice of you," Lindsey said.

"What can I say? Unrequited love makes a man mean," he said. "You think you've found your mate but, no, she's all tangled up in some sailor's knots and you're left high and dry without the girl. It's positively galling."

Lindsey smiled. From the sheer amount of bluster coming out of him, she knew Robbie was going to be just fine.

"I recently read something about unrequited love," she said. "It went something like, 'Love from afar is an unopened letter, to leave the contents unknown makes nothing better—'"

"'For love that is worthy does not make a straight line, rather it encircles two hearts and two minds.'"

Lindsey whipped her head in the direction of the voice. Brian Kelly was standing in the doorway to the library. A small smile turned up the corner of his mouth as he leaned against the doorjamb.

"Nice poem," he said. "One of my favorites, actually. The author was just young and brash enough to make an ass of himself and not care. The arrogance of youth."

"How did you know the words?" Lindsey asked. "I just read that recently in an old yearbook. It was written by a student at the local high school. How could you . . ."

And then she knew. Looking at Brian Kelly, she suddenly saw the boy he would have been twenty years ago.

"Matthew, is it you?"

CHAPTER

25

BRIAR CREEK
PUBLIC LIBRARY

Brian winked at her. Then he turned on his heel and disappeared into the library.

"Matthew? I thought his name was Brian," Robbie said. "Met him at the Anchor a few nights ago. Interesting chap. He's lived all over the country, most recently in Oregon, if I remember right. Full of great stories."

"Was one of them about how he killed his teacher Candice Whitley?" Lindsey asked. She shoved the flag into Robbie's arms and raced after Brian.

"I think I would have remembered that!" Robbie cried as he hurried after her.

They dashed into the building. Lindsey glanced left then right. There wasn't another unalarmed exit in the building. The only way out was the front door.

She spun around and grabbed Robbie by the arms. "Stay here and guard the door."

"But what if he's dangerous—" he began to protest.

"Just do it!" Lindsey yelled.

She turned and raced into the fiction area. The stacks of bookshelves were perfect for hiding and Matthew had a healthy head start. She ran down the main aisle, snapping her head back and forth looking for him. Other than a few patrons browsing books there was no one. She hurried over to the non-fiction side and did the same.

"Oh, Lindsey, perfect timing. Do you know where I can find a vegan—" Becky Delaney asked. She was seated on the floor amidst a stack of cookbooks.

"Sorry, can't talk now," Lindsey said. "Did anyone run by here in the last few minutes?"

"Other than you? No." Becky frowned. "Is everything all right?"

"No, not even close," Lindsey muttered.

She ran out of the stacks. The only other place Matthew could have gone would be the hallway that led to the meeting rooms. The doors were kept locked, so if he ran this way he should be trapped.

"Ms. Cole, did anyone run by here?" she cried as she raced past the desk.

"No! Of course not! There's no running in the library!" Ms. Cole shouted as Lindsey ran past.

Even knowing that the lemon was probably going to have a cow, Lindsey didn't slow her pace. She had to catch Matthew if he was here. He was the key to so many of their questions. She was sure of it.

The doors to the meeting rooms were all closed. Lindsey tried the first two. They were locked. She grabbed the last door-knob and prepared to fling it open but then stopped. If Matthew was in there, which seemed most likely, he could be waiting for her. Despite his alibi, he could still be a murderer.

She exhaled slowly, trying to calm her racing heart. She turned the knob. It wasn't locked. She eased the door open. There was no noise from inside the room. She did feel a breeze stir the hair that had fallen about her face. It was a cold, stiff gust, the sort that accompanied an incoming storm.

"Damn it!" Lindsey shoved the door open and strode into the empty room.

A window on the far side of the room was open. She had no doubt that this was how Matthew Mercer had made his escape. She crossed the room and peered out the window, knowing as she did that he was likely long gone.

"Hello, love," Robbie said from below the window. It had just begun raining and he was getting wet.

"I told you to stay by the front door," Lindsey cried. "He might be getting away."

"No." Robbie shook his head. "He was way ahead of us."

He pointed to the ground where a pair of footprints showed clearly in the mud as leaving the building via the window. Lindsey tapped the sill with her fist. She'd lost him.

Lindsey leaned down and held her hand out to Robbie. He clasped her wrist with his hand and she locked her fingers around his wrist and hauled him through the open window and back into the library.

"Well, Sherlock, it looks like we need to report the discovery of Matthew Mercer's alias to our police chief," Robbie said. He didn't look the least bit reluctant, which Lindsey thought spoke well of him since Emma struck fear into the hearts of most people, including Lindsey occasionally.

"Not just yet, Watson," Lindsey said. "I happen to know that Brian Kelly is renting a room from Peter Harwood."

"And you're thinking to go and pay him a visit?" Robbie

shook the rain off his reddish blond hair, sending droplets of water across the room.

"I clock out in ten minutes," Lindsey said. She wiped a few drops from her face. "Meet me in front?"

Robbie grinned. "You're letting me go with you without an argument?"

"Don't look so surprised, Watson," Lindsey said. She closed the window and locked it. "Every good detective needs a sidekick."

"Sidekick?" Robbie frowned. "I don't think I really thought the character assignments through."

"Too late," she said. "You already gave me the hat."

"Just so," he said.

Lindsey led the way out of the room, locking the door behind her. If Emma wanted to come over here and check for any sort of fingerprint evidence that showed Brian Kelly to be Matthew Mercer, then she wanted to leave the room as uncontaminated as possible.

Back in the main room of the library, Lindsey went to close up her office and grab her umbrella while Robbie cooled his heels by the front door. Lindsey knew where Pete Harwood lived because his was the only house in town that sported a toilet as a petunia planter. It made Eloise Schaffer, his across-the-street neighbor, crazy, and she'd spent hours in the library poring over the local zoning ordinances to see if she could make him remove the toilet. She could not. Lindsey was quite sure Peter had taken an absurd delight in thwarting Eloise. Either that or he just really loved the petunias in his toilet, as he replanted them every spring.

Lindsey handed Robbie an umbrella she had fished out of lost and found. Together they stepped outside into the windy wet. Lindsey led the way as they trudged down the sidewalk toward Peter's house.

A grizzled old man with a perpetual five o'clock shadow, his silver hair was always unkempt and the end of his bulbous nose pulsed with the sort of capillary-busting red only found at the end of many gin bottles. Pete was harmless so long as you didn't get on his bad side. Lindsey wondered how Matthew Mercer had managed not to do that all these months when he was clearly living a lie.

She walked through the center of town and then turned on a small side street. At the end of the cul-de-sac, Peter's house faced Eloise's in a stare down that could be felt all the way down the street.

Eloise's home was an immaculately kept cape, white with a forest green trim, surrounded by a classic picket fence. Purple and white flowers exploded from the front garden beds, while not so much as one stray leaf marred the perfection of the green lawn.

Across the way, Pete's place seemed to mock Eloise's perfection by being an explosion of colorful bushes and trees, all leggy and wild. The lawn was uneven, leaves were scattered across the high grass and odds and ends filled the front porch and the yard. A squashy couch was on the front porch along with a noisy collection of wind chimes. Lindsey was betting the noise drove Eloise batty. And sure enough, at the base of the front steps was the much-maligned toilet.

Lindsey hurried up the walkway with Robbie at her side. He paused at the base of the steps to study the purple flowers gushing out of the toilet.

"What sort of statement do you think he's making with this?" he asked.

"The sort where he wants his busybody neighbor to mind her own beeswax," Lindsey said.

"You got that right!"

Lindsey and Robbie spun around to see Peter Harwood walking around the corner of the house. He was smoking a cigarette that he paused to stub out on the bottom of his shoe before tucking the butt into the bottom of the petunia pot. He wore a bright yellow raincoat with the hood up.

"You're the librarian, right?"

"That's me," Lindsey said. She stepped forward and held out her hand. "This is my . . . associate Robbie Vine."

"Good day," Robbie said and shook Pete's hand next.

"You're the actor."

"You've heard of me?" Robbie looked flattered.

"Eloise across the way had a lot to say about your performance in the play last fall. She seemed to think you weren't committed to your craft, that perhaps you lacked confidence, if you chose to die onstage."

Robbie frowned. He glared at the tidy house across the street and then looked back at Peter. "I can get another toilet for your front yard if you need one. We can make it a low flow."

Peter busted out a laugh, which quickly rolled into a meaty smoker's cough. While he hacked, Lindsey and Robbie exchanged concerned looks.

"I may take you up on that," Peter wheezed. He gestured for them to follow him up onto the front porch. Wicker chairs were scattered across the narrow area but Peter sat down on the big, squashy sofa that looked more worn than the others. His favorite, Lindsey guessed.

"What can I do for you?" Peter asked. He pushed the hood back from his face.

Lindsey closed her umbrella and perched on the edge of her seat. She was edgy and poised to run should there be any sign of Matthew Mercer in the vicinity.

"We're looking for the man who is renting a room from you," Lindsey said.

Peter gave her a dubious look. "Why? Did he not pay his library fine? Is this guy going to shake the money out of him for you?"

"Now I'm an enforcer," Robbie said. "I quite like the sound of that."

Lindsey gave him a quelling look. He shrugged.

"No, nothing like that," Lindsey said. She wasn't sure what to say given that she didn't know what Peter Harwood knew. "How long have you lived in Briar Creek?"

"All my life," he said.

"A native," Lindsey said. "Well, that does change things."

"How?"

"Because now I know that you know we aren't here to talk to Brian," Lindsey said.

"I do?"

"Of course you do, mate," Robbie said. "Because you know we're actually looking for Matthew Mercer."

Peter visibly paled. He swallowed hard and said, "I don't know what you're talking about."

"Yes, you do," Lindsey said. "We know that Brian Kelly is Matthew Mercer. We need to find him."

"He didn't kill Candice," Peter said. He jumped to his feet with his fists balled at his side, looking like he wanted to take a swing at someone.

"We didn't say he did," Robbie said. He rose to face Peter. His voice was deceptively even until it went flat and cold. "Why did you?"

Lindsey took out her phone and dialed Emma's direct number. "I'm calling the chief of police. I imagine she's going to want to talk to you."

Peter looked back and forth as if trying to find an escape route.

"Don't, just don't," Robbie said.

Peter lowered his head and charged him like a bull. Robbie let out a whoosh of air and dropped to the ground. Lindsey went to grab Peter but he bolted out into the rain. She knew she could chase him or tend Robbie and finish her call to Emma, but she couldn't do all three. She crouched beside Robbie.

"Are you all right?" she asked him.

He was curled up with his knees against his chest, sucking in air like a fish out of water.

"Lindsey, what's going on?" Emma's voice demanded from her phone.

"Robbie and I are at Peter Harwood's," Lindsey said. "You'd better get over here right away."

"Why? What's happening?"

"We found Matthew Mercer," Lindsey said.

"Damn it, I told you to butt out," Emma snapped. "I'll be right there."

The call ended and Lindsey pocketed her phone. She grabbed Robbie by the arm and hauled him into the nearest chair.

"Scale of one to ten with one being Emma unconscious and ten being Emma volcanic, how much trouble are we in?" Robbie asked.

"That depends."

"Upon?"

"What's worse than volcanic?"

CHAPTER

26

BRIAR CREEK
PUBLIC LIBRARY

"What were you thinking?" Emma asked. She didn't wait for an answer but kept pacing across the porch as if she might explode if she stopped moving.

"We were just taking the flags down," Lindsey said. She figured the best way to calm Emma down was to let her think this was all just happenstance.

"But then our investigative powers kicked in," Robbie said. He stood and planted his hands on his hips as if he were a superhero.

Lindsey shook her head at him. Emma was not one to be trifled with when she was in a temper.

"Investigative powers?" Emma rounded on Robbie. She was a head shorter than him but not at all intimidated by his height, good looks, fame or anything else for that matter. "I'm sorry, did I hire you recently? Because I am pretty sure I didn't, and if I didn't you have no business chasing down leads in *my* investigation."

"What's the matter, love?" Robbie asked, leaning in. "Does it really bother you that I am such a natural at this?"

Emma closed one eye as if warding off a headache. "Is he for real?"

Lindsey nodded. Yes, Robbie was obviously very proud of himself. What Lindsey found interesting was that he seemed very determined to make Emma see him that way as well. Interesting.

"Chief, I have the warrant," Officer Kirkland said. He strode up the walkway with purpose in his stride.

"Excellent," Robbie said. He rubbed his hands together, as if eager to search the house.

"Sit!" Emma barked at him.

He raised one eyebrow at her, as if amazed by her temerity in talking to him in that tone.

"No," he said. "We found Mercer and we tracked him here. I'm going in."

"No, you're not," Emma said. She glanced at Lindsey, who was still seated. "Neither of you is to set foot in this house. This is now an official police investigation. While I am grateful that you discovered Brian Kelly's real identity and confirmed that he's been living here, you are not to do anything further on this case."

"Bloody Nora!" Robbie protested.

"Are you calling me names?" Emma asked. They were still standing nose to nose and she looked like she'd have no problem kicking him in the privates if she felt it was warranted.

"No, it's just an expression of . . . outrage," Robbie said. He must have sensed Emma's ire, because he turned so that his side was facing her and his privates were protected.

"Well, can it," Emma said. "And if you put one toe inside the door of this house, make no mistake: I will shoot it."

Emma spun on her heel and stormed the house with Kirkland right behind her. They knocked. No one answered. Not a big surprise. Emma reached for the doorknob and found it unlocked. Pulling out her service revolver as a precaution, she led the way into the house.

"Hell of a woman," Robbie muttered. The admiration in his voice was impossible to mistake.

"It's about time," Lindsey said.

"For what?" He turned reluctantly from the door to face her.

"For you to figure out that you have the hots for Emma," Lindsey said.

"What?" he squawked. "Don't be daft."

"I'm not," she said. She checked the time on her cell phone. It was fifteen minutes until Sully was supposed to pick her up for their date. She jumped to her feet. "Oh, no, I have to go!"

"Date with the seahorse?" Robbie asked. His usual disparaging tone was replaced by something else, something without rancor. Lindsey thought it might be acceptance.

"How did you know?" she asked.

"Because you've had the look of a woman anticipating seeing the man she's in love with all day," he said.

They stared at each other for a heartbeat and Lindsey smiled. "You seem awfully okay with it."

"I've come to realize that in my life, Lindsey Norris, you will always have a special place in my heart," he said.

"I will?"

"You will always be the one who got away," he said. He stepped forward and kissed her forehead. The contact warmed Lindsey all the way down to her toes because she knew that it meant they had turned a corner; that no matter what, Robbie Vine would always be her friend.

"I like that," she said.

"Good."

"What are you going to do?"

"Stay here and badger information out of the chief until she tells me all," he said. "It's quite thrilling, this crime-solving thing."

"Some might even say addictive," Lindsey agreed. "Please be careful and don't get arrested."

"I'm too charming to be incarcerated," he said. "Now go, and for God's sake, Norris, put on a short skirt and tight top and bring that man to his knees."

Lindsey grinned. "Will do."

She didn't bother to go back to the library to retrieve her bike. She figured she and Sully could pick it up later. But even at a fast jog, it took Lindsey all fifteen minutes to get home. She arrived on the porch sweaty and disheveled after the last of the afternoon's rain shower had decided to pelt her under her umbrella all the way home.

Mercifully, Sully's truck wasn't there yet. She raced inside and pounded on Nancy's door. Heathcliff started barking and greeted her with his usual exuberance when Nancy opened the door, wiping her hands on her apron.

"Lindsey, what are you doing here?" Nancy cried.

Violet popped up behind her. "You're supposed to have a date!"

"With my brother!" Mary cried, joining the group. "Do not tell me you called it off. I swear I will have an aneurysm."

"What? No!" Lindsey said. "I'm just running late. I was just with Robbie—"

"What?" Nancy and Mary gasped while Violet frowned.

"No, not like that," Lindsey said. "We were following up on a lead— Listen, it's not important. What is important is that I need to shower and change. Can you stall Sully? He'll be here any minute."

"Of course we can," Nancy said. The rumble of Sully's truck sounded outside on the pavement. "We've got this! Go!"

Lindsey turned and bolted up the stairs. She got up three steps before she turned and called, "Violet!"

Violet appeared in the doorway, "Yes?"

"I know you wanted Robbie and I to hook up so that he would stay in Briar Creek."

Violet sighed. "It was selfish of me. You and Sully are a perfect pair. I am happy for you."

"Thank you," Lindsey said. "But don't despair. Robbie gave me his blessing tonight to date Sully, and I think it's because his heart is pulling him in a new direction."

Violet clasped her hands together in front of her chest in a hopeful gesture.

"I don't want to speak out of turn, but don't be surprised if you find he has a sudden interest in the criminal justice system."

The sound of someone stepping onto the porch made them both jump.

"Go!" Violet squealed.

Lindsey did not need to be told twice. She raced up the three flights of stairs with Heathcliff by her side.

"Come on, buddy. Mama has a date," she said.

It was the fastest shower of Lindsey's life. There was no fighting the humidity, so she defrizzed her long blond curls as best she could but accepted that they were going to run amok whether she liked it or not.

She took Robbie's advice and went with her highest heels—a ridiculous pair of forties-style black and white stilettos that she had bought because they were on sale—her shortest charcoal gray pinstripe skirt and a crisp white blouse. It was the sort of outfit that screamed professional, but she wasn't sure of what.

She wished she had her purple vest, the one she had loaned to Beth. It always made her feel better and right now she could use a little fabric courage. Maybe it was because they hadn't seen each other since this morning, maybe it was because everyone in town knew they were together again or maybe it was because she was no longer pushing aside how she truly felt about Sully, but she felt as if tonight was going to be different between them, and it made her nervous.

She felt as if they had been dancing around each other for months. Robbie was right. It was time to either go big or go home. She had just finished putting on her lipstick when she heard him knock on her door.

Heathcliff charged the door and Lindsey followed, smoothing her hands over her skirt as she went. Maybe she should change. Maybe they weren't ready for a big date night. Maybe this was not as big of a deal to him as it was to her. Suddenly, the urge to go into her room and hide was more tempting than reading just one more chapter in a really good book when it was already the wee hours of the morning and she knew she needed to sleep. Yes, the urge was that strong. She shook it off.

"Here goes," she said. She blew out a breath and pulled open the door.

Sully in a suit—a frigging suit—stood there grinning at her.

"Phew," he said. "I was beginning to think you were going to stand me up."

"Not a chance," she said.

As she stood there taking in the sight of him—really, how had she never guessed how good he'd look in a suit?—he took a bouquet of red roses from behind his back and held it out to her.

"Thank you. They're lovely," she said. She breathed in their scent and smiled at him.

"I stopped by the flower shop on my way here," he said. "I told Kelsey at the counter that I was coming here, so the news that we are out on an official date should have circulated through town"—he paused and glanced at the watch on his wrist before adding—"about thirty minutes ago."

"So, we're officially a thing?" she asked.

She took the roses and led the way inside. He caught her hand in his when she would have disappeared into the kitchen for a vase and pulled her back to him. Then he kissed her with a thoroughness that left her breathless and made her ears ring.

"Officially a thing," he said. He seemed content just to stand with his hands on her hips, holding her close, breathing her in. "Darlin', you look stunning."

"Thank you," she said. "You look pretty wow yourself."

He grinned. Done with being ignored, Heathcliff joined the huddle and Sully let go of Lindsey so he could crouch down and scratch the dog's ears.

Lindsey continued on her way to the kitchen and grabbed a vase off of the shelf.

"Speaking of rumors, I heard Emma was investigating Peter Harwood's house this afternoon," he said.

"I can verify that," Lindsey said. She filled the vase and then took the roses out of their paper wrapper and put them inside. She glanced at him across the narrow counter and said, "Because Robbie and I were the ones to call her when we figured out that Peter's tenant Brian Kelly is actually Matthew Mercer."

Sully opened his mouth to speak but then shook his head. "How did you figure that out?"

"That's the weird part," Lindsey said. "I have a feeling he wanted us to figure it out. I was quoting a poem about unrequited love to Robbie—"

Sully ran a hand over his face as he sank onto a stool at the counter. "Maybe we should have drinks while we have this conversation."

Lindsey laughed. "Here, let me ease your mind. Robbie is okay with us. In fact, he was the one who recommended that I wear my shortest skirt."

Sully sat up straighter. "Huh, I may actually become fond of the overactor."

"I think he's over me and besotted with Emma," she said. "Which is why I left him at Harwood's house with her while she investigates."

"Clever," he said. "Encourage the romance and have him in the loop to report back to you."

"Am I that obvious?"

"Only because I know you," he said. He reached across the counter and took her hand in his. He pulled her gently around the counter until she was standing in front of him. A small smile lifted the corners of his lips as his gaze held hers and he said, "And because I love you."

CHAPTER

27

BRIAR CREEK
PUBLIC LIBRARY

Lindsey felt her heart skip a beat in her chest. Then it pounded double-time to catch up, making her lightheaded and a little woozy in the best possible way. So this was the moment, the moment when the "L" word arrived in their relationship and changed everything.

"I have loved you since the day I first saw you riding your bike through town on your way to your new job as the librarian," he said. "I will forever remember the way the sun shone on your hair and how you smiled at everyone you passed, including me, with a nervous, hopeful look that sucker punched me right in the heart."

Lindsey opened her mouth to speak but no words came out, which was fine, as Sully, her quiet one, had more to say.

"I've wanted to tell you how I feel for a long time, but we always seem to have one big drama or another happening, and I didn't want to say it after a near-death experience or some other traumatic event and have you thinking that I was saying it because of an emotional fallout. I wanted to wait until it was just you and me and things were calm—well, relatively calm—so that you would know that I mean—"

"I love you, too." The words burst out of her.

"—it," he said.

They stared at each other for a moment and then they both laughed. Lindsey knew it was a relieved sort of laugh, the kind that celebrated the fact that they both felt the same way and that no one was going to get their heart shredded by their confession.

The humor in Sully's eyes was quickly replaced by an intensity that made her toes curl. Then he kissed her. The kiss was as hot as the look in his eyes and Lindsey knew, once again, that everything between them was different.

This kiss staked a claim. It was thorough and possessive and let her know with no doubts or second-guesses that if their relationship didn't work out this time, they would not be parting as friends. It was an all-or-nothing situation now.

She twined her arms about his neck, pulled him close and kissed him back with the same vulnerability, the same commitment, the same heat.

When they broke apart for air, Lindsey was surprised to find they weren't fused together permanently and she was a little disappointed. At the very least she had expected some sort of magical moonbeam keeping them bound together. Then again, maybe she'd been reading too many fairy tales lately.

"It's different between us now, isn't it?" he asked.

He laced his fingers between hers and she felt it, the connection between them. It was as tangible as the feelings she had for him. Maybe the magical moonbeam existed after all.

"Yes," she said. She squeezed his fingers.

He blew out a pent-up breath. "Good. I feel as if I've been holding a lid on all of that for a very long time."

"Me, too," she said. She leaned against him, and he wrapped an arm around her, pulled her close and kissed her head.

"But now we're in a dilemma," he said.

"What dilemma?" she asked. She tried to think of what could be wrong. Robbie had clearly accepted things and she knew that their friends would be happy with the outcome. What could be wrong?

"The dilemma is that if we don't leave here soon, I'm going to get distracted." He turned her to face him and took the opportunity to kiss her. "See? Distracted. And if I get distracted, I'm going to do my best to distract you, and then we'll both be . . . distracted, and we'll miss our first official date in public, which I think is overdue."

"I'm not sure that I really care," she said. She leaned against him and hugged him close. "Then again, I know our friends well enough to know they'd have no problem showing up here to find out what happened to us, which would be embarrassing."

"Mostly for them because we'll be, you know, distracted." His grin was wicked and made Lindsey reconsider their dinner plans.

"Oh, my," she said. Her brain was beginning to flatline and she shook her head, trying to jostle her common sense into functioning again. "Clearly, before we get distracted, we should fortify, because I plan on distracting you for a very long time."

"Mercy!" Sully said. He shook his head, too, and Lindsey laughed when she realized he was suffering from the same fuzzy-headedness that she was.

"That's it!" He grabbed her hand and pulled her toward the door. "Any more talk like that and I may never let you leave this apartment, and I have waited entirely too long to show you off as my girl to let the opportunity pass. Let's go."

Lindsey let him pull her out the door to begin their date, knowing that after this evening her world would be altered. She would be a part of an official couple and not two people who met covertly when they thought no one was looking. As she led Heathcliff out the door to go to Nancy, who was dog-sitting him for the evening, she couldn't stop smiling.

The unfamiliar weight of an arm across her side woke Lindsey up in the early hours of the morning. The gentle rise and fall of the chest at her back was comforting. Sully. She rolled over carefully and glanced at his face.

Reddish brown curls fell over his forehead. His dark lashes fanned out across his cheeks and his lips were slack with sleep. He looked as peaceful as she'd ever seen him. She wanted to hug him, but she resisted. Knowing he had a full schedule at work that day, she didn't want to wake him.

Instead she was content just to watch him sleep. Was that love, then? When just being near the person that you loved was enough? It sure felt like it.

What if when Sully had told her that he loved her, she hadn't returned the sentiment? How would he have handled it? It was Sully, so she knew he would have been gracious. Being the quiet man that he was, she imagined he would have closed up his protective shell and disappeared into his work on his boats, and she would rarely, if ever, see him again.

The thought made her insides clench in mild panic. Thankfully, that had not been the case. She flipped it around. What if she had been the one to say "I love you" first and

Sully hadn't returned the feeling? Oh, horror. What if he had thanked her and then ignored her feelings as if they were a big gassy elephant in the room that he was hoping would go away? The mere idea of having her feelings not be returned by Sully was the stuff of nightmares.

Unrequited love—was there anything more devastating or painful? Again, the urge to hug Sully was almost more than she could resist. Lindsey pushed aside her covers and slid out from under his arm and out of the bed.

She grabbed her cotton robe from the foot of the bed and slipped it on over her tank top and pajama bottoms. The early-morning air was chilly and even Heathcliff didn't rouse from his spot at the foot of the bed when she slipped out of the room to go make herself a cup of tea in the kitchen.

Once she had her tea, she went to the table where she'd tossed the file folder of pictures that Hannah had copied from the high school archives for her. She had looked at these pictures so often she had memorized the expressions on the subjects' faces. Mostly, they were happy or distracted. A few were candid, caught when the person was talking or listening.

When she looked at Matthew Mercer's picture, she couldn't believe she hadn't recognized Brian Kelly sooner. They had the same stubborn chin and sardonic smile. And his eyes, the twinkle in his eyes that she'd seen when he finished reciting his own poem, was very much in evidence in the high school pictures.

She held the picture out at arm's length. She studied his face. Was this the face of a killer? Had he strangled Candice because she didn't return his romantic feelings? Was Matthew Mercer a murderer?

Lindsey shook her head. She didn't believe it. It made no

sense. Why was he here? Why had he let her know that he was Matthew Mercer? Surely, he had to know that if he blew his cover to her, she was going to go to the police. Why would he do that?

Unless he was a stone-cold sociopath who enjoyed playing with all of them, the only conclusion Lindsey could make was that he was innocent. Then why was he here? The only thing Lindsey could think was that something had made him come back to confront his past. But what?

She glanced back at his picture. Maybe it wasn't a significant event so much as it was just being tired of having everyone in his hometown think he was a killer. She couldn't imagine living with that for twenty years. Perhaps Matthew Mercer was innocent and he wanted everyone to know it and the only way to prove it was to come home.

Four houses had been robbed but nothing of any real value had been taken. Why those four families? Why the four that had the closest connections to Candice outside of her own family? But Lindsey knew. It was the book. It was no coincidence that the book had been returned on amnesty day just after all four robberies had been committed. Whoever had been robbing those houses, they had been looking for the book. But why return it to the library, unless they had wanted someone to notice it and make the connection?

A chill rippled through her and she took a long sip from her mug and let it warm her from the inside out. They still had weeks to wait until Detective Trimble and the state police could test the book for evidence. In the meantime, there had to be something in the pile of pictures in front of Lindsey that could offer her a clue.

She sifted through the old photographs. There was

nothing—just regular people doing regular things, having no idea that one among their number would be strangled to death.

Lindsey studied the picture of Judy and Candice during play rehearsals. At the time of the photo, they were both in their midtwenties and they looked so serious in their conversation, with both of them clutching the rolled-up pages of the play they were casting.

Judy was listening to her friend with an interested look on her face while she absently played with the top button on her sweater. Lindsey looked at the sweater. The black-and-white photo made it impossible to determine the color, but it had pearl buttons. Not that cardigans were that unusual, but Lindsey couldn't help thinking about what Daniels had said when he described finding Candice.

He had said she was lying perfectly still with her hands clasped and her blue sweater buttoned all the way to the collar, as if she'd been taking a nap. What if the sweater Judy was wearing in the photograph was the blue sweater? Just like Ann Marie had thought Beth was Lindsey when she caught sight of her purple vest through the stacks, maybe someone had thought Candice was Judy—that is, if the sweater belonged to Judy, which meant Candice had never been the target at all.

Lindsey knew it was a long shot but Candice and Judy had been best friends, much like she and Beth. If she loaned Beth her favorite vest, wouldn't Judy and Candice do the same? She had to talk to Judy and ask her. Of course, if it turned out that the sweater in the photo was purple or red then the whole thing was a bust, but if it was the blue sweater, maybe, just maybe, the reason they had never found Candice's killer was because they'd been looking for the wrong person. Maybe it hadn't been someone in Candice's life but rather someone in Judy's. Lindsey felt her heart thump hard in her chest. If it was someone after Judy, was that why the book had reappeared? Was that why Matthew Mercer was back? Had Judy been his target all along? Or was Lindsey just being paranoid? Probably.

Lindsey rinsed her cup and put it in the sink. She tucked the picture into her purse and decided she'd have to pay Hannah a visit at the high school. And if she ran into Judy, all the better, even if she had to stake out Judy's classroom to do it.

She slid into bed beside Sully, noting that he took up more than half of the surface area. As she curled herself up against him and he pulled her in close without waking up, she realized she didn't mind. Not a bit.

Sully was gone when she woke up but had left her a love note and a fresh pot of coffee. At first she was hard-pressed to decide which gesture she appreciated more, but then she read the note. Always a man of few words, he got right to the heart of it, committing to paper the words he'd spoken the night before, making the note the hands down winner.

Lindsey tucked it away in her jewelry box, grinning like an idiot as she did so. She had to admit, she really liked this new level of affection in their relationship.

She wasn't due at the library until later in the morning, so she took Heathcliff out for an early jog on the beach before turning him over to Nancy to keep her company for the day. Then she headed over to the high school to see if she could talk to Judy before she started her classes.

She arrived twenty minutes before school began. Having retrieved her bike from the library the night before while on her date with Sully, she locked it onto the main bike rack in front of the school and strode into the office.

"Hi, Michelle," she greeted the receptionist. "I'm here to see Hannah."

"She just signed in," Michelle said. "You can probably catch her on the stairs if you hurry."

"Thanks," Lindsey said. She signed the book and then hurried upstairs, turning in the opposite direction of the library when she got to the top.

Most of the doors to the classrooms were still closed as the teachers were still arriving. She hurried to the English wing, hoping that Judy was an early riser. Sure enough, the door to her classroom was open.

Lindsey knocked on the doorframe and heard Judy call, "Come in."

When she entered the room, Judy was standing in front of the window, looking out at the football field. It was the same position she had been in the last time Lindsey had found her. She wondered how often she stood there, staring out at the place where her best friend had been found dead.

"Morning, Judy," she said. "Sorry to interrupt."

"No, it's all right," Judy said. "I'm already prepped for my day. I was just fortifying with my favorite vitamin, caffeine."

She raised her coffee cup and then took a long sip.

"I understand," Lindsey said. "I doubled up on my vitamin today already."

"What can I do for you?" Judy asked. She gave her a wary look and Lindsey remembered the last time they spoke she had told her that she thought Candice's killer was at large.

How had Judy processed that over the past few days? It couldn't have given her any peace.

Lindsey figured it was best to get it over with. She opened her purse and pulled out the black-and-white photo of Judy and Candice. She held it out to Judy, who took it reluctantly with a puzzled look on her face.

When she glanced at the picture, Judy gasped. "Oh, wow, I haven't seen this picture in years."

"From the date on the back of the original, I'm guessing it was taken a few weeks before Candice died," Lindsey said.

"We were working on the school play," Judy said. Her fingers were shaking as she ran the tips of her fingers over Candice's face as if she could reach into the photo and touch her friend. "Where did you get this?"

"The school archives," she said. "I know this sounds crazy, but do you remember the sweater you're wearing in the photograph?"

Judy glanced at the picture. She tipped her head to the side. "Yes, it was blue, one of my favorites actually, until . . ."

"Until?" Lindsey asked.

A tear leaked out of the corner of Judy's eye. She brushed it away with the back of her hand.

"I lost track of it," she said. She glanced away and Lindsey knew she was hiding something.

"Judy, I don't want to alarm you, but do you know if you loaned that sweater to Candice?"

"I don't know," she said. "It would have been over twenty years ago. Although come to think of it, I don't think I ever saw it after she died. Huh. I thought I lost it somewhere . . ."

Her voice trailed off and Lindsey studied her face. What was she thinking? Judy wore such a closed expression that Lindsey couldn't hazard a guess.

"Why are you asking me these questions?" Judy asked. Her

chin jutted out and Lindsey knew her guard was up. She was going to have to explain it very carefully so as not to antagonize her.

"When former police chief Daniels described the scene of Candice's murder to me, one of the things he mentioned was her blue sweater with pearl buttons being buttoned up to her throat without a snag or a tear, nothing that showed a struggle on it."

"So what?"

"When I saw the picture of the two of you and saw you in a cardigan with pearl buttons, I thought maybe it was blue and that the sweater Candice was found wearing was really yours," Lindsey said.

"Maybe it was," Judy said. "We were best friends. We shared clothes all the time. So what if the sweater was mine?"

"Because maybe the person who murdered Candice didn't mean to murder Candice at all," Lindsey said. "Maybe they saw the blue sweater and thought it was you. Maybe whoever murdered Candice was really out to get you."

CHAPTER

28

BRIAR CREEK
PUBLIC LIBRARY

**"I** s this some kind of sick joke?" Judy asked. She looked furious. "How can you come into my classroom and say such a horrible thing? Candice was my best friend. How could I live with myself if someone harmed her because they thought she was me?"

"Which I am guessing is why you left town," Lindsey said.

Judy paled and Lindsey knew she was right.

"You know who killed Candice, don't you?" she asked.

"No!" Judy shook her head.

"Fine," Lindsey said. "Maybe you don't know for sure, but you suspect you know."

"You need to leave. Now," Judy said. "School is about to start and I can't listen to this ridiculous nonsense."

"Judy, stop it," Lindsey said. "Don't you see? Candice's murderer is back. You disappeared after she was killed. Likely the murderer left town, too. But now you're back and so is he, which is why he returned the library book. He wanted everyone to know he is back."

"No, no, no." Judy sank onto the edge of her desk and lowered her face into her hands. "The sweater. I left it in the back of . . . someone's car. Candice must have gotten it for me. It was cold that day in October, if she put it on to keep warm . . . Oh, God, there really is no escaping the past, is there?"

"Not when you sleep with someone else's husband there isn't."

Judy and Lindsey turned toward the door. Karen Larsen stood there, wearing an expression that was so brutally cold it made Lindsey shiver.

"Michelle said you were going to the library to see Hannah," Karen said to Lindsey. She wagged her finger at her. "But you lied and came here instead. You've been poking around, snooping, sticking your nose where it doesn't belong. I knew I had to follow you and see what you were up to, and I'm so glad I did."

She turned and looked at Judy. The malevolence on her face would have been impressive if it weren't so terrifying.

"Karen, it's not what you think," Judy said.

"Oh, I'm guessing it's exactly what I think," Karen said. "You and James. Huh. I didn't really see you as his type."

Lindsey met Judy's gaze and shook her head. If Judy confessed to the affair, who knew what kind of crazy it would unleash in Karen? For now, it was best to deny, deny, deny.

"All this time, I thought I'd gotten rid of the bitch who was trying to steal my husband, but it turns out it was really you," Karen said. "That was your blue sweater that I found in my husband's car after a 'school board meeting' ran late." She made air quotes with her fingers.

Judy's face flamed bright red and then deathly pale. It

couldn't have been more clear if she had verbally confessed to having an affair with James Larsen.

"So, poor Candice died for your sins," Karen said. "Bad luck."

"You strangled her," Judy said. Her voice was raspy, as if she couldn't quite form the words because they were so awful.

"After I found the sweater, I confronted James. I asked him who it belonged to but he said he didn't know. Here's the thing: James is a terrible liar. But you probably already know that since you slept with him. Surely, you must have seen how his lips quiver when he tries to lie. Honestly, it's pathetic.

"Of course, I pretended to believe him and then I waited. It took several weeks, but then I saw her wearing the sweater and I knew that she was the one James was having an affair with and I knew what I had to do."

"You killed her. You killed her because of me." Judy gasped and then dissolved into tears.

"I did, and you know, it was quite satisfying strangling the life out of her, knowing that she was the whore who thought she could steal my husband." Karen closed her eyes and a small smile lifted the corner of her mouth as she mentally revisited snuffing the life out of Candice Whitley. "But now that I know the truth, killing you is going to be so much more rewarding."

"Karen, there is nothing to be gained by killing Judy," Lindsey said. "The affair is long over and James is with you and he always has been."

Karen turned to look at Lindsey. Gone was the mild-mannered reading teacher. In her place was a woman with vacant eyes who, while standing in the room with them, was obviously tuned in to some alternate channel otherwise known as the crazy voices in her head.

"I'm sorry," she said. She pulled a petite yet lethal-looking handgun out of her purse. "But it looks like I'm going to have to kill you, too."

Now Lindsey felt her skin flash scorching hot and then bitterly cold as panic made her heart stop and then pound triple-time.

"Not here," Judy said. Her voice was faint. "Not in front of the students."

"Of course not," Karen said. "Let's reunite you with your friend under the football bleachers. It's a lovely place to die."

Lindsey tried to swallow around the lump of terror lodged in her throat but she choked on it instead.

"Let's go," Karen said. She gestured for them to walk toward the door. When they hesitated, she snapped, "Move it! Unless you want me to shoot you in front of your first-period class."

Lindsey and Judy walked to the door, giving Karen a wide berth. The halls were still deserted, for which Lindsey was grateful. She was terrified that Karen might lose her grip completely and start blasting them when students were nearby. She most definitely did not want to live with endangering any kids, assuming they survived this at all.

Karen ushered them down the hall to an emergency exit. It said it was alarmed but when they pushed through it the absence of noise made the caution sign a lie.

"The student smokers like to hang out in this stairwell," Karen said. "One of the many perks of being here for so long is that I know all of the school's secrets."

Lindsey wondered if she caught the irony of her own statement in that her murdering Candice was the school's biggest, darkest, ugliest secret of all. Glancing at Karen's face, she guessed not.

Karen stayed at their backs with the gun pointed at them and instructed them to walk beside the brick building toward the football stadium. A narrow service road ran between the music department and the stadium. They only had about twenty-five feet of open area to cross before Karen would have them out of sight under the bleachers.

"So, why did you do it?" Lindsey asked.

"Duh, I thought she was sleeping with my husband," Karen snapped.

"No, not that," Lindsey said. "Why did you return the library book you took from Candice's body? Did you really think no one would notice a book that was twenty years overdue?"

"I didn't," Karen said. "Candice didn't have a book on her when I strangled her."

Lindsey glanced over her shoulder to see if Karen was telling the truth. The woman was glaring, looking like she'd be happy to shoot Lindsey on the spot. She turned back around. If Karen didn't return the book, then who did?

"Do not try and draw attention to yourselves or call for help," Karen hissed as they crossed the narrow road. "I will shoot you."

Judy was a step ahead of Lindsey. Her shoulders were slumped and she seemed resigned to her fate. Lindsey supposed the guilt she was feeling at finding out that her friend was murdered because of her own affair with the principal had taken the fight right out of her.

Lindsey understood, she did, but she had also just gotten her boyfriend back and he had popped out the "L" word. If Karen thought she was going to shoot Lindsey and prematurely end her relationship with Sully by killing her, she was seriously mistaken.

The underbelly of the bleachers was open on the sides but

blocked by a cement wall along the back. As they stepped into the side of the stadium seating, Lindsey started scouting for a weapon. There had to be something. Didn't they have groundskeepers who maintained the garbage that got dropped down here with rakes and shovels? Lindsey was betting that a good slap upside the head with a shovel would take Karen down. Unfortunately, there was nothing.

Lindsey started to feel panic swell up inside of her. She leaned close to Judy and hissed, "If she kills us, she gets away with Candice's murder as well as ours. We're the only ones who know what she did. We have to stop her."

Judy turned a sad face toward Lindsey. She met her gaze and then gave her a small nod.

"That's far enough," Karen said.

They were at the midpoint under the bleachers. No one could see them here. Lindsey glanced down at the tufts of dead grass, candy wrappers and broken glass at her feet. She was not going to die here. No way in hell.

"How do you plan to explain the town librarian and the high school English teacher dead under the bleachers?" she asked. It was part stalling and part curiosity to see just how crazy Karen was.

Karen snorted. "Easy. What everyone will find out is that Judy killed Candice in a jealous rage over Benji, and you, the nosy librarian, figured it out. The two of you had an altercation, which resulted in you killing each other. At least, that's what will be surmised after I make it look like you fought over the gun, resulting in both of you being fatally shot in the tussle," she said.

"No one's going to believe that," Judy said. "Benji was my friend, nothing more."

Karen shrugged. "When I get done spinning my tales and planting my bogus evidence, they won't believe anything else."

Lindsey would argue that no one would believe that she was a nosy librarian, but yeah, that wasn't going to work. She had to get Karen to see that her plan was flawed.

"Your lies will fail," she said. "And I'll tell you why."

Karen didn't seem inclined to listen to Lindsey as she raised the gun, assumed a shooter's stance with a two-handed grip and sighted her target—Lindsey—with one eye. The gun was pointed right at Lindsey's chest, which suddenly felt so tight she couldn't breathe.

Lindsey was going to die. Karen was going to pull the trigger and kill her and there was nothing she could do to stop her. A terrified paralysis took over Lindsey's whole body and she stood there, unable to think, speak or move.

"Stop!" Judy cried. "You can't do this. Lindsey has nothing to do with what happened between James and me and your anger with us."

"So what? She's in the way," Karen said. She looked so smug, so sure of herself. It really pissed Lindsey off.

"You're going to die in prison," Lindsey said. "Because whoever turned in that book did it to draw you out, and they're never going to believe that Judy and I killed each other. That's entirely too convenient. You know it, I know it and the person looking for Candice's murderer knows it, too."

A flicker of doubt crossed Karen's face. She relaxed her stance for just a moment and it was all that was needed.

"Get down!" a man shouted.

Lindsey and Judy threw themselves to the ground just as two big, dark shadows dropped from between the bleacher seats above. Karen's gun went off and there was a piercing scream and then a sickening crunch as the two shadows took Karen down to the ground under their full weight.

Lindsey heard the gun skitter across the ground. She rose from her crouch and hurried to grab it. Once she had it wrapped in her shirt in an effort to preserve Karen's fingerprints, she turned to see Brian Kelly—rather, Matthew Mercer—with another man she didn't recognize, pulling Karen Larsen to her feet.

She was scratching and biting and clawing at them until the stranger punched her right in the face, knocking her out cold. She slumped into Matthew's arms and he let her drop to the ground as if he couldn't bear to touch her. The stranger shook out his hand and the two men looked at each other and exchanged satisfied nods.

"Lindsey, this is my friend Benji Gunderson," Matthew said.

"Oh, hi," Lindsey said. It occurred to her that he looked an awful lot like his brother, but she didn't dwell on it. Relief was making her a bit weak in the knees and light-headed. "Your timing is excellent."

"Benji?"

They all turned to see Judy still sitting on the ground, holding one arm into her chest while blood gushed out of a wound by her elbow.

"Judy!" Benji yelped and raced toward her. "You've been shot. Come on, let's get you out of here."

He went to pick her up, but she shook her head. Tears were coursing down her cheeks and she sobbed.

"Candice is dead because of me," she said.

Benji shook his head at her. "No, she isn't. She's dead because of Karen and only her."

"But the sweater . . ." Judy said.

"Doesn't matter," Benji said. "Karen Larsen chose to kill her. That has nothing to do with you. And now she is finally going to pay for her crime."

He scooped Judy up into his arms and carried her out from under the bleachers. Lindsey walked toward Matthew. She was still shaking from the aftershock of thinking she was going to die, but the sweet sense of relief that she felt was beginning to sweep over the fear.

"Lindsey!"

She glanced up to see Sully running toward her. Behind him was Emma, limp-running with Robbie's assistance.

"Here!" she cried. "I'm here!"

Sully hit her like a train, picking her up and clutching her close, knocking the air out of her with the force of his embrace and then a lip-lock that took what little oxygen she had left. She didn't care one little bit. He cupped her face and stared into her eyes as if reassuring himself that she was all right.

"Careful," she said. "I've got a gun."

"I'll take that," Emma said. She held open an evidence bag and Lindsey dropped the gun inside. Then Emma muscled her way in between Lindsey and Sully and gave her a one-armed hug that about cracked Lindsey's ribs. "Do not ever scare me like that again. When the call came in over the radio, I thought I was going to have a stroke. For real."

"Same goes for me, love," Robbie said. "You're giving me a head full of bloody gray hair."

He gave Lindsey a quick squeeze and then turned her back over to Sully as he joined Emma by Matthew, who was still standing guard over Karen's unconscious body as if she might come to and escape.

Sully opened his arms and Lindsey stepped into them.

She pressed her cheek to his chest and listened to his heart thunder behind his ribs.

"This," she said. She leaned back and looked at the face that was so dear to her. "When Karen pointed that gun at me, I froze and the only thing I could think about was this. You and me. Having that taken away. I've never been so scared. Ever. I love you."

"I love you, too," he said. She could tell from the tight grip he was maintaining that he was just as rattled as she was. And that's when she knew; she knew she couldn't put them through this ever again.

She leaned back and met his gaze. "I promise I will never investigate, snoop, be a buttinsky, get involved in police business or anything like this ever again. I swear on my favorite detective books. I will mind my own business from now on."

Sully hugged her close and she relaxed against him. She breathed in the ocean smell that was uniquely his and felt the last of the terrified trembles leave her. It was going to be okay. She was newly committed to a nice, quiet, appropriately librarian way of being that would no longer invite danger into her life. Truly, she was reformed.

It took her a second to notice that Sully was shaking. Maybe he was having a delayed reaction of shock. She stepped away, preparing to call for help until she looked at his face.

"Are you laughing?" she cried.

CHAPTER

29

BRIAR CREEK
PUBLIC LIBRARY

**"L**indsey, wait!" Sully cried.

She ignored him. Here she had poured out her heart to him and he was laughing. She continued stomping away from him, mindful only of not smacking her head against the steel bars around her that held up the bleachers.

"It was the shock!" he said.

She gave him a look over her shoulder that told him where he could shove that. She marched ahead, following Robbie and Matthew as they half carried, half dragged Karen out from under the bleachers, leaving Emma to hobble after them.

Sully caught up to her and grabbed her hand, forcing her to stop, then he turned her around to face him.

"Hey," he said. "I'm sorry. It's just the thought of you not . . ." His voice trailed off as if he knew better than to continue this line of discussion. "Listen, I love you as you are, even if you get yourself into situations that scare the snot out of me. You don't have to change for me or for us, because now that I've got you, I'm never letting go."

And just like that, the fight went right out of her. Lindsey threw herself into his arms and hugged him tight. What she didn't tell him was that she meant what she said. She was never going to put either of them at risk again. What they had was too special to be taken for granted. Now that she had him, she was never letting go either.

It was clear Sully wasn't ready to hear that she was going to change, so she would just have to show him. Thankfully, since Karen hadn't blown a hole right in the middle of her chest, Lindsey had nothing but time. Her days of investigating anything more taxing than a patron's reference question were over and she was going to happily spend the rest of her life proving it to Sully.

The crafternoon room was pleasantly crowded. Violet, Charlene, Nancy, Mary and Beth had been happy to open up the group to new members. Hannah and Paula had joined the group and as promised Paula was leading the discussion on *The Catcher in the Rye* while Hannah brought her chai tea to share with the group.

"I enjoyed the descriptions of New York City," Violet said. "It reminded me so much of when I arrived there and started auditioning for parts back in the sixties."

"Everything was so glamorous back then," Nancy said.

"It didn't sound glamorous to me," Mary said. "It seemed seedy and creepy and sad."

Paula rolled her eyes and Hannah laughed.

"What?"

"I told you not everyone was going to love the book as much as you," she said.

Paula tossed her purple braid over her shoulder. She had an intense look on her face, a look Lindsey had come to learn was her determined face.

"Holden Caulfield is a post-war rebel," Paula said. "His entire journey is an anti-conformist one. He doesn't want to be a part of the newly minted shiny fifties. He is drawn to authenticity and is undone by innocence. He is the inappropriate gritty underbelly of the youth of his time."

The room was silent as they all looked at her, waiting to see if she was done.

"What?" she asked. "Too much?"

Lindsey laughed. She put her arm around Paula and gave her a half hug.

"Not at all," she said. "I love your enthusiasm."

"But you still don't love the book," Paula said. She held up her craft project. "And I bet you're just going to love the bead project I was planning to share."

Lindsey glanced at the chain of beaded daisies Paula held in her hands. It looked hard. Mercifully, she was saved from having to answer by the arrival of their newest member.

"Am I late?"

They all turned toward the door to see Matthew Mercer hurry into the room. He was carrying a Crock-Pot and had lost his ubiquitous beanie, which freed his unruly black hair to swirl about his head in dark waves.

"Yes, but if you brought food all is forgiven," Mary said. She moved items on the buffet table to make room for Matthew's contribution.

"Not only did I bring food, I brought meatballs in marinara sauce and fresh-baked bread."

He set the Crock-Pot down along with a paper bag that had a warm loaf of Italian bread sticking out of it. He glanced around the room and took an empty seat beside the elephant, which was actually Beth still in her story time costume. The fact that Beth's outfit, which included a hefty trunk that hung over her face, didn't even faze him made Lindsey think he was a natural fit in their book discussion group.

"Matthew, if I wasn't already happily married, I'd propose to you," Charlene said as she lifted the lid off of the Crock-Pot and breathed in the delicious aroma of homemade sauce and meatballs.

"And I'd say yes," Matthew said with a grin. "Now how far along in the discussion are we?"

"I am trying to convince them that Holden is the poster boy for antiestablishmentarianism," Paula said.

"Totally," Matthew agreed. "It starts when he runs away from prep school and is maintained as a constant theme throughout the book."

The two of them beamed at each other in perfect accord and Lindsey exchanged a grin with Beth.

"I think having a man in the crafternooners is going to broaden the opinions quite nicely," Violet said. "Can he knit, though?"

"Probably better than me," Lindsey said. While the group went to go and fill their plates, Lindsey moved to sit beside Matthew. "I'm glad you joined us."

"Me, too," he said. "I think I bring a much-needed infusion of testosterone to the group."

"Matthew, is it true that Principal Larsen resigned from his position at the high school?" Beth asked. "I heard a rumor but I figured you're closer to the whole situation and might know the deets."

"Yes, he did," he said. "You all know Karen murdered Candice because she believed that she was having an affair with James Larsen?"

Violet and Nancy nodded while the rest of the room went silent to listen to Matthew's recap of the events.

"Thanks to Lindsey, here, who noticed a picture of Judy wearing the sweater that Candice was found in, the identity of the killer was revealed."

"Because I'm an idiot and led her right to Judy," Lindsey muttered. "It's a good thing you and Benji happened to be sitting up in the bleachers, contemplating what to do to draw the killer out, when we arrived."

"Yeah, we started meeting at the bleachers every morning to talk over our search for the killer and, I suppose, in some small way to be with Candice," he said.

"It was almost deadly, for all of us." Lindsey shivered at the memory.

Matthew patted her arm in a comforting gesture. It was a nice effort but Lindsey knew she would never forgive herself for almost getting Judy killed, not to mention putting her own life in jeopardy, especially when she had so much to live for.

"Anyway, the nitty-gritty of it is that Principal Larsen suspected his wife had killed Candice in the mistaken belief that he was having an affair with her," he said. "His guilt at being the one to cause his wife to commit such a heinous act kept him quiet. He told Judy to leave town, although he didn't explain why, just that he thought it was for the best. Heartbroken at her closest friend's death, Judy went.

"Meanwhile, Benji Gunderson and I became the most likely suspects because of our closeness to Candice. We both felt the need to leave Briar Creek. I bounced around for a while, but finally, I realized I was never really going to move forward with my life if I didn't get some closure on the past. I tracked Benji down through his brother's social media posts, and we started messaging back and forth. We started talking about how lousy it was to be driven from our hometown for a crime we didn't commit. That's when I decided to return to Briar Creek in disguise and see if I could figure out who really killed Ms. Whitley."

"You are a very brave young man," Nancy said.

"No. Stubborn maybe, not brave," he said. "I'm just glad we caught her. Now that Judy is on the mend, she is planning to create a scholarship in Candice's name for students with an interest in literature or theater, and I'm going to help."

"We all will," Violet said. The rest of the crafternooners nodded in agreement.

"Well, it looks like Karen will be in jail for the rest of her life," Mary said. She raised her glass in the air. "Justice has been served."

They all raised their glasses of iced tea and lemonade in return and toasted her words. The small group went back to dishing their food and the conversation broke off as they discussed the possible future that Karen would be enjoying in prison.

Lindsey turned to Matthew. "I know we've hashed all of this out, but I need to clarify something."

"Sure," he said. "Anything I can do to help."

"Okay, here's the thing," she said. "Why did you return the copy of *The Catcher in the Rye* that Candice gave you on amnesty day?"

Matthew put his hand on the back of his neck. He looked uncomfortable, but Lindsey wasn't about to let him off the hook. When they had gone to the police station after he and Benji subdued Karen, he admitted to returning the library book while Benji had admitted that he had been the one to burglarize the homes of those people with a connection to Candice. So far no charges had been filed, and Lindsey doubted any would be.

"Why return the book to the library?" she pressed.

"For years I kept that book with me," Matthew said. "Ms. Whitley and I met right outside the library on the day she died, and she gave it to me, telling me to read it because I would relate to Holden Caulfield. Sadly, I related to him much more after her murder than I would have before. I would have preferred not to."

A faraway look came into his eyes and Lindsey knew he was thinking about the last moments he'd shared with Ms. Whitley.

"When she was killed, I felt like it was the last thing I had of her. I kept it with me through all of my travels and all of my moves. I tried to keep it in pristine condition out of respect for her and her belief in me. I read it once a year faithfully, but then . . ."

He paused and after a few moments, Lindsey nudged him with her elbow, and said, "But then?"

"After I returned to town as Brian Kelly, and I got to know a few people, I learned that a certain librarian had a reputation for figuring things out. It occurred to me, and Benji agreed, that if we returned the library book that Candice had checked out right before she died, you would be curious and start asking questions."

He gave Lindsey a side eye, as if checking to see how mad she was.

"It's okay," she said. "I'm aware that I have a reputation."

"Well, it proved out," he said. "If the burglaries hadn't been enough to start up interest in the old case, you deciding to turn the book over to the police did. And even better than that, you started asking questions. Karen never would have been caught if it weren't for you, Lindsey. Benji and I are so very grateful."

"You're welcome," she said. "And I was happy to help, but this is the last time I am ever going to do anything like that ever again."

"What do you mean?"

"I've learned my lesson," Lindsey said. "I need to change my ways and respect the limits of my position as the town librarian. Karen scared me straight. I will not be doing any more investigations. From now on I am going to mind my own business and let the police handle things."

The room went silent. Lindsey turned away from Matthew to find all of her friends staring at her as if they didn't recognize her.

"What?" she asked. "Why are you staring at me?"

"Because getting information is what you do," Beth said. "It's like hardwired into your DNA or something."

"I'm not turning in my reference credentials, just my snooping ones," Lindsey said.

"But you're like an information superhighway all on your own," Violet said. "I'm not sure you can just switch that off."

"Besides, you know Sully loves you just the way you are," Mary said. Then she clapped a hand over her mouth.

Now they all went wide-eyed, except for the newcomers because, of course, they had no idea that the "L" word had been the topic of last week's crafternoon meeting.

"No way!" Beth jumped up and down, sending the elephant trunk on her head bouncing until it slapped her in the face, forcing her to calm down. "Who said it first?"

Lindsey felt her face go hot. "I never said . . . I'm not . . .

Hey, did you know that *The Catcher in the Rye* was the most censored book in the U.S. from nineteen sixty-one to nineteen eighty-two?"

"He totally said it first," Beth said to Mary, who giggled.

Lindsey rolled her eyes. Then she noticed that everyone in the room was grinning at her. They were happy for her. It was impossible not to respond and Lindsey beamed back at them, unable to keep her newfound happiness contained.

"Yeah, he said it first," she admitted. "And it was pretty great."

"'I like it when somebody gets excited about something,'" Paula said to Matthew.

He laughed and added, "'It's nice.'"

"Hey, that's from the book," Violet said. She glanced from them to Nancy. "Looks like we have a couple of smarty-pants in our crafternoon group."

"Excellent," Nancy said. "If Lindsey really is going to quit being a buttinsky, we're going to need some new recruits to keep things interesting."

She glanced at Lindsey with one silver eyebrow raised. Lindsey knew she was trying to get her to recant her declaration of no more investigations, but Lindsey wasn't going to be swayed so easily.

Life was feeling pretty perfect at the moment, and she didn't plan on doing anything to mess it up, which included unraveling mysteries that were none of her business. Surely, that couldn't be too hard, right?

# The Briar Creek Library
# Guide to Crafternoons

The crafternooners would love to help you kick-start your own crafternoon. It's pretty simple in concept and execution. All you need is a gathering of friends to share good food, a craft and a conversation about a really good book. So here you go!

# Readers Guide for
## *The Catcher in the Rye*
### by J. D. Salinger

1. Do you find the character of Holden Caulfield likable? Why or why not? Is he a typical teenager?

2. What does the title *The Catcher in the Rye* refer to? How is it used in the novel?

3. Why does Holden go to New York City? What is the significance of the setting?

4. Why does Holden Caulfield see everyone as "phony"? Is his perception of others accurate? Is Holden himself a phony?

5. Why is the character Phoebe special to Holden? Why is she the only one he seems to care for?

# Craft:
# Paula's Beaded Daisy Chain

*Thread*
*Needle*
*3 colors of beads (the directions will use white petals,*
*    yellow centers, and green leaves)*

To start cut a six-foot length of thread and thread the needle
so that you have a double thread three feet in length.

Start by making a ring of beads for the clasp. For this, string
six green beads and two white beads, then pull all eight beads
all the way down the thread until they are two inches from the
end. Then bring the needle through the first bead, going in the
side of the bead closest to the two-inch tail, then go through
each bead and pull the thread tight to form a ring. Tie a knot
with the thread and the two-inch tail to keep the ring of beads
secure.

Now the first daisy will be formed by bringing the needle and thread back through the two white beads. String six more white beads and bring the needle and thread back through the first white bead, forming a ring of white beads. String one yellow bead and bring the needle and thread through a white bead on the opposite side of the ring, at the top of the daisy. This creates your first daisy in the chain.

The next step will make leaves and the beginning of the next daisy. String two green beads, two white beads and two more green beads. Bring the needle and thread through a white bead at the top of the previous daisy and pull tight so that it forms a ring. String one green bead to fill the center of the ring and then pull the needle and thread through one of the white beads on the ring. Now your leaves are done.

Repeat the directions for the first daisy and the leaves until your beaded daisy chain is the desired length. End by stringing six green beads and forming a loop just like the first one. Tie off the string in between beads.

# Recipes

## VIOLET'S HAM AND CHEESE SLIDERS

*¾ cup melted butter*
*1½ tablespoons Dijon mustard*
*1½ tablespoons Worcestershire sauce*
*24 smalls rolls*
*1 pound sliced ham*
*1 pound sliced Swiss cheese*

Preheat oven to 350 degrees. Line a 13x9–inch glass baking dish with parchment paper. In a small bowl, mix together the melted butter, mustard and Worcestershire sauce and set aside. Slice the rolls, placing the bottom halves onto the parchment paper in the baking dish. Layer the ham on the rolls and then the cheese. Put the tops of the rolls onto the sandwiches. Brush the mustard mixture evenly over the rolls and bake for 20 minutes, until the cheese has melted and the rolls are golden brown.

# MATTHEW'S CROCK-POT
# MARINARA MEATBALLS

*2 (14.5 ounce) cans diced tomatoes with basil, garlic and oregano*
*1 (14.5 ounce) can tomato sauce*
*2 tablespoons tomato paste*
*1 tablespoon sugar*
*1 teaspoon garlic powder*
*1 teaspoon onion powder*
*1 teaspoon kosher salt*
*36 meatballs, uncooked (recipe below)*
*2 bay leaves*

In a large blender, combine all ingredients, except the meatballs and bay leaves. Blend until your sauce is the consistency you prefer, chunky or smooth. Pour half of the sauce on the bottom of the Crock-Pot. Put aside remaining sauce to pour on top of the meatballs. Place uncooked meatballs in Crock-Pot. Pour sauce over top, until covered. Add bay leaves. Cover and cook on high for 3–4 hours, or low for 6–8 hours.

## MEATBALL RECIPE

*1 pound ground beef*
*½ cup Italian breadcrumbs*
*½ cup red wine, such as Chianti*
*¼ cup fresh-grated Parmesan cheese*
*1 teaspoon garlic powder*
*1 teaspoon onion powder*

    *1 tablespoon dried Italian seasoning*
    *½ teaspoon salt*
    *½ teaspoon black pepper*
    *1 large egg, lightly beaten*

In a large mixing bowl, combine all ingredients until well blended. Roll the mixture evenly into 36 meatballs.

# HANNAH'S CHAI TEA

*8 cups water*
*1 cinnamon stick*
*6 green cardamom pods*
*8 whole cloves*
*1 (½ inch) piece of ginger root, peeled and thinly sliced*
*6 black peppercorns*
*2 tablespoons loose-leaf black tea*
*¼ cup brown sugar*
*1 cup milk*

In a medium saucepan, combine the water, cinnamon, carda-mom, cloves, ginger and peppercorns; bring to a boil for five minutes; remove from heat and let sit for ten minutes.

Add the tea, return to the stove and bring to a boil, then lower the heat to simmer for five minutes. Use a wire strainer to strain the spices and tea leaves from the liquid into another saucepan and return the liquid to the stove. Over low heat, use a whisk to stir in the brown sugar and milk until well blended. Serve while hot.

*MAKES 8 (1 CUP) SERVINGS.*

Keep reading for a special preview of
Jenn McKinlay's next Hat Shop Mystery . . .

# ASSAULT AND BERET

*Coming January 2017 in paperback
from Berkley Prime Crime!*

"You know everyone says that French waiters are rude, but I don't think our waiter is rude at all," I said to my cousin Vivian Tremont. "He seems very pleasant."

"That's because he's trying to sleep with you, Scarlett," Vivian said. "Why do you think our bottle of Cheverny La Bodice was on the house?"

"Seriously? Free wine for a tussle in the sheets? Do I look that easy?" I asked. "Well, that is rude."

"Uh-huh," she said. Which was only slightly better than *I told you so*, but not much.

It was late evening in Paris, the city of light, and we were enjoying a nosh—as Viv, who is British, would say. We were seated inside the Bistro Renee on Rue de Javel.

The bitter wind that whipped down the street from the Seine River could not get us here. We had ducked inside to eat but also to get warm.

Thankfully, the food did not disappoint. I ordered quail

with roasted spring onions while Viv indulged in suckling pig with salsify, which is a lot like a parsnip, and we shared a baguette seasoned with the mellow heat of the espelette pepper from the Basque region, or so our waiter, David, informed us when asked.

He was very charming and quite good-looking with his wavy dark hair and golden eyes. He told us his father owned the Bistro, which was named for his mother, Renee, who had passed away when he was just a boy. Honestly, he broke my heart a little with that story but not enough to have a sleepover with him.

The small restaurant was everything a late meal in Paris should be. Candlelight, soft music in the background, an exotic blossom of some sort in a blue bottle on our small square table swathed in a pristine white cloth with matching napkins.

The crumbs of the baguette and the near-empty bottle of sauvignon blanc sat on the table between us. We had scraped our plates clean. We did share as only cousins who live together like sisters can, with some squabbling over what exactly was equitable and over who had ordered the tastier dish. I had, but Viv refused to admit it because I am her younger American cousin and she refuses to acknowledge that I am just as cultured as she is.

I glanced out the window. It was beautiful, but it was not exactly the Paris of my dreams. Instead of sitting on an outside patio enjoying the warm floral-scented breeze of spring, we were swathed in scarves and sweaters, sitting inside a small café watching a January snowfall.

Why were we here? Here's the short version. Viv is an acclaimed London milliner hired to teach a one-week hat-making class at the local art school. I am Scarlett Parker, not just her cousin but also part owner in our millinery business housed on Portobello Road in Notting Hill, London, which we inherited six years ago from our grandmother Mim.

Now, because I know you're going to ask, since everyone does, the answer is no, positively, unequivocally no. I can't make a hat to save my life. So what am I doing here with her?

I'm sorry, did you miss the part that we're in Paris? Yes, even in January it's still Paris. Besides, the fact is that while Viv is an amazing artist, she's not the best with people. That's where I come in.

Viv, being a creative type, is known to occasionally be impulsive. I am generally the voice of reason when this happens but unfortunately when she decided on a whim to elope, she neglected to mention it to me, thus I couldn't stop her. This was a couple of years ago while I was busy ruining my own life in a bad relationship.

In hindsight, we were both reeling from the loss of our grandmother Mim and neither of us were making good choices in our grief. Why is hindsight always so much clearer than foresight?

Anyway, after a few weeks of marriage, Viv ditched her husband without properly ending her marriage and last she knew he was in Paris, so my mission, if I chose to accept it—which I did—was to find her husband and get him to agree to an annulment. Easy peasy, right?

Right. In the meantime, I needed to scrape off our waiter.

"Well, I'm not going to sleep with him," I said. "But I will finish off the wine."

"Naturally," Viv said.

I poured the remainder into our two glasses. Viv raised her glass and I did the same. We gently tapped them together.

"To finding your husband," I said. She blanched.

Okay, that was me being a buzzkill but also keeping her on task. Viv can be sly when she wants to be, as is evidenced by the fact that she got married and never told me. I mean, honestly, who does that?

"How about to returning home happier than when we arrived," she offered instead.

"I like that," I said. "It leaves it nice and open-ended for all possibilities."

"Precisely," she said.

We drained our glasses.

We declined coffee and a dessert, although I was tempted by the lemon cannoli, and a request for my phone number. In all honesty, I really felt that David must be vision impaired, as I have the fiery hair and freckles of my dad's ginger-infused DNA while Viv has the milky complexion and long blond curls of our grandmother. In a beauty competition, Viv beats me hands down every time—yes, even when I put in great effort. Good thing I learned to get by on my personality years ago.

When we stepped outside, the chill wind was relentless, pushing us down the street like we were wayward teenagers being forced home before curfew. I tightened the scarf about my neck and jammed the cuff of my leather gloves up into the sleeves of my jacket. I really despise the cold.

It was a short walk to Madame Leclaire's apartment building where the Paris School of Art was housing us for the duration of Viv's class. It was a charming place located on the edge of the fifteenth arrondissement, within walking distance of the Eiffel Tower. It was built of white stone with a blue mansard roof and was four stories tall, containing eight small apartments with the added bonus of a communal living room and dining room on the main floor, where Madame

Leclaire served a continental breakfast every day and a night-cap in the evenings.

The furniture in our apartment was a mash-up of antiques and modern accessories. We each had a twin bed and a large armoire in our rooms, which were connected by a sitting room with a kitchenette. We were on one of the upper floors and our apartment had large windows with narrow wrought-iron balconies. Mostly, our view was of the similar building across the way and the street below, but if I pressed my body against the glass and angled my head just right I could glimpse a sliver of the Eiffel Tower to the north of us.

The house was warm and safe and Madame Leclaire was lovely and charming and always seemed to have the best wine and cheese on hand. That is a wonderful quality in an apartment building owner.

With our scarves wrapped around our heads, conversation was impossible as we hurried down the street. The snow was getting sharper as it pelted my back, pushing me toward my fluffy, soft bed. I really didn't need the encouragement.

The lights were on in the front room of Madame Leclaire's. Viv and I picked up our pace. We dashed up the steps and hurried into the vestibule. Viv pressed the intercom and called a cheery, "Hello, we're home."

The inside door opened with a click and we pushed through with the eagerness of schoolgirls looking for cookies after a long day. Warmth washed over us and Madame Leclaire popped her head out of the communal sitting room on the first floor.

"Girls, you look frozen. You should come and sit by the fire." She gestured for us to follow her. Honestly, with her alluring French accent I would have followed her anywhere, but the fire seemed like an excellent suggestion.

We did not need to be asked twice. Well, Viv might
have—she's British and they do hem and haw a lot in a show
of good manners, but I am American and I do not. I walked
right into the cozy room without hesitation and plopped
myself in a darling chair right in front of the fire.

"This is heaven," I said. I peeled off my short wool coat
and let the heat from the flames wash over me.

"Would you care for some hot chocolate?" Madame Leclaire
offered. "Usually I serve something stronger in the evening but
with the snow I felt like chocolate was most appropriate."

"Oh, we don't want to trouble you," Viv said at the same
time I said, "Yes, please."

Madame Leclaire glanced between us and smiled, amused
no doubt by how different we were. She was much too polite
to say so, however.

Madame was tall and lithe, with a cap of dark curls about
her heart-shaped face that was just beginning to go gray. Her
lips were wide and generous and her eyes a rich, trustworthy
brown. I had liked her immediately when we arrived the day
before and she had been nothing but gracious and kind to
us, which just reinforced my first impression.

This evening she wore tailored black slacks and a crisp
raspberry blouse, which was mostly covered by the charcoal
gray cashmere wrap she had draped about her shoulders,
giving her a look that was both chic and comfy at the same
time. You simply cannot out-dress the French, and I would
never be stupid enough to try.

Viv perched on the edge of the seat across from mine as
if getting ready to bail the moment she felt her presence was
an imposition. I burrowed deeper into my seat.

A silver pot with a random collection of mismatched china
cups sat on the table in front of the couch, where Madame

Leclaire resumed her seat. A cup of half-drunk chocolate sat on a coaster and beside it a French novel was facedown on the highly polished wooden table.

Now I wondered if we had intruded upon Madame Leclaire's quiet time. But I thought not because the other cups on the tray indicated that she was open to company.

As if she were reading my thoughts, she took a delicate china cup and poured the piping-hot chocolate into it. She placed it on a mismatched saucer and handed it to me. The steam rising out of the cup smelled a little like I've always imagined heaven would smell, assuming of course that there is one and that I am invited.

Madame Leclaire looked at Viv as if trying to determine if she wanted chocolate or if she was about to flee the room.

"Yes?" she asked as she held up the pot.

"Thank you, Madame Leclaire," Viv said. "You are most kind."

"Please call me Suzette," she said. "Most of my tenants do."

"Most?" I asked. "Which ones don't?"

"The ones I don't like," she said.

Viv and I both laughed at the wicked gleam in her eye.

"We are very honored that you like us," I said. Then I added, "Suzette."

Viv sipped her hot chocolate and I saw her spine relax as she melted into her chair. There really is nothing a good cup of cocoa can't cure.

"You start your classes tomorrow?" Suzette asked.

"Yes, bright and early," Viv said. "Monsieur Martin said he would be by to escort me."

"He is very attentive," Suzette said. "Do you both teach millinery or do you teach something different, Ms. Parker?"

"Scarlett, please," I said.

"And I'm Vivian, or Viv, if you prefer," Viv chimed in.

"I don't teach anything," I said. "I have no artistic ability at all. The last hat I tried to make looked like a very bad brioche."

Suzette covered her mouth with one delicate hand and laughed. "I am sure that is not true."

"Oy, it's true," Viv said with the candor only a cousin could manage without it being a slam to the ego.

"What will you do with your time, then, Scarlett, while Viv is teaching?"

"I am going to be looking for her husband," I said.

Viv gasped and Suzette's perfectly arched eyebrows rose almost to her hairline. Even surprise looked good on her.

"I am afraid I do not comprehend," Suzette said. "You are looking for a husband for your cousin?"

"No, I'm actually looking for *her* husband," I said. "She misplaced him."

Viv glowered at me and I shrugged.

"What?" I asked. "You did. Besides, maybe Suzette can help me figure out where to start."

"But of course. If there is anything I can do to help, I will do so gladly," she said.

"See?" I said to Viv. She continued to glower at me and I was pretty sure she growled deep in her throat, but then she sipped her cocoa and seemed to settle back down again.

"But do explain to me how you misplace a husband," Suzette said. She smiled over the edge of her own cup. "I may need to know how to do that one day."